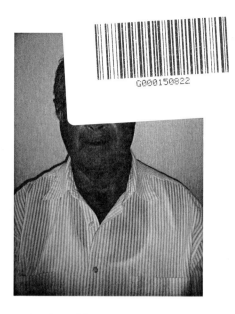

After leaving school at fifteen, James Harley served a five-year engineering apprenticeship before joining the merchant navy as an engineer officer for six years then returning to the MOD(N) PAS, still working as an engineer officer on their ships. He had to retire at age fifty-five on health grounds.

He didn't start writing books until he was seventy, when he wrote his unpublished autobiography, *Three Score Years and Ten: The Life So Far of an Ordinary Man*, under his real name, Harley Jones.

He has been married to the same lady, Betty, for sixty years and has two grown-up children, Wendy and Ian, who between them produced three grandchildren and two great grandchildren.

He now spends his time enjoying DIY, gardening, playing bowls and writing novels and poetry for pleasure.

I dedicate this book to my grandchildren, Catriona, Olivia and Heidi; great grandchildren, Connor and Ethan.

I wish them well and hope they have a healthy, happy, enjoyable and successful future and that they remember me with affection in years to come.

James Harley

BEYOND THE CANE

To
Claire
and

The Sunshine Day Centre
Waterlooville

with best wishes

from the author

James Harley

October 2022.

AUSTIN MACAULEY PUBLISHERS™

LONDON • CAMBRIDGE • NEW YORK • SHARJAH

A CIP catalogue record for this title is available from the British Library.

ISBN 9781528997553 (Paperback)
ISBN 9781528997560 (ePub e-book)

www.austinmacauley.com

First Published 2022
Austin Macauley Publishers Ltd®
1 Canada Square
Canary Wharf
London
E14 5AA

I would like to give a big thank you to Glynis Perkins for reading my original manuscript and notating the alterations she found necessary to be made. Her time and patience taken up in doing so is much appreciated.

I also thank my wife, Betty, who had to watch the television on her own while I spent time writing this novel.

Other Novels published for the Author by Austin Macauley Publishers are:

Crime on a Queen
The Smuggling Leg

Chapter 1

James Royston and Fred Baker had done very well over the last fifteen years since starting their private detective and investigation agency. So much so that James and Susan, his wife, had decided to send their son to a private boarding school for boys. Fredrick was twelve years old and the local school he was attending was not of a very high academic standard, so it was decided that, with his consent, he would be a boarder at Radcliff's Boarding School in Monkshire, about a four-hour drive from where they lived. His twin sister was at her local girls school that was a good standard, and seeing she was doing so well, it was best for her to remain there. Fredrick started in May and it wasn't until he came home for the summer holiday that his parents were aware that things were not as they should be. His first night home, he wet the bed that was not like him at all. Knowing there must be a good reason for it, his father questioned him, which brought him to tears.

He said he had been caned many times by one of the teachers and bullied by the prefects led by the head prefect who went by the nickname Flashman, from the book Tom Brown's School Days. James wanted to know who the schoolmaster was and why he kept giving Fredrick the cane.

He said the teacher was his form master and the one who coached the schools' rugby teams. He gave his name as Mr Walter Brent. He said he took part in the rugby training sessions and was very spiteful when playing with the boys, especially the younger ones. He is a sadist because he likes hurting people and seems to enjoy caning. He keeps the cane in his desk and gets it out directly when he comes into the class. It takes very little for him to pick on a boy for caning. He makes whomever it is he has picked on to stand with his hand out to its full extent and then brings the cane down with as much force as he can muster. He not only canes one hand but always both and sometimes two on each. There are occasions when he chooses to cane a boy on his backside that he does with the same venom over a desk with the minimum being four strokes. It is the look on his face that makes us boys realise he is getting enjoyment out of it.

'Why are you being caned so often?' James wanted to know and was told he didn't really know, it was for silly things like talking when you weren't or a spelling mistake in an essay, any excuse to use the cane!

It was the evening of the second day he was home when James walked into the bathroom, not knowing Fredrick had just got out of the bath and was drying himself, that he noticed the bruising and wheels on his backside; some were fading out, but there were a couple of relatively fresh ones which Fredrick was trying to cover with the towel. When his father questioned him, he said he had got them playing rugby and that the teacher had tackled him hard and had caused them. James asked his son why he hadn't complained on the occasions they had spoken to him on the phone, and he just told his father he didn't want him to be ashamed of him by seeming to be a wimp that couldn't take his punishment. James cuddled his son in, nearly in tears himself, for what he had caused his son to suffer. He told Fredrick he or his mother had never laid a hand on their children, so they were not going to stand by and let someone else punish them. He told Fredrick to finish getting dressed and he would see him downstairs.

They had the meal Susan had prepared and talked about anything but school, excepting for a mention of the homework they had both been given. Their mother made the suggestion they both get it done in the first few days, or as much of it as they could, so that the rest of the six weeks could be their own to do what they liked without having to worry about homework. Both Fredrick and Joyce thought it a great idea and said they would start on it that evening.

It was when they went to their rooms that James told Susan that he had seen Fredrick's bruising and how he had tried to hide them from him. He said if he could get hold of Mr Brent, he would give him a hiding.

Susan said, 'And when you have finished with him, give him to me, and I will finish the job.' Susan became upset, as James had become, to think the boy had suffered in silence because he didn't want his parents to be ashamed of him. James said he was going to do something about it, starting tomorrow. He and Fred were not private investigators for nothing, and they would get to the bottom of what was going on at the school.

James phoned his partner Fred Baker that evening and told him they were going to do an investigating job they would not be getting paid for. Fred reminded James that they didn't work for nothing, to which James said they would be on this occasion. He said he would see him at the office in the morning.

Getting to the office, Fred had already put the kettle on and was reading last evening's local newspaper. When the kettle boiled, Fred made the tea, and while they drank it, James explained about Fredrick's school and how he had been treated. Fred was as angry as James had been, and being Fredrick's godfather, he was not going to stand by and see him being ill-treated. What he intended doing about it, he asked James and was told they were going to investigate all there was to learn about the school and how it is being managed and run.

'We are going to start by going to the school at Monkshire, which is a four-hour drive from the office, and see what we can learn.'

James told him that Susan was coming into the office later and would help to get them started. She will come in her own car so she can finish when she likes or if we get held up and don't get back until late. He explained he had only been to the school once and that was the day Fredrick was enrolled, so he was going to see if he could find anyone he could talk to while the school was closed down for the summer holiday.

They had only just got started when Susan arrived and, going through the mail, told them one of the letters was from a client that was threatening them with legal action if they didn't complete the job they had taken on within a week. James knew immediately who the gentleman in question was and suggested to Fred that he had better look out the file and complete what they had not, up until then, been able to complete for lack of one piece of evidence they had only just last week acquired. Fred frowned, but James said he had better get this chap off their backs or he would carry out the threat he had made, of that he was sure. He was a nasty piece of work and, turning to Susan, asked her to take him off their clients' register. Picking up the telephone, he rang the number on the letterhead and, on the call being answered, asked to speak to the client in question but was told he was out of the office. James asked her, assuming she was his secretary, to pass on a message to him that his case was being dealt with and would be passed to the police within the next two days. They would be notifying him in writing as soon as the police had received it and would be sending him the bill that he wanted to be paid within a week. Any further delay he would experience would be the fault of the police and that the case was dealt with and closed as far as Royston and Baker were concerned. The response, from whomever he was speaking to, obviously annoyed him for he just said "Talk to the police" and put the phone down.

While Fred got the file out, swearing under his breath because he wanted to be in on the school enquiries right from the start, James and Susan started on a suitable route to get to the school in the quickest time. James worked it out that by the time he got there, spent two or three hours, making enquiries and getting back home, it would be nine or ten o'clock. Susan reminded him that the school might be shut with nobody there. James said he would take a chance on that and if he found it shut, he would make enquiries elsewhere in the locality rather than have a wasted journey. He got his briefcase and a notebook together with some other papers he thought might be useful, ready to set off, leaving Fred being assisted by Susan putting the finishing touches to the outstanding case the letter and phone call had been about.

Susan asked before he left what he would be doing about having something to eat and drink, to which he said he would manage something and not to have a meal ready for him when he got home. By the time he actually managed to leave the office, it was ten o'clock. He called into the nearest garage and topped up with petrol before getting on his way. The route they had mapped out got him to Monkshire village in less than four hours, and on getting there he had to ask directions to the school. It was nearly two o'clock when he stopped the car, finding the school gates closed. However, there was a car he could see parked inside through the railings, so parking in the nearby pub car park, he went in and asked if he could get a spot of lunch.

The pub only had a few customers, mostly at the bar, but there was a couple sitting at a table, eating. The landlord said he was only just in time for they would be closing in an hour's time.

He ordered a half pint of cider and a ham and salad lunch that did not take very long to be brought to the table he had chosen to sit at. It was before three o'clock when he left the pub having asked if he could leave his car in the car park for a couple of hours. He picked up his briefcase and walked the short walk across to the school gates. The main gates were locked but the side gate was not, so, supposing that the owner of the car inside was about, he entered the school grounds. The school building had originally been a very large country mansion that was now looking tired, but certainly not falling down.

He knocked on the very heavy oak door with the very heavy lion's head knocker and waited. It seemed an age that he was standing there waiting for the door to be opened before it was by a very tall gentleman dressed in overalls. He said the school was closed for the summer holidays, and that he was the art teacher doing some work prior to the school reopening in six weeks' time. James introduced himself and asked if he was a teacher, could he spare some time to speak to him. The teacher asked him in and said they could talk while he was finishing off what he was doing. They went to what was, obviously, the art room after the front door was closed. Getting there, James was offered a chair to sit on while the teacher got on with what he was doing before being interrupted by James' visit. He introduced himself as David Wise and said he was the senior art teacher. He asked what did James want to talk to him about.

James asked how long he had been at the school, and having said 'ten years', he was asked if he had seen many changes in that time. He said his reason for being there was because his son attended the school, and as he was passing on his way home, he thought he would just call in and see if he could speak to anybody. David Wise said he had very nearly had a wasted journey for it was only by chance that he had chosen to come in that day to do what he was doing. James asked if he had taught his son at all, for he was interested in art albeit he wasn't very good at it. Mr Wise said he had seen Fredrick a couple of times, and if he remembered rightly, he was a nice lad and was quite good at pencil drawing.

Getting back to what changes David Wise had seen over the past ten years, he said quite a lot. The school had a respected reputation when he first joined under an excellent headmaster by the name of Dr John Mountford. He said that back in those days, there was a waiting list to get a place at the school, as it was a matter of dead man's shoes so to speak.

You had to wait for those that had to leave for university or whatever other reason the pupils had to leave for before vacancies arose.

'What about now?' James wanted to know and was not surprised when told, he was thinking of retiring early to get out. He explained that two years ago, the school was bought by a private purchaser from a consortium of men that had shares in the property and formed the board of school governors. It was then that things started going downhill.

'In what way?' James wanted to know.

'The first thing that happened was the board of governors were replaced without any consultation, and when Dr Mountford complained about it, he was told it was not his place to challenge it. So, he called a meeting with his senior members of staff. I was unable to attend because I was on holiday but was told that those that agreed with the headmaster, were given their marching orders, and because he felt responsible for them being sacked, he resigned. His replacement, Gerald Good, was appointed by the head of the new board of governors, and from what I have seen of him, he couldn't manage a kindergarten, let alone a school of this magnitude.'

'Where did he come from?' James wanted to know. David just raised his shoulders before saying he didn't know, but he came to the school as a junior master about six months before Dr Mountford tendered his resignation.

Finishing what he had been painting, David Wise asked James if he would like a cup of tea. On saying he would, he said he would go to the kitchen and put a kettle on. While he was away, James looked around the art room and was very interested in what he saw. David came back with a tray with some mugs on and some biscuits, explaining they might be a bit soft for he didn't know how old they were. He asked if James took sugar and apologised that if he did, he was sorry but he couldn't find any, however, the milk was fresh because he had brought it with him that morning. As they drank the tea, James asked what the masters were like that replaced the senior masters that had been sacked. David explained that none of them had much experience, hence why, in his opinion, the standard of education was falling. James then asked about a teacher by the name of Walter Brent.

'Oh, him?' David gave a little grimace. 'I steer clear of him; I think he could be trouble.'

'He is a very unsocial man who thinks a great deal of himself and seems to think he owns the place. I have heard complaints have been made about the way he treats the boys, especially the younger ones that are boarders, and some parents have taken their boys away from the school because of him. Mr Good, although he is the headmaster, is frightened to death of him.' They talked on for another half an hour before David said he had to get home, as his wife would start worrying about where he had got to. They went to the kitchen together to wash the mugs up, and while doing it, James asked if he knew who the new board of governors were, especially the owner of the school. David said he couldn't help him with that but would give him the name and telephone number of the school secretary.

James took out his notebook and wrote down the name and phone number David read out to him from his diary. Thanking him for all the information he had given him, they left the school together, David locking the front door behind them. As they walked towards his car, he asked why James had been asking all the questions he had tried to answer, and James told him to keep it under his hat, but that he was a private investigator and was going to do something about the way the school was being managed. He assured David things would improve in the future so not to seek early retirement yet. David said he wouldn't say a word to anyone and hoped James was successful, for something had to be done.

As they got to David's car, they shook hands and bid each other good day. David said he would lock the gates when he left and hoped James had a safe journey home.

Chapter 2

Getting back to his car, James headed for home. Nearing five o'clock and knowing he had a nearly four-hour drive in front of him, he decided to stop for a meal on his way. He had been on the road for two hours when he came to a public house that had an appeal about it, and so, he drove into the car park. Entering, he could see there were a lot of customers eating, and he asked at the bar if he could have a meal as well as a drink. The man he spoke to was obviously the landlord for he called a lady over and told her to see to this gentleman, indicating who he was referring to. He was politely shown to a corner table set for two and asked if he would like a drink while he studied the menu. He said he would and ordered a pint of bitter. While the waitress was gone, he studied the menu and ordered his meal when she returned with his drink.

The meal came and was very enjoyable, and James asked for their card when he paid his bill; not forgetting to ask for a receipt to go against expenses, of course. Leaving the pub, with traffic now not nearly as busy as when he left the school, he was now able to get home in less than two hours.

Getting indoors, he found Susan washing up the dinner things, and giving her a little loving slap on her backside, he kissed the side of her neck.

'Hello,' she said, 'What kept you?' She turned and kissed him and offered him the tea towel. As she carried on washing and him drying up, she asked if he had had a good day. He said he had, and that he had to make a phone call before it got too late; so, on finishing and putting the tea towel away, he got his notebook from his briefcase and rang the phone number David Wise had given him.

It rang half a dozen times before a lady's voice said, 'Hello, Stella here.'

'Is that Stella Boulton?' James asked.

'Yes,' replied Stella.

'Who wants her?' James explained who he was and asked if he could see her. She reminded him it was quite late and that she was enjoying a school holiday, but James persisted and told her he would only need a couple of hours of her time if she would be kind enough to spare it. He said he would meet her at the school or at her home if she preferred and would let her set the time, but he insisted it must be tomorrow. She said she would be having a late-night that night so could it not wait for the next day rather than tomorrow. She suggested they meet at her home rather than the school and gave him a time and her address. She asked what he wanted from her, and when he said it was to do with the school and her job, she became very nervous; James could feel it down the line. He told her not to be concerned as it was only information he wanted and it would be nothing that would get her into trouble. Before he rang off, he hoped she would have a good night and that he would see her the day after tomorrow.

After putting the phone down, he called Fredrick downstairs and told him who he had seen that day and asked what Mr Wise was like as a teacher. Fredrick said he was a very nice man but had not been in his art class much, that he had spent most lessons with his deputy. He then asked his son if he knew the school secretary and was told she was quite young and very attractive. He said the prefects used to do anything they could to have the excuse to visit her office, especially Flashman. They very rarely saw her, as she spent most of the time in her office. He said her office was next to the headmaster's and said he thought there was an adjoining door between the two. He asked his dad why he went to the school, to which James said he would tell him everything in a couple of weeks' time. Thanking Fredrick, he said he could go back and play with his electric trains, and that he would be up to play with him before he went to bed.

James rang Fred and asked him if he had passed what they had done onto the police and was told yes and how grateful he was for the help Susan had given him before she went home.

He said he would see him in the office in the morning when they could talk through what had been done and the reaction the police had when they received it. James told him quickly how his day had gone and what he wanted them to do tomorrow as Susan would not be going in. He put the phone down and suggested to Susan that she take the kids out for the day, shopping, knowing they needed new school shoes for a start. She said she thought that was a good idea and would take them into Southampton. They sat together and had a glass of wine while James told her in detail what had gone on at the school.

He went up to Fredrick's bedroom as he had promised to play with the electric train set that he had painstakingly built on shelving around three walls of his bedroom, with the control desk setup at the foot of his bed. Like with his son, once he got started with it, time just flew by, and it was only when he looked at his watch and saw what the time was that he asked Fredrick to shut it all down because it was time for bed. They got downstairs where Joyce was watching television with her mother and seeing her dad asked if she could spend some money on some new clothes as well as just shoes.

He said to both of them, 'As long as your mother agrees with what you want to buy then, of course, you can, but there is a limit to how much you can spend, but that is up to her.'

James didn't sleep very well and got up earlier than usual. He made tea for himself and Susan and sat and read the previous day's Times. He always looked for articles written by Joyce Sheen who he knew well from the Queen Mary days. If he felt there was a need to expose anything that they found with the school investigation they were making, he would be on to her to get The Times to print it as an exclusive. After glancing through the paper, he went and got shaved and dressed, and by the time he got back downstairs, Susan was well underway with a cooked breakfast. She told him to start on the serials and that his eggs, bacon and trimmings would be ready in a few minutes. They sat and ate their breakfast together and talked about what he and Fred would be doing that day. He explained roughly what he wanted them to do and promised he would be home earlier than he was yesterday. Giving Susan a peck on the cheek, he went out to his car.

The traffic was already quite heavy, but getting over to Fred's house didn't take long. Fred was surprised when James said he would give him a lift as they would not be going out anywhere that day, and so he thought they could save some petrol by only taking one car. He said hello to Amy, Fred's wife, and Elizabeth, her sister, who were both dressed ready for the day ahead. James asked Elizabeth how business was going in the sweet shop that she managed below their office and was glad to hear it was doing well. He asked if she wanted a lift as well, but she declined saying she wasn't sure what time she was going to be finished, for she had some deliveries coming and wanted to do a bit of a stock take, but she thanked him for the offer.

They got to the office and started discussing their plan of action after James had learnt how yesterday had gone for Fred, who said he had taken all the paperwork and photographs to the Southampton Police Station himself and what the chief superintendent had had to say about it all. He assured Fred the police would now take the case up and to watch this space as prosecutions would be being made and he could see jail sentences looming for at least two of those named and involved in the case. Fred warned him of their client, telling him about the letter and phone call to which the chief superintendent smiled.

'We know just how to deal with blokes like him; he will be no trouble, but thanks for the warning.'

It was as James was finishing telling Fred what his day had been like that the phone rang on his desk. He answered it and was surprised to find it was Stella Boulton on the other end. She said her late-night out had been cancelled and seeing he had left his phone number when he had rung her, she thought she would see if he wanted to see her today after all instead of tomorrow. James said that would be fine, in fact, perfect. She explained how to get to her house, when they got to the village she lived in, that was three-quarters of an hour nearer to them than the school. She said they could come at any time that morning because she wouldn't be going out until the late afternoon. James looked at his watch and worked out they could be there within about two and a half hours so gave her eleven o'clock as arrival time. She said that would be fine but observed that he had said "we" and not just "him". James explained he would be bringing his business partner with him if that was all right with her. She said it was, but she didn't sound too happy about it. James tried to ease the tension she must have been feeling by telling her he is a nice man, to which she said she was sure he was.

Putting the phone down, James turned to Fred and said, 'Change of plan; we are going to see the school secretary this morning and not have to wait until tomorrow.' James took his briefcase with his notebook and Fred took the road map and they left the office right on half-past eight.

The traffic was busy on the main roads but quieter when they got out into the country. It was just after eleven o'clock when they drove into the village, and following the directions Stella had given, they pulled up in front of a quaint country cottage. She must have been looking out for them for the door opened as they walked up the path. She smiled and held her hand out as they got to her and invited them into her humble home as she called it. It was very cosy with low ceilings which Fred realised when he didn't duck quite low enough as he went through the front-room door. She asked them to sit down and if they would like a drink. James said a cup of tea would be nice after their drive, so she went out to what must have been her kitchen to make it. Her home was lovely, it had "live alone" written all over it and some of the pictures and ornaments were really tasteful. She asked Fred if he would mind moving the coffee table so she could put the tray she was carrying onto it. She asked if they wanted milk and sugar and did the honours after pouring the tea out.

James introduced Fred after himself and explained they were making enquiries into what was going on at a school that had been highly recommended to him before he had enrolled his son. She enquired if his son was Fredrick Royston, and when it was confirmed, she said he was a nice lad and very well-mannered. James said he was proud of him, and that Fred was his godfather, which brought the subject back to the school.

The first question James asked was how long Stella had worked at the school?

She said, 'Nearly five years.' It was the job she got when her husband was killed in a road accident. He asked if she was still as happy with the job as when she first got it? In answer to this, she gave an emphatic "no". He asked when the change started to happen and was told when Dr Mountford left the school. She said he was a wonderful man who ran the school like a well-oiled machine. She said how helpful and patient he had been with her and that he was a pleasure to work for. The masters respected him and the senior masters were left to teach their subjects in the way they saw fit and with the success rating they had up until he left was very high, hence why parents were cuing up to get their sons into the school. What has changed, Fred wanted to know, not to be left sitting, twiddling his thumbs. The answer she gave was somewhat like what James had learnt from the art teacher; this time they were able to follow it up. James asked her if she got on with the old headmaster's replacement and was told,

'Not really, for he is such a negative man.'

'What about all the other masters that have come in to replace those that were sacked?'

'Some of them are a waste of space,' she said, 'especially Fredrick's form master Mr Walter Brent who gives me the creeps. He thinks he runs the school and Mr Good, the headmaster, is frightened to death of him. He is the main reason I would like to leave, but getting jobs like mine are very difficult to get, and being a widow, I have to work.'

'Why does Mr Brent make you feel how you do?' James asked.

'Whenever he comes to my office, he makes suggestive remarks implying he wants to get into my knickers and is a proper pest. I have complained three times in the last six months to Mr Good, but he does nothing. Dr Mountford would, by now, have given him enough warnings to have been able to throw him out on his ear; that's if he had ever employed him in the first place.'

James wanted to know about the Board of Governors' appointments.

Stella said she knew nothing about them other than their names, addresses and phone numbers, but she was sure there was a strong link between the head of the board, the owner of the school and the governors he appointed. Did she have any of the details she had just mentioned at home, Fred asked, to which she replied "No". She never took work home, all that information and more was in her office at the school. James put her to the sword when he asked if she would be prepared to help them get to the bottom of what was going on. She said she had no loyalty left to the school but did not want to see it go to the wall, so she would give them all the assistance she could. This was music to their ears. He asked her if she had time to take them to the school and her office so they could get any information she had that they could use. She said if it meant saving her job and it going back to what it used to be, she would help them in any way she could. She suggested they go in her car, as people living near the school knew it and would not be surprised if she unlocked the gates and went in. She always parked in the same place so they would think she was on school business even though the pupils were on holiday.

On the way, James asked if she knew of any complaints made about Walter Brent from the parents. She said she did because of the discipline he was supposedly activating. Some of the younger boys had already been taken away. She said the school nurse had spoken to her on several occasions when he had dealt out punishment. She said she should report him to the authorities but knew if she did, she would lose her job, and like her, Stella, could not afford to do that, so she kept quiet.

'I think your son's name was mentioned on a couple of occasions when he had been too severe. He bullies them on the rugby field, I believe.'

'How long had he been at the school?' They wanted to know and were told he arrived soon after Gerald Good. She said a punishment book was kept in her office and all punishment dished out was in it or was supposed to be, from detention and lines to canings. She said at this point that no punishment book was ever needed while Dr Mountford was the headmaster; any punishment required was always dealt with by him and rarely was a cane required.

As they got to the school gates, they were just being opened by a man she obviously knew, for he waved and indicated he would leave the gates open for her. Fred asked who it was, and she said the groundsman who was responsible for all the outside maintenance of the school.

She drove in and parked in her usual place before going back to shut and lock the gates. They entered the front door when she opened it with the small bunch of keys that she had brought with her. After shutting it, she led them to her office where she asked what they wanted to see. The first thing James asked for was the names and addresses of the board of governor members, whilst Fred asked to see the punishment book. James took down all the details she had on the board of Governors, as Fred fumed as he looked through the punishment book. As James finished, Fred said if he ever had the misfortune to meet Mr Walter Brent, he would do him serious harm.

'Fredrick's name is in this book over the last three months more than any other pupil, and all canings signed by Brent.'

'What about prior to Brent's arrival?' James wanted to know.

'Very few,' Fred replied, 'and most of them were lines or detention.'

The next thing James wanted was the names and addresses of the masters. Stella opened a filing cabinet and took out a file containing the information he required. He asked if there was anything that had Dr Mountford's address and telephone number on. Stella took out a notebook from her desk draw and passed it to him, saying those were details of past staff, but she could not guarantee that they would still be correct, as some of them might have moved to get other jobs in other parts of the country or gone abroad. He wanted a list of the pupils attending the school as of when they broke up and asked her to point out the name of the prefect that went under the nickname "Flashman". Stella pointed it out and he wrote down the name "Edward Andrews"; he asked her who the other prefects were and noted them too. She asked if it would help if she gave him spare copies of the lists he had been looking at. He said it would be very helpful. She said about Edward Andrews that he was a spoilt brat and a bully that came from a rich family.

James and Fred between them looked at all the files albeit very quickly not to take up too much time, and when satisfied they thanked Stella and said she could close everything up, but that if it was the headmaster's office next door, did she have the interconnecting door key for it so they could have a quick look inside. She said she had but could not open anything in his office because she didn't have any keys, but James told her not to worry. There were several photographs on his desk that James took a look at and asked Fred to look at them too. All his desk draws, including the one filing cabinet, were locked, but then again, James thought that is how it should be. He took note of the sort of locks they were and also that there was a wall safe set into the wall behind his desk.

Satisfied, they could do no more at that time, James thanked Stella and asked her to keep mum on what they had been doing. She said she had never seen them and smiled.

On the way back to her house, James asked her to stop at a flower shop and, going inside, came out with a large bouquet. They drove back to the cottage and refusing her offer of another cup of tea or coffee said they wanted to get back home. James gave her the flowers and thanked her for all that she had done for them. She blushed and said he shouldn't have gone to the trouble but thanked them both and told them that if she were ever needed for anything else, they would know where to find her.

They shook hands again, and this time, being almost old enough to be her father, Fred gave her a little kiss on her cheek. She waved from the front door as they drove off with James telling Fred he was a dirty old man. But Fred was not put out and just said, 'When an opportunity presents itself, you shouldn't waste it,' and laughed saying, 'Fredrick was quite right, she is a very attractive young woman and probably older than she looks.'

It was approaching five o'clock when James dropped Fred off, saying they would need to do some research in the office tomorrow, on what they had learned today, and could go from there to make further enquiries. On getting home, he found the family had not long been home from their shopping expedition. Fredrick and Joyce were watching television, and Susan was preparing the evening meal. James went up and changed out of his suit into something more casual before going down and getting a beer for himself and some sherry for Susan. He then went into the garden for a look around, having left his beer in its bottle. He looked in the pond and found one of the smaller goldfish laying on the surface. He got the net and fished it out before making a hole in one of the borders and burying it. He stayed out there until the sun was low in the sky and finished his beer, putting the bottle in the bin before he went back indoors. He told Susan he had just hooked another fish out of the pond and wondered what had caused it to die.

After they had washed up, Joyce asked if they could play monopoly and went to the cupboard to get it out and set up. They played it the short way so that they would have a winner before it got too late. Just before ten o'clock, Joyce was declared the winner, having made the rest of them bankrupt. Being quite tired after five hours or so of driving, James said he was going to bed and was soon followed by Susan who said she and the kids had had a great day shopping and been very careful what they had purchased. She said how expensive the shoes were getting but they had to have them. James gave her a quick rundown on what he and Fred had achieved and said he wanted her in the office to help them in the morning. He turned out the bedside light, gave her a quick kiss and went straight off to sleep.

They all went to work in separate cars, Susan getting to the office half an hour after the men, who, when she got there, were already pouring over the road map. They had decided on a plan of action and were finalising who was going to visit whom if they could get hold of anybody on the end of a phone line. James said he wanted to go to Fraisborough where Gerald Good lived because he wondered why he had two phone numbers, one for while the school was open and another when it had broken up. He had asked Stella, but she said she didn't know, but what she was told was that she was never to get them mixed up.

Going by the map, Gerald Good and Walter Brent lived in the same direction, less than an hour's drive apart, so they decided they would go in different directions; James would visit Gerald Good's and Walter Brent's houses, and Fred would go in the other direction and speak to Dr John Mountford.

While they discussed what they were going to try and find out, Susan busied herself setting up files for those they were going to visit.

They started off by using both office phones to try and contact those they were going to visit. James telephoned the number for Gerald Good during school time, which Stella was forbidden to do, and when the phone was answered by a female voice, he asked if he was speaking to Mrs Good. He asked if her husband was there and was told "No". He then went on to ask if he could still make a visit as he was in the area and wanted to let them know about the improvements her husband had spoken about to him two months ago. She said she knew nothing about it for being a council house, she thought the council dealt with such matters. James had to think quickly and said he worked for a company that was contracted to the council and that he had been chosen to visit that area. He emphasised that she didn't have to make any decisions but to save him a wasted journey later, he asked if he could just make a call.

She said reluctantly, 'Yes, I suppose so, but when?' He told her that day if she would be at home. She said she had to do some shopping that morning and so it would have to be that afternoon. They agreed on a time after one o'clock and thanking her rang off. On putting the phone down, Susan asked,

'Where did all that come from?' James said he had to think of something to get her to see him, and he played it as it came into his head. The Goods live in a council house and so I had to think of something.

Before he telephoned Brent's number, he said it would be much the same, as he didn't know who was going to answer the phone, man, woman or child, if it was answered at all. He dialled the number, and again, it was a woman that answered. He asked if he could speak to Mr Brent, and was told "No" because he was away fishing. Asking how long he would be away for, she said she didn't know, but it was usually for a week, it depended on how long the men he went with stayed. He decided on the same cock and bull story he had given to Mrs Good and it worked, even better this time, and when was it that he wanted to visit. James said he would be in the area that day if that would be convenient. She said it wasn't, for she was going to be away from the house that day until late but would see him in the morning if that would be suitable. He asked if nine-thirty would be too early and was told that time would be fine. This settled on, he put the phone down. This time Susan said nothing other than she supposed he would be spending the night away rather than coming home and going back the next day. With the time it would take and the petrol it would use, he thought her idea was a splendid one and that it took a woman to think of it. She just nodded. He asked her if she would look out local builders merchants that he could visit to get pamphlets and literature that he could take with him to make what he was doing look authentic.

Fred had managed to get through to the number of Dr Mountford, the previous headmaster, but was told by the man answering the phone that the Mountfords had moved, but that he had a phone number for him that he could try, but the address he was reluctant to give, saying that if he got through to John, he would tell him where he lived. Fred thanked the man before ringing off. He then rang the number he had been given and was soon answered by a lady. She said indeed she was Mrs Mountford and would get her husband to the phone.

After a very short time, John Mountford said hello and asked to whom he was speaking.

Fred gave him his name and explained who he was and what he wanted to speak to him about. John said he would like to help and agreed that if Fred could get to their home today, he would be pleased to accommodate his request. He gave Fred his address and local directions from Marymarch, a small village not far away and just before Torquay in Devon. Fred thanked him and asked him if it would be all right if he didn't give him a definite time that he would arrive because he didn't know how long the journey would take, but that he should be able to do it in three-and-a-half to four hours, depending on traffic. John said he was not going anywhere that day and so any time would be suitable. Fred went back to the road map and worked out the distance and agreed with himself that he should be able to make it in the time he had said and would be able to get back home that night.

By the time he was ready to go, James and Susan had returned from their travels around the builders merchants, and building companies they had looked up. James was almost ready to leave as well, having called into their home to pick up his overnight bag, a pair of overalls and a few other bits and pieces he thought might be useful, torch, measuring tape, gloves and a few tools.

Fred said he must get off after ringing Amy to tell her he would be late home but couldn't give her a definite time.

He left the office with briefcase and notepad at ten-thirty and, with a full tank of petrol, was sure he would be with the Mountfords by three o'clock at the outside. Sticking to the A roads as much as he could and with not too much heavy traffic, he made good headway until he got to some of the villages where the roads were quite narrow. He got to the Mounsfords in slightly less time than he thought, and on pulling up outside of the address he had been given, he was in a cul-de-sac of well-appointed bungalows, all with garages and neat gardens. Going up to the front door, he could see how well-maintained this garden was, it was obvious that a lot of time and trouble had been put into its layout and tendering. He rang the doorbell and, when opened, was faced by a man of quite a small stature with grey to white hair and a small beard. His brown eyes were bright and attentive with a pair of spectacles covering them. He asked if it was Mr Baker, and when Fred said it was, he offered his hand and said he was pleased to meet him. As he moved into the bungalow, with John shutting the front door behind them, he pointed to a door on Fred's right.

'Please go in,' he offered, 'and meet my wife Hazel.' As Fred entered a beautifully decorated room that was tastefully furnished, Mrs Mountford got up from her chair.

'Please don't get up,' he said, shaking her hand, 'it is Hazel, I believe.' She said she was pleased to meet him and asked if he would like a cup of tea or maybe something a little stronger after his drive. Fred said tea with one sugar would be fine. John asked him to take a seat, indicating where, and sat alongside him in his armchair.

'I hope I have not been presumptuous, but I have got some paperwork out that you might find useful from what you told me on the phone this morning,' he said, 'and I would like to know more about what you are endeavouring to do with regard to my old school.' With the tea brought in for all of them by Hazel, they talked while they drank and ate the delicious homemade cake she brought with it.

Fred told him about his Godson Fredrick, how he had been punished by his class master and the deterioration of the school in general since he'd resigned. Dr Mountford said nothing for a few minutes, trying to compose himself before he continued.

'That school was my life,' he said. 'I attended it as a boy and went back to it as a teacher, after I had got the degrees I wanted at university. As you know it was rather more than just a Bachelor-of-Arts Degree, hence the Doctorate. I served for ten years as a mathematics and English teacher before becoming the headmaster, that was the proudest day of my life. I am now, after all that happened prior to my resignation, a very bitter man but have principles that I had to abide by. I do not regret what I did, but it broke my heart having to do it. The man that purchased the school is wicked and should be put in prison for what he has done.'

Fred said that was what his visit was for because apart from being his godson, he was also the son of his partner. He said they intended going into every aspect of why the school was like it is now to what it was when John was the headmaster. He asked if he could tell him how the selling of the school came about in the first place. John started going through the papers he had by the side of him.

It all started when one of the shareholders died. He had a twin brother, also a shareholder, and a member of the board of governors. They were both very nice men. Their father, when he died, left them equal shares in the ownership of the house as it was then before it was turned into a school. When his brother died and he inherited his brother's shares from the will, George decided he would like to sell the combined shares and distance himself from the board of governors.

Bearing in mind, the whole board was getting on a bit, the youngest being in his late fifties, a crack appeared in the ranks so to speak. The twin that died belonged to the freemasons and it must have been through them that Mr Anthony Oliver came on the scene. He is a businessman who owns Oliver's, the transport company. It is a massively large firm that has operations in countries all over the world, including Russia and the United States, under other names, of course. He apparently contacted George and, after seeing the buildings and grounds, asked him if he wanted to sell his shares and that he would give him a good price for them. It was at one of the board meetings that George tendered his resignation and told the other board members what he intended doing. I was in attendance and was surprised when he told the others what he had been offered for his shares that were nearly two-fifths of the total holding. The oldest member said if he could get the same deal, he would sell out so that he could give the value of his shares to his children and grandchildren. This really started the rot, and by the end of the meeting, they had all agreed to sell their shares at the price offered to George, I was the only one that held out, but mine were minimal to theirs.

In the end, having talked it over with Hazel, I decided to keep mine, for I would have some say in any future developments and as headmaster, I could have a bit of influence in the running of the school.

It was after many weeks that a meeting was called in Mr Oliver's head office board room, and the board of governors and myself were invited to attend. His head office is near Oxford.

None of these people knew anything about Mr Oliver, not even George, only through the Masonic contact. However, when George filtered it back through his contact, Mr Oliver telephoned him. He said he would like to meet him and discuss in more detail what he was buying. According to George, it was then that it was mentioned that the other shareholders were prepared to sell if they could get the same offer as him, all but one that was, but he would be no trouble to get around; that was where the big mistake was made, for George didn't realise how much the school meant to me.

The date and time were arranged, and the meeting took place.

'I have the notes I made right here if you would like to look at them.

Mr Oliver came across as a charming man, and his secretary Carol Jarvis was efficiency its-self.

They welcomed each member including myself, when we were ushered into the board room, with a handshake and the offer of a drink, Carol doing the honours. Mr Oliver or his secretary had done a lot of work before calling the meeting for he had quite a large file on the table where he was going to sit. They were offered cigars if they smoked or cigarettes if they preferred. We were all offered seats around the table with Carol Jarvis sitting at a desk a little way away.

Mr Oliver started off by asking if all those attending wanted to sell their shares in the school. They all put their hands up except me.

'What about you, Mr Mountford?' he asked, looking at me.

'I don't want to sell mine,' I said.

'And why not?' he interjected.

'Because unlike these other members, the school means a lot to me, and I don't want to give up my part of it.'

He said, 'In that case, we would be partners with you having very little to say in what I decide to do.'

I said, 'Yes, but you will have to have my signature on any major changes you want to make to the school and the grounds.'

And that was when he showed his true colours. The other governors looked at each other, but all they could hear and see was money and lots of it. Oliver had got contracts drawn up and, after Carol had distributed them, he asked them to read the contents and sign them if they agreed with the terms and wording. This they all did except me, although I read it. It turned out that I held five per cent of the total shares with Oliver owning the rest.

I had done my best to dissuade the others before we got anywhere near to Oliver's buy out, but they could only see a big fat cheque heading their way.

I asked if all the board members wanted to step down as school governors and was promptly told by Oliver that he would appoint new ones to replace those that were stepping down. With everybody satisfied with what they had done, he wrote them cheques for the amounts their shares had cost him. He must have already known that his offer was going to be accepted for it is not normal for a man to write cheques totalling half a million pounds, which is what the total came to. To keep that amount of money in a current account was ridiculous if the cheques were not to bounce. I shook each of them by the hand as they left the building to get in their cars, and hoped they would enjoy their money. Talk about Judas Iscariot, he had nothing on these guys.

On getting back home, I told Hazel what had gone on, and on her advice, I called a meeting of my senior masters the next day. Fred asked the names of the masters he called on to attend that meeting, and John wrote them down and gave them to him, asking why did he want them.

'Because I think one of them was responsible for letting Oliver know what you had done, and those that were agreeing with you in not wanting the school to be taken over by this man. How else would he have known who to sack?' John put his head down and looked at the floor, feeling guilty for not thinking of that. He said he had to resign after seeing some of the best teachers he had ever worked with sacked and for no other reason than trying to support the headmaster and the school.

Fred asked if he still held his shares in the school. He said yes, he was the only person who could put any brake on what Oliver could do with the school.

'How do you know about the sackings?' John asked and was told they had spoken to Stella Boulton.

'It is a wonder she is still working there,' John observed, for 'she was very supportive of me'.

Fred asked if he could borrow the paperwork John had looked out so he could take it back to his office to go through it in detail with his partner. John said he was welcome, but he would like it returned just in case any of it was needed in a court of law. Fred asked what he knew about this new owner.

John said, 'He is a ruthless businessman who will do anything to make money. After I resigned, I am sure he thought he would force me to sell my shares to him for he offered me twice as much as he bought the other shareholders shares for, but he was dealing with me and not them. I will not sell to him if he offers me ten times more. I am the only one who can queer his pitch, and we both know it. I think all those who sold to him realise their mistake but, of course, can do nothing about it now. The man that started it all, more than the rest, realised what a fool he had been and, it is supposed, felt so bad about it he committed suicide.'

They say: Money is the root of all evil, well, in this case, that is the truest statement that has ever been uttered. Fred asked if he knew what the other shareholders had done or were doing? John said not only did he not know but never wanted to. He said they were friends for years but directly Oliver bought them out he had not seen or heard anything from one of them. He only knew of the suicide because his obituary was in the local evening newspaper before they moved home.

Hazel Mountford had listened to all that was said but never once interrupted until she asked Fred if he would like to have dinner with them before he made for home. Fred said that was very generous of her, and yes, he would because it was going to be late by the time he got home. She got up and, before leaving, said she would call them when the meal was ready. Fred and John carried on talking, Fred finding out what more he could learn of the retiring school governors and the little there was to tell about Anthony Oliver.

It was half an hour after she had left the room that Hazel called them both to the dining room where they sat down and had a very enjoyable meal together and a rather nice glass of wine.

It was Hazel that asked Fred what he and his partner wanted to do about what was going on at the school, and Fred said they were going to investigate what was going on and try and get something done about it. He said there was more to it all than what was first thought, and that if they could get to the bottom of it all prove that Mr Oliver was the root cause of it, they would make as much trouble for him as they could. Regarding Mr Brent, they would try to get him put in prison, adding that it would be very difficult for his partner James Royston to interview him, for he was sure he would want to beat the living daylights out of him; as would he. But that was in the future, and there was a lot to be done before they came to him. The time was getting on when Fred thanked Hazel for the meal and John for all the information that he had given him but said he must go now or it would be so late when he got home. He asked if he could phone his wife and use their toilet before he left, and phoning Amy, he told her where he was and that he would be home as soon as he could and was leaving then.

Shaking hands with them both at the front door, he said they probably wouldn't be hearing from him again for a while but that he would return John's paperwork as soon as they had finished with it. He took his leave of the Mountfords and had a non-eventful journey home, making it in quicker time than going. It had just got dark when he drove onto his drive and went indoors, taking his briefcase with him. Amy had not gone to bed and wanted to know what sort of day he had had and how he had got on. She asked him if he would like a bedtime drink, but he said he would prefer a glass of scotch to unwind before going up to bed. He flopped down in his favourite armchair while Amy poured the whisky and bringing them over, hers and his, they sat and chatted over his eventful day. He said what a nice couple the Mountfords made and how sorry he felt for John, if for no other reason than he would be doing his best to bring Mr Oliver in particular to justice. He said there was much more to this than met the eye, and he was going to do his best to get justice for not only Fredrick but for the school as a whole. He had acquired written information that he and James would be going over in the morning that might really get them going.

Finishing his whiskey, he said he thought it was time for bed because he wanted to get up early to get to the office and get started.

Chapter 3

It was over two hours after Fred left the office to visit Dr John Mountford that James got himself sorted out and left, heading to Fraisborough. He didn't have to travel as far as Fred, and not needing to get there until after lunch, he had plenty of time. He decided to have a bit of lunch when he got there, as it would help him to kill a bit of time if he needed to. He was not sure how big a place he was going to, for on the map, it seemed quite spread out. It took him a couple of hours to get to the village or town centre, he wasn't sure which, and found the police station. He called in, and the desk sergeant, asking him what he wanted, got out a local area map and showed him exactly where the address he was looking for was. James thanked him and headed to where he had been directed. When he got there, he drove around after seeing no car outside, looking for somewhere to have something to eat. He found a tearoom on the edge of the estate and on parking up went in and ordered what he fancied from the menu he was given. It was a nice little place, big enough to seat eight people and was spotlessly clean. The young lady that served him was aptly dressed and very polite. He ordered a light lunch and a pot of tea. There was only one other person eating and reading a newspaper when he sat down, but before he finished his lunch, the place was nearly full. It was two o'clock by the time he left the tearoom after paying his bill and leaving a small tip.

He drove back to Mrs Good's address, and this time there was a car parked outside.

Being a terraced council house, there were no garages and not too many cars parked in the road. Hers, if it was hers, had seen better days but looking at those that were around, so had they. He parked behind it and, taking his briefcase, went and knocked the front door. It was opened by a quite tall, middle-aged lady, with bottle-blonde hair, smoking a cigarette. James asked if she was Mrs Good and when told "Yes", he said who he was. She asked him in and showed him into the front room. The room reeked of stale cigarette smoke, and the furniture was quite tatty, the curtains hadn't been cleaned since they had first been hung up by the looks of it, but she seemed quite content with it all as it was. There was an empty glass on the coffee table next to a half-filled ashtray and a half-empty bottle of gin on the sideboard. Behind the quite decorative fire screen, the grate still had the ashes from the last fire in it, and being the summer, he wondered when that had been.

Getting out some of the literature he had brought and his notebook, he asked her what she thought needed doing in way of upgrading the house. She gave a little laugh and said,

'Where do I start?'

'Well, Mrs Good—' he continued.

'Oh, please call me Judith,' she interrupted, 'Mrs Good all the time will be much too formal.'

James continued as to where she would like him to start. She said that the room they were in needed re-wallpapering to start with and painting. James said that that didn't come under his remit because wallpapering comes under the responsibility of the occupant.

She said, 'Let us begin in the kitchen then.' It was when they got to the kitchen that he realised this lady didn't like housework, in fact, she didn't like work of any kind by the look of it.

He asked casually where her husband was and whether he worked away. She said he was a schoolteacher, a headmaster, at a private boys' school, so during school time he came and went as the job demanded. James said that the schools were on holiday for the summer so why was he not on holiday. She said he was on a six-week course in Manchester this time and telephoned normally once a week to let her know how things were getting on.

'You said Manchester this time, isn't it always Manchester?'

'No,' she said, 'it can be anywhere in the country, even Scotland one year. I do rather think the teaching profession is unfair, for he has to go on courses most times the schools break up. I do get a bit fed up with it sometimes.'

James went through the motions of noting things that had to be renewed in the kitchen, and then going up to the bathroom, he did the same there. The wiring looked in bad condition in places, and in one bedroom, there was an obvious sign of damp where the wallpaper was coming off the wall. Judith said they never used that room and didn't know where the damp was coming from. He asked her if he could see in the loft, and getting up there, he used his torch to find a leak in the water tank that was right over the bedroom wall that was damp. He got down, closing the hatch behind him, and explained to her what he had found and told her she should get a plumber in and send the bill to the council, for this again was not what he was there for.

Having gone right through the house, they went back to the front room to discuss what had to be done and what was their responsibility. He said there were other houses he had to visit in the area, so she wouldn't hear from the council for quite a few weeks, for they had to prioritise where the money had to be spent and what on. Judith offered him a cup of tea or coffee, but after seeing the state of her kitchen, he declined. He had taken note of all the photographs she had around which gave him a mental picture of what Gerald Good looked like. Pointing to one on the sideboard near the gin bottle, he asked if that was her husband. She said it was, the poor sod. Why did she say that, he enquired?

'Because he is such a nice man really, and from what he says about the school, he is not happy at his work.'

'Why is that? If he is the headmaster, he can surely run the school how he sees fit, can't he?' She asked why James was so interested in her husband when he was not there. He said he had been a schoolteacher before getting the job he had and wondered if her husband was experiencing the sort of problems that he had that made him give up teaching. Saying that opened Judith up a bit thinking she was talking to someone that understood. She said Gerald hated one master in particular that kept on undermining him but when he had tried to get rid of him the head of the board of governors would not hear of it. This master, his name he has never mentioned, must have found out about his complaint and has since put himself out to make Gerald's life a misery.

47

He asked her if they had any children, to which she said no, not together, although she had a son from her previous marriage.

'He is in the army,' she said, 'And is doing very well; he is serving abroad at the moment and wants to go for a commission.' He asked if it was Gerald's second marriage too, and she said 'Yes, his first wife died.'

He asked if her husband had always been a teacher and was told as far as she knew, yes, since leaving university.

James had been in the house for nearly two hours when looking at his watch, he said he had to go because he had another call to make before going home. She said she hoped he could do something about getting some changes made and would tell Gerald he had called when he gets home.

She said, as they got to the front door, that she would have to get some housework done as the place was beginning to look a bit of a mess. During the time James was with her, she must have smoked at least five cigarettes if not more, but she didn't touch the gin bottle. She seemed to be a nice lady that was missing out on the sort of life she would have liked, but she was being held back by her husband's job; he felt sorry for her.

She closed the front door as he was walking down the path, and getting into his car, he drove off.

He got to the edge of the estate and stopped in a pull-in and got his road map out from his briefcase. He worked it out that it would take him less than an hour to get to where Walter Brent lived, so he would be there by five o'clock, although he couldn't call, he could find out where the house was and have a look around the area. He got to Bayford without going wrong and found himself in a quaint unspoiled little village.

He stopped outside the paper shop and general store and going in, asked the lady behind the counter if she could tell him where the road that he was looking for was. She gave him directions and asked what house number he was looking for. He told her number 14.

Looking up in her newspaper delivery book, she said, 'That will be Mr and Mrs Brent, is that who you are looking for?'

James said it was, and asked if she could recommend anywhere he might get a bed for the night. She said there was a "Bed and Breakfast" not far away from Mr Brent's house and was quite near the local pub if he would be wanting an evening meal, adding, 'Their steak pies and puddings are the best you would have ever tasted.'

He purchased the evening paper and, thanking her for the information, said he would be on his way.

Before he got to the door, she said, 'Be warned; Mr Brent is not the nicest man you will ever meet.' James thanked her for the warning.

He drove in the direction he had been given, and on passing the pub she had recommended, he took a turning right and then left to get to the address he wanted. The house was quite new compared to the others he had seen in the vicinity. The outlook from the back of the houses looked over open fields and dry stone walls. He could see they were all well-kept with nicely laid out gardens. Number 14 had a garage bigger than the rest, maybe because it was the last one in the road. Being quiet, he got out of the car to have a look around just to get a feel for the place. After seeing what he wanted to see, he got back in the car and made his way to the address of the Bed and Breakfast. He got to it after passing the pub again, and parking outside, he went and rang the front doorbell. On being opened by a rather rotund lady with a happy-looking face, she said she had a room available when asked. He said he would only be staying one night but would like to see the room. She introduced herself as Mrs Moore but said he could call her Trixie.

After the available room was accepted, she apologised for not being able to supply an evening meal but recommended the local pub; she was also saying how good the pies were. Going back downstairs, she gave him a front-door key in case he got back after ten-thirty when she closed down for the night. He got his night bag and went up to his room to read the newspaper he had purchased. He got onto the bed to have a read and woke up, suddenly realising he had fallen off to sleep. Looking at his watch it showed half-past seven. He got up and rinsed his face in the bedroom sink before going to the pub for a meal.

He decided to walk to the pub for the exercise and the fresh air would do him good, and on getting there, he found the public bar had a darts match in progress, so he went into the lounge. There he found it a lot quieter with only a couple of men and woman in it. He got to the bar where the barman asked him what he wanted to drink. Before answering, he asked if he could have a meal and was directed to the restaurant that was set apart from the bars. He asked for a pint of bitter and asked if it could be brought to the table he chose. The barman was, he thought, the owner of the pub or the manager by the way he got a young lady to show him to a suitable table. She asked him if that would do, and when told "Yes", she said she would bring his drink to him together with the menu. Looking across to where a couple were already eating, he nodded as a "hello" gesture, and they, in return, smiled back.

His beer arrived with the menu, and looking at it, he said that he would have crab meat fish cakes, steak pie and would choose a sweet if he had room after the main course.

The young lady went away with his order after saying he wouldn't have to wait very long as the restaurant wasn't very busy yet. James just smiled after what she had said and took the first sip from his beer. While he was waiting for his meal, the man that had been behind the bar came over to his table. He was indeed the owner and introduced himself, saying he must be a visitor as he hadn't seen him before and hoped he would enjoy his meal.

James said, 'Your steak pies and puddings have been recommended to me by two separate villagers, so how could I not try one of them?' The landlord smiled and asked who the people were that had made the recommendation. James told him the lady in the paper shop and the lady in the B&B he was lodging in. He said he was in the village to visit Mrs Brent tomorrow. The mention of the name "Brent" had an immediate effect on the landlord. James noticed this and asked if Mr Brent used the pub.

'Mr Brent is banned from this public house,' he said, 'I won't allow people like him across my doorstep.' He added that he hoped James was not a friend of his. James assured him he wasn't and asked why he was so hostile towards the name.

The landlord asked if he could sit down and he would tell him.

James welcomed him to sit down and became very intent on listening to what he had to say.

'That man came to the village a few years ago, and is if not the most obnoxious man in the world must be well up there. He thinks he owns the place and treats his wife like dirt. She is a very nice lady, as you will find out for yourself if he is not home, which I don't think he is because he is either playing golf or fishing with some friends of his who are also barred from this pub. How his misses puts up with him, we don't know, when I say "we", I mean the villagers. No one is certain, but we think he knocks her about and her son is frightened to death of him.

He is a bully and a real nasty piece of work. I banned him and his mates because of their behaviour on these premises because it got so bad I was losing customers. It was when he started a fight the last time he was home that I had to get the police in to have him and his cronies ejected that I put the ban on which the police will enforce if they have to.' James put it to him that he had just said, 'When he is home.'

'Did he work away?' The landlord said he was a teacher at a private boys boarding school and stays over during the week, adding, he felt sorry for the boarders.

'He may be different there than he is in the village, but I doubt it. He is a detestable man. It seemed an age that he was talking although it was only a few minutes and the landlord apologised for taking his time when his food arrived. He said he hoped he enjoyed his meal, and if he was going to have another drink, it would be on the house. Excusing himself, he went back to managing his pub.

James had another pint but didn't have a sweet, as the steak pie was as good if not better than had been recommended. He left the pub just as the darts match was finishing after paying his bill and saying cheerio to the landlord, who wished him luck. The walk back to the B&B in the darkness was enjoyable and with a contented stomach. He got in just as Mrs Moore was about to lock up for the night. She asked James what he thought of his meal and was not surprised when he said he had not eaten a better steak pie ever. He asked her if she had time for him to have a word with her before she went to bed. She said he could and invited him into the sitting room. On sitting down, James told her of his conversation with the pub's landlord and asked her if he was perhaps exaggerating a bit. Mrs Moore said no, he was not, everything he said was true, and that the villagers would do anything to get rid of him.

'His wife is a lovely gentle soul and the son is a nice lad, but him, words can't describe him.' She said as far as she knew, it would be Mrs Brent he would be seeing, for her husband was away playing golf or fishing somewhere in the north of England or in Scotland. James thanked her and bid her good night and asked what time breakfast was in the morning. She told him breakfast would be between seven-thirty and nine o'clock. James thanked her yet again and went up to bed.

He slept well and woke when his travelling alarm clock went off at seven o'clock. He had a wash and got dressed in a clean shirt and went down for his breakfast.

Mrs Moore asked if he would like a full English when he had finished his cereals and was told, 'Yes, please!'

On its completion, he paid her, and going back up to his room, he collected his overnight bag and his briefcase and left saying cheerio to her as he got to the front door and telling her he had left the key in the bedroom door lock.

It was nearly nine-thirty when he rang Mrs Brent's doorbell and heard her call out to wait a minute. He, of course, didn't know why, but there could have been many reasons.

When the door was finally opened, James introduced himself and asked if she was Mrs Brent? She said she was and apologised for keeping him waiting. He explained the company he was representing, and as a result, she invited him in. She was quite a slight lady who was heavily made up for that time of day, but it had not completely covered the bruising around her left eye. She invited James to sit down and asked if he would like a cup of coffee or tea. He said he had only recently had one and so declined. He said it was really her husband he wanted to speak to, but seeing he was in the area, he was sure she could deal with what he had called for.

She said her husband had only gone to Scotland two days ago to go fishing with some of his mates, but if he gave her some idea what he wanted to know, she might be able to help. Like in the Good's home, James asked similar questions and was shown around the house, room by room, and also into the attic where the water tanks were. It was in the small bedroom that James asked about all the aeroplanes and who had made them? They were well-made models and everywhere, on shelves, windowsills and even hanging from the ceiling. They were all different sizes and all military planes. She said her son was mad on them and was in the ATC and was at this moment away with them, he is desperate to become old enough to join the RAF and become a pilot. James wanted to know if he was good at school, and he was told "Yes".

'My husband wanted him to go to the school he teaches at, but he will not go.' Did she know the reason he wanted to know. She said he adored his real dad and is not yet over losing him in a hit and run accident that killed him.

'Does he get on well with his stepfather?' James asked and was told he disliked him intensely. Was there a reason for that, he wanted to know and was told her husband wasn't very nice to him. It was only after she had remarried that her new husband had started to show his true colours, especially after he had been drinking. Her son would go to his bedroom and lock the door when he knew his stepfather had gone out drinking as he feared the possibility of getting punished in one way or another if he was around when he got home from the pub or wherever he had been drinking.

As they were coming downstairs, James noted the framed photographs adorning the walls, mostly of men in uniform. As they entered the front room, James quickly took a mental note of its contents. There were photos in frames all over the place, once again, mostly of military men. James asked if they were of her first husband or the one that she was married to now. She said he had got rid of most of the photos of her first husband, saying she didn't need them around now that she was married to him.

James excused himself for asking but asked all the same if he was ever violent to her. She asked what all the questions were for regarding her husband when he had come to discuss what needed doing to the house.

It was then that James came clean and told her what he was really doing and why he had come to see her.

James explained that his son was at the school her husband taught at, and that he was being ill-treated. He said that was not the only reason, but that the school was going into decline, and he wanted to find out what the cause was.

She said her husband rarely talked about the school while he was home but often mentioned a man by the name of Andrews, who he was in the army with and who was responsible for getting him the job at Radcliff's.

'What sort of things does he talk about?' James asked.

'Oh, mostly about what a good man he is, and what a good officer he was, and about how well-off he is, and all that sort of thing.'

She showed him one of the photographs and pointing said, 'That's him.' They both looked resplendent in their uniforms, both with their medals on display.

'Why did your husband leave the army if he enjoyed it so much?' James asked, to which she said,

'He was asked to leave, or should I say, told to leave or he would have been dishonourably discharged.'

'Do you know what for?'

She said he never talks about that.

'How did he get into teaching?' the next question came.

She said, 'It was again, due to Mr Andrews.'

Mrs Brent asked him again if he would like a cup of coffee or tea, as she wanted one herself. He said he would like coffee but only if she was making one for herself and not just for him. As she got up to go to the kitchen, she was obviously in a lot of pain. She tried to disguise it and said she was suffering from a bit of stiffness. With the amount of make-up that she was wearing and now this, James was sure she was being knocked about, and this was why her son locked himself away in his bedroom. While she was out of the room, he got up and looked at the photographs more closely. This guy thought a lot of himself but not too much about others. As he heard her coming back, he sat back down in his chair, ready to drink the coffee she had brought in. Sitting down herself, she asked if James was going to be able to do anything about the house, and James had to admit again, it was only an excuse to get in the house to speak to her.

He explained why he and his partner were investigating the school and its management and hoped she would not mention to her husband when he returned that he had been there. She said she understood what he was saying and would go along with it. James was relieved to hear her say this because otherwise, his chances of being successful in what he wanted to do would be gone.

If Brent got even the slightest inkling of what was going on, it would soon get back to Oliver, and who knows what would happen then? James said he realised it was making her disloyal to her husband but was surprised when she said it was going to help her get the divorce she was going to apply for soon. Not only for the good of herself but more for the benefit of her son. She said she liked the village and the people in it, but she knew of the reputation her husband had got himself, together with the cronies he hung about with when he was home.

Before leaving, he asked Mrs Brent if she had a recent photograph of her son as he could not see one on display. She said she did have one that she kept hidden so that her husband would not destroy it. James asked if it would be possible to see it. She said yes and left the room. He heard her go upstairs, and on returning, she held out a postcard-sized photograph of him. On looking at it, James immediately knew why Fredrick was always getting caned, for Fredrick was a spitting image of the boy in the photograph. It was uncanny, for although slightly different in age, they could almost be taken as identical twins. He asked if he could take the photo away but was told emphatically 'No' and with a touch of venom. On handing it back to her, she immediately took it upstairs and presumably put it back in its hiding place. When she came back down, James was ready to leave and thanking her and squeezing her hand when shaking it said goodbye and assured her nothing would cause her any retribution from her husband.

Getting to his car, he sat for a few minutes, thinking on what Mrs Brent had told him, and having seen the photograph of her son looking so much like his, he thought Brent was not punishing Fredrick with the cane but his wife's son who he could not punish, albeit whenever he tried his wife reminded him he was not his son but hers and to leave him alone. This might well be why she was getting knocked about. This angered James even more if what he was thinking was correct, for from what Mrs Brent had told him, neither boy deserved what he was dishing out to Fredrick.

It took him nearly three hours to get back to the office where he found Fred still working. They sat for an hour, talking over what each of them had discovered and decided they would start looking into what Fred had got from Dr Mountford the next day.

Chapter 4

Getting home, Susan asked him where he had been to smell like he did. She said he smelt like an un-emptied ashtray. He said he would tell her all about it after he had had a shower and got changed into fresh casual clothes. Having been all over Mrs Good's house, it was not surprising his clothes smelt, and going into a house that had never had a smoker in it, it must have stunk to high heaven. He told Susan he would have to have his suit dry-cleaned and wrapped it up in a large bag when he took it off and emptied the pockets when he got undressed for his shower.

The children were both watching television when he got downstairs, so he joined them. The film they were watching was a humorous one, and so, the three of them sat together and laughed their heads off, so much so that Susan went in to see what they were laughing at. It was good for James, for it took the tension off what he was feeling and it was good for Fredrick and Joyce to see their Father enjoying himself in their company.

It was after they went to bed that night that James told Susan how his day had gone and why his clothes stank of cigarette smoke. He said how nice both Mrs Good was and how he found Mrs Brent.

He said he had to locate the second Mrs Good, but that would have to wait until another time. Susan was confused until it was explained to her that it appeared Gerald Good was a bigamist, or that is how it seemed; it would be confirmed when they had done some more research. If they found this suspicion to be true, then this could be the hold Brent had over Good if he knew, and how he was able to give him such a hard time.

The next morning, it was nearly nine o'clock by the time James, with Susan, arrived at the office to find Fred's car already outside. He was well-engrossed with what he was doing when they went in, so, they only got a grunt and 'Good morning' from him when they went in. It was only after Susan had opened the office up so to speak, and James had got the things he wanted from his briefcase that Fred put his pen down and apologised for not speaking properly when they arrived. He said he had been so engrossed in what he was writing he didn't want his train of thought interrupted. He said he was going through all the written information that John Mountford had supplied him with and was making notes and checking names, addresses and phone numbers of the old and new board of governors as well as the teachers that had been sacked by Oliver.

Susan asked if they both wanted coffee, and while she made it, they both sat at Fred's desk and started looking up the locations in an AA map book. They decided what ones they would do together and those they could each do separately to save a bit of time, for they really wanted to get a result for their efforts within the school holiday period. They thought that although they had information about the old board of governors, that was in the past, and that it is the present and future they were more interested in, and so they decided they would do the together visits first and fit the separate ones in whenever they could, as long as the whole thing was prioritised.

Although they decided this, James said he was going to go to Oliver's head office on his own purely so that anybody working there would not see Fred and would, therefore, think he was working alone, which might be a help further down the line of their enquiries. Fred agreed and said he would follow up on the other Mrs Good.

This made Susan smile and say, 'This all sounds too good to be true,' which, of course, made the two of them laugh. Fred looked up Mrs Goods address and said he could make that visit in a day and so would get on his way which he did, leaving James to spend the rest of the day finding out as much as he could about Anthony Oliver and his companies and what he traded in.

He first looked up Oliver's company offices in Oxford to get a telephone number so he could arrange the first contact. He realised what he was going to do was not going to be easy and maybe dangerous, but he had to start somewhere and thought it might as well be the best to go for the hornet's nest. He made a call to the number he had found and got a charming voice telling him he had got through to Oliver's Haulage. When asked who he wanted to speak to, he was a little discouraged because, of course, he didn't know, so he asked to speak to the senior person available.

He heard a little buzzing noise before the lady he spoke to said, 'You are through to Mr Conrad, the assistant manager.'

Before he could thank her, a voice said, 'Conrad here.'

James, thinking quickly and not knowing why, gave a false name, saying he was Edward Miles. Asked what he wanted, James said he wanted a very large load transported to Germany and was getting quotes from firms to do it. Mr Conrad, in a rather pompous-sounding voice, said there was no need to go to anyone else as Oliver's were the biggest and the best and would meet the lowest quote that he had so far acquired. James asked if he could call and see him and was told he could, but that it would have to wait for some time because he was being transferred to another section of Oliver's company as from tomorrow and therefore it would be a wasted journey. James said he wanted to speak to someone so who would it be. Mr Conrad suggested he speak to Mr Oliver's secretary tomorrow and she would be able to help him. James asked if it would be possible to speak to Mr Oliver himself and was told Mr Oliver was out of the country and would, he suspected, not see him personally even if he wasn't. He asked for the secretary's name and extension and said he would telephone later and rang off.

Not being satisfied with this, he decided to ring the secretary, and calling the number he had been given, together with the extension, he got through to a woman.

'Hello, Carol Jarvis speaking can I help you?'

James again gave his name as Edward Miles and told her he had spoken to Mr Conrad who gave him her number. She asked what he wanted, and on telling her what he had told Conrad, she gave a little sort of cough, saying if it was really important business that he wanted to discuss, could he come and see her today if it was possible. He said it was, and that he could make it after two o'clock. She said two o'clock would be fine, and so it was arranged.

Satisfied he had got his foot in the door, James had some thinking to do before setting off to Oxford, telling Susan he would drop her home before taking the car to Oxford. She just nodded, handing the road atlas to him and said the rest of the day off would be fine for her for there were lots for her to do at home.

By the time they got home after picking up some petrol, it was well into the morning before he got on his way to Oxford. He told Susan he might be late home but not to worry about it.

It was nearer three o'clock than two by the time he had found the offices he wanted and felt a little bit edgy when he found how large they were, this was obviously not a little tin pot company. He asked at reception if he could see Carol Jarvis and was asked who wanted her. The receptionist picked up a telephone and pressed a little lever and speaking into the phone asked if a person named Mr Edward Miles was expected. On getting an answer, she put the phone back in its cradle and gave James directions on how to get to Carol Jarvis's office.

Using the directions that he had been given, James found himself on the second floor at the front of the building. Getting to the door, that had quite a large embossed nameplate on it saying whose office it was, he knocked and was asked to go in. On opening the door, he walked into a very spacious room that was fit for any high executive rather than just a secretary. The lady sitting behind the desk was very attractive in what James' guess was in her early thirties. She stood up as James approached her desk, and moving around from behind it, she offered her hand before asking him to sit down on the chair she indicated. Not only was she attractive, she also had a figure that did plenty for her. After shaking hands, she went back behind her desk and sitting down asked James what he wanted. Being a hot-blooded man, he could imagine being in bed with this woman, but he just said what his business was.

He went over the conversation he had had with Mr Conrad and asked if she could help with what he wanted to do. She told him similar to what Conrad had told him but went into much more detail.

James mentioned how large the office building was for just a haulage company that made Carol smile. What was funny, he wanted to know and was told it was the offices for every enterprise Mr Oliver owned or had an interest in. James put on a green coat when asking what other companies Mr Oliver was involved in, as he had already researched some of them. To this, Carol became Mr Oliver's personal secretary. She indicated as politely as she could, that that was none of his business. However, she gave him the name of the gentleman who was going to be taking over from Mr Conrad and told him he would not be available until next week.

She told him where his office would be and gave him the extension number he would have to use. She asked if there was anything else that she could help him with, as she was a very busy lady especially when Mr Oliver was out of the country.

Getting up, James thanked her for seeing him and said he could find his own way out. Shaking hands and taking a slightly more detailed look around the room as he did so, left her to get on with what she was doing before he went into her office.

As he left Carol's office, he decided to have a look around to see what he could learn, if anything, before leaving the building. Starting from the second floor that he was on, he went around that, and then to the upper floor where the offices seemed occupied by more than one person. He took a mental note of the name plaques on the doors for he could not stop outside and write them down. Getting to the bottom floor and looking for Mr Oliver's office, he bumped into a young man who was carrying an armful of dockets. He asked him where Mr Oliver's office was and being told he was just going there; he could follow him. This he did, and on getting to it, he realised it was directly below the office he had just left. Going in, the young lad handed the folders to a lady and closing the door behind him left leaving James standing outside, taking no further notice of him. He wondered if he should knock the door but decided that would be futile, for what could he say that would justify him being there. He just checked the rest of the ground floor that included a very large and comfortable-looking canteen. The canteen staff members who were obviously closing it down for the day, were just doing what had to be done before leaving for home.

He had been in Oliver's offices for just over an hour, and other than having a good look around he had achieved nothing, or so he thought. He stopped for something to eat in Oxford before making his way home, that he did in just over two hours. Getting there, Susan asked if he had had any success and what were the offices like. He said not very successful other than knowing what Mr Oliver's head office was all about. She asked if he had eaten, and when being told yes, she started clearing their meal things away. While she did that, James telephoned Fred to find out if he was home yet and what his day had been like. On answering it, Fred said he would tell him all about it tomorrow as he was just having his evening meal. Satisfied with that, he put the phone down and spent the rest of the day spending time with his children until their bedtime.

Getting to the office the next morning, James decided he would try and get to see where Edward Andrews (Flashman) lived and what sort of background he came from. He was looking up the direction to the address that Stella had given him when Fred arrived quickly followed by Susan. On getting themselves sorted out, James stopped what he was doing and asked Fred what his visit to the other Mrs Good had achieved. Fred went through what his visit had been like and how he was sure his Mrs Good was absolutely clueless about her husband being a bigamist.

When he got to the house, he found that Gerald Good was away on a fishing trip with a neighbour for a couple of days, but Mrs Good let him in after he told her he was from the education department and he was writing a book about teacher's wives, and hers had come up as the wife of a headmaster at a private school.

'She asked me in and to take a seat in her lounge. I told her that most of the ladies I had so far spoken to were the wives of teachers from all levels of teaching, but she was the first of a headmaster. She said she was very interested and would like to know how other wives found it being the wife of a teacher. She seemed to be quite upper crust and her home was classy. She had not held back on spending money on what she liked.' The furnishings were all quality, just the opposite of how James had described how the other Mrs Good's was. She explained that because she had never been able to have children, she had spent a lot of her time doing charity work, mainly with the elderly. She said her husband had been quite happy at all the schools he had taught at until he went as headmaster to the private school he was at now. He spent time having to go to meetings, but it didn't put her out very much as she had got used to it; she had plenty of friends, and she entertained them a lot while Gerald was boarded at the school. She said that at holiday times, they spent time together, but her husband wasn't a very social man and didn't enjoy the women she associated with very much.

He asked how long they had been married and she just smiled and said, 'Quite a long time.' It was when she got around to talking about the charity work that she did, it came up that she was wealthy enough not to go to work in a paid job, or have to rely on Gerald's salary. She said she had a private income left to her by her father when he died. She said her father was a very shrewd man and left her mother with the house and a pension income, her brother with the very profitable business and her with the savings he had put in trust for her when she became twenty years old.

Fred couldn't remember how it got around to who her brother was, but she said her mother lived with him and his wife and was becoming quite frail. He said it came quite out of the blue that his business was mentioned and that he had taken over from his father and had grown it substantially since their father died.

She never said anything else other than it was mainly haulage and he lived near Oxford. Fred asked if she got on well with her sister-in-law and was told, not very well, and that she was the reason she didn't see her brother very much, in fact, hardly at all these days.

Getting back to Gerald, she said it was her brother that got him the job at the private school as a teacher, but then when a vacancy arose, he was promoted to headmaster. She mentioned that he no longer entertains like he used to, which she supposed was one of the ways he had changed, but he helps her when she entertains and he was at home.

To break away from the subject of school, he asked about holidays they have at school holiday time, to which she said most of the time, they go on different holidays as their interests were completely different for instance, she liked the sun, hospitality and company abroad, and Gerald liked a quiet life and the occasional game of golf, mainly in our own country.

'It suits us both, and perhaps it is good for us both being that way.'

It was at this point that she said, 'I am so sorry, we have been sitting here talking and I haven't offered you a drink. Would you like one, and if you would what would it be?' Fred said, 'Coffee would be very nice.' He was asked what type of coffee? Being given a verbal list of what was available, black or white sugar, etc., he chose what he wanted and how he wanted it, and she got up and left the room.

Learning from James, he took the opportunity to look at the photographs that were scattered around the room, mostly all in silver frames. One he particularly took note of was what he assumed was of the direct family, mother, father, her, a sister and her brother. There was also one of a man dressed in army uniform and another with the same two men as in the family photo together, displaying their medals.

Fred, hearing the cups rattling, quickly sat back down in his chair as if he hadn't moved. When Mrs Good came in with the tea trolley, he moved to accept the cup and saucer she offered him and brought a little table from the nest nearby and put it beside him.

Taking her own, she said, 'Now, where were we?'

Fred said, 'We were talking about holidays.'

'Oh, yes,' she said, 'I have had some great ones and have travelled a lot over the years since my father died.'

Fred said it got to the point where he wanted to get away as this woman wouldn't stop talking about herself. However, before he left, he managed to ask her who were in some of the photographs she had on display.

'I am not so sure that was a sensible thing to do, for she went into so much detail in who they were and their life story. However, it was confirmed who the family group were, and that I was correct assuming who those in uniform were, but it was by, "My Father" and "My Brother" and not by name. However, I have a mental picture so that if ever we bump into her brother, I will know who he is.'

It was over three hours before Fred got the opportunity to leave and, thanking her for the chat and hospitality, left for home. James asked what the house was like and was told not over large but in a very posh area and, by what he could make of it, not very old. He said it looked as if it had been designed and built to order rather than just a house they had found. James asked how much he had managed to find out about Gerald Good.

Fred said, 'Believe it or not, not very much, it was established that he does his own thing and she does hers most of the time, and they just get on in the meantime. He spends the school holidays at home, but according to his wife, he is not as he was before becoming the headmaster but never once mentioned the school by name. She said there is one particular master that is upsetting him, but he doesn't or will not mention his name ever. I am convinced she doesn't know he is married to another woman that has a son. I didn't go into why, when she said she couldn't have children, or the reason for it.'

In Fred's opinion, his trip was worthwhile in as much as they should not bother to follow up on her, as they would be wasting time that could be better spent in other ways.

Chapter 5

The discussion between them now was what would come next. James couldn't make up his mind whether to go to Andrews' house on his own or if they should go together, before starting to visit the current board of directors. He decided with a bit of persuasion from Susan, who apologised for butting in, that it would be more productive to both go together.

Fred said he had brought his overnight bag with him just in case he had to use it, but James said it wouldn't be needed as they should get the visit done in a day easily.

This agreed, they set off in James's car to the address James was looking up when Fred and Susan had arrived. He said he didn't know how long it would take to get there, but they should be able to get back to the office that day so that Fred could pick his car up.

'What are we going to use as a reason for the visit?' Fred asked, to which James, on thinking about it, said, 'I think what you used as a reason to get to see Mrs Good was a good one, but not to write a book. We will be conducting a survey of schools in the area, for the address we are going to is only about twenty miles from the school.' This was agreed, and knowing that they would have to play it by ear and think on their feet as they went, they made the journey in good time and without going wrong with their directions.

The house they arrived at was large with iron gates and a long drive. Fred got out of the car and went to the call box. He pressed the button as instructed on the instrument and waited for an answer.

He didn't wait long before a voice asked who he was and what he wanted. He said he was from the Education Authority and wanted to speak to Mr Henry Andrews.

The voice said, 'The gates will open and shut automatically behind you, and don't leave your car until you get to the house as there are guard dogs on patrol in the grounds.' With that, there was a little click, and the gates started to open. Getting quickly back in the car, Fred said he didn't think this was an ordinary house.

Driving up the drive, passing a couple of gardeners on the way, they parked outside the house where a man was standing outside the front door. With him, he had one of the biggest Doberman Pinschers they had ever seen.

'Good morning,' the man said and asked who did they want to see.

Fred said, 'Mr Henry Andrews.' The man asked them to follow him, telling the dog to stay…and guard. As the dog lay down, they followed him into the house. He led them through the entrance hall, past the billiard room that had the door ajar and out into a rather large solarium.

The man asked them to take a seat in one of the wicker chairs with palatial cushions while he went to find Mr Andrews.

It was quite a time before the man came in from the garden, followed by another man dressed in riding attire and carrying a riding crop. He told the man to get the stable lad to sort out the horses and to report to him when he had finished, giving him the crop to put away.

'Yes, sir,' he said with a slight bow and left.

'Now, gentleman, I am Sir Henry Andrews, what do you require of me?' James answered by saying they were from the Education Authority and had got his address from a list of board of governors and thought he might help them by giving them some information about the Radcliff Private School for boys at Monkshire.

'What sort of information?' he asked. James was thankful he had not been asked for anything to prove they were from the EA for, of course, he had nothing and would have had a problem. He said he was on the board of governors at that school and two others, but he had had to be persuaded to go on the board at Radcliff's.

Sitting down himself, he said he had been asked by Oliver to become a school governor after he had placed his son Edward at the school, just having to mention as a bye the bye that Edward had been made head prefect. He said he refrained from accepting the offer in the beginning because it wouldn't seem right in the eyes of other parents who had boys at the school, but that he was persuaded, using the argument that it would give the school more credibility if it became known that one of the board of governor's son was a boarder. James asked if he was a friend of the owner or just an acquaintance.

He said, 'A friendship of sorts was formed while we were in the army together. I tell you what, come with me to my study and I will tell you more there, where we can have a drink if you would like one?' They got up and followed him through the house into a quite large room where they were invited to take a seat in two comfortable chairs while he sat in the one behind his desk that he pulled out and sat on. He picked up his telephone and pressed a button on it. He waited a short while and spoke into it, asking someone to come to his study. He asked if they would like a beverage or gin and tonic as it was gin and tonic time for him, as he put it, looking at his watch and invited them to join him and keep him company. James said,

'That would be a good idea.' Fred nodded too.

It wasn't long before there was a knock at the door and a man came in.

'Will you bring me three gin and tonics, ice and lemon and ask the cook to make some sandwiches for three?'

'Yes, sir,' the man said and left. While they waited for their refreshments, Fred asked if they would be able to speak to Edward if he was home. He said he was out in the grounds somewhere, so Fred said he would go and find him after they had eaten.

James asked how long had he spent in the army and what rank had he reached when he left. He said, 'Let the photographs tell you.' It was then that they saw all the photographs around the room. Inviting them to get up, he showed them his career in picture form, explaining who was who and what was what as they went around. James was particularly interested in a few of them as he had seen them before in Walter Brent's house. There was one that had the man in it that James said met them when they arrived.

'Oh!' he said, 'Yes, that was my batman that is now my butler Harry; he is a good man. He was appointed to me when I was made a major and stayed with me until I was invalided out with heart trouble just before I was about to be promoted to major general. I went into the army as an officer cadet after leaving the grammar school and worked my way up. I was promoted quite quickly because I worked hard, passed all my examinations and became the best cadet at Sandhurst. I was a camp commander by the time I was thirty as a major. When I was next promoted, I became office-bound in London and remained there for the rest of my army service. It was mainly in an advisory capacity and with a vast amount of responsibility. I started the business I run now when I came out of the army, but I work close to them in retirement from it.'

'What business is that?' Fred asked and was told armaments and weaponry, but would not enlarge on that. He said he owned a large company now and had received a knighthood two years ago.

The door was knocked and when told to enter, Harry came in with a large tray containing all that he was told to supply. He put it down on a table and did all the serving out from it to the three of them, as they told him what they wanted and how they wanted it. When this was completed, he went to leave the room, but before closing the door, he said, looking at Henry, the groom was seeing to both horses, but he had told him to wait until your visitors had gone before he reports to you, sir. Harry was told that was fine and that he had done well.

While they ate and drank what Harry had brought in, the discussion returned to the school and how he had got involved in it. Henry said it was when he joined the Freemason's that he met Tony Oliver again, after not seeing him since he left the army.

'He was a good officer under my command and was ruthless when he undertook the tasks he was given. He came to me in London and I put him on procurement. He came from a rich family, and since his father died leaving him with the family business, he has and is still, doing well. He has taken the haulage business into all sorts of directions, buying up companies as time has gone on. It was a surprise to me when he told me he had bought a private boys school and it was then that I told him I would put my son there. He said he was doing a clear-out of the old board of governors and asked if I would like to become one. I eventually agreed and as a reward for that support, he supposed, Edward Andrews was made the head prefect.'

They had finished their lunch when Fred said he would like to find Edward and asked if he could be excused. This agreed, he left James with Henry still talking while he went back to the solarium and out into the grounds. It was not just a garden for there were acres of it, hence the stables and the horse riding. He went around the stables, glancing inside as he went. There were three horses in it, and the place was spotless. He could see the groom scrubbing out and another man in what Fred could only imagine was a small forge attached to the stables.

It took him nearly a quarter of an hour to find Edward, who was shooting with a rather lethal-looking rifle. He did not see Fred coming, being so intent on shooting at anything that moved.

It was only when the dog he had with him barked that he turned to see Fred coming. He heard him tell the dog to stay, and standing the rifle down, he asked Fred what he wanted or was he trespassing.

Fred told him who he was, and that he wanted to know about the school he went to. Edward was a big lad, much like his father, and had the same sort of arrogance about him. Fred asked him if he liked the school and the staff and how much longer he had to do at it. Edward answered he was the head prefect and as such had certain privileges that other students didn't have, he said it was a position of power. Asked if there was any particular master he got on with, that he admired and tried to emulate, he immediately said without hesitation, 'Mr Brent.' Fred was not surprised to hear this but asked if there was any particular reason for it. Edward just said, 'He is a disciplinarian, and I like that, everybody seems to be frightened of him.' Fred asked about the younger boys, and how they were dealt with. He just said, 'If they step out of line, they are punished, and Mr Brent sees to that.'

'Are the prefects able to give out punishments like fagging in the old days?' He said no, but he was working on it. He said, all they could do was give out lines, and if the kids don't do them, the prefects report it to Mr Brent who deals with it. Fred asked if there had been much change when Dr Mountford left and was told there was, for that silly old fool was only interested in education and getting boys to university. He said he was glad he had left, and that it gave him and his fellow prefects, who he was now able to choose, more authority than they had been given by the old headmaster.

Fred asked what he thought about Dr Mountford's relief. Edward never hesitated, he just said he was a weakling and didn't know how he got the job, for it would have been far more sensible to have given the job to Mr Brent. He asked if he knew what school Mr Brent came from, to which he said, 'No, but from snippets of conversations I have overheard, when I had heard my father talking, it seems it is through the army and being a Freemason.' It was then that Edward asked what all the questions were for, and Fred had to explain it was all to do with the information the Education Authority required from all the schools in the area.

Seeing a movement, Edward picked up the rifle and fired at a rabbit that lept up in the air before dropping dead on the ground. Fred asked if he got enjoyment out of killing living creatures, and the answer he got was, 'It was much more satisfying than firing at a paper target.' Fred asked him if he enjoyed being cruel, to which he failed to answer. He just said, 'His father had given him the rifle, so why not use it for what it was made for…? Killing. Fred asked how easy it was to make friends at the school,' to which Edward answered, 'It was easier before Mountford left, but now no one gives a toss.'

Fred asked if his father went to all the board of governors and parent-teacher meetings and was told that he goes to the first and not to the second, probably just to meet up to find out how the other governors were getting on. He went on to say that the teachers and parents thing was a waste of time because his father would tell him if there was anything worth telling, plus the fact, I can't leave school fast enough. This led Fred to ask what he wanted to do as a job when he left school?

'I'm not really interested at the moment, but I will probably join the family business, for when my dad snuffs it, there is nobody else to take it over.'

'What about your mother?' Fred asked.

'She wouldn't have a clue how to run anything, so it would have to be up to me.'

'What does your mother think when you talk like that?'

'She can think what she likes, but it won't make any difference to me, for when I leave school, I will do what I like.'

Fred thanked him for being so frank and wished him all the best for the future, with tongue in cheek, leaving him to kill the next thing that moved.

As he walked back to the house, he realised what a spoilt brat he had been talking to with a rich boy's attitude, and what he must be like at school and to his godson.

Passing the forge, he called in and spoke to the blacksmith or farrier, he was not sure which. He was making horseshoes when Fred drew his attention to his presence.

'Hello, mate, what can I do for you?' Fred just said he had always fancied working with his hands and asked how long he had worked there. He said for five years and how much he liked working there. He said he did both jobs, with the odd roof thatching repair. Did he get call-outs from other people in the area who own horses? He said he had a full-time job, trying to keep up with the work coming in from outside customers as he called them. Fred asked what it was like working for Sir Henry Andrews. He said he was all right but ruled with a rod of iron if he didn't mind the pun. He said it was his son he couldn't get on with.

'He is the most spoilt, ignorant obnoxious sod, he is detestable, and if I didn't think I would get the sack he would get a hinding from me. It is, however, his mother, the lady of the house that I feel sorry for, as the pair of them treat her like dirt. She sometimes comes in for a little chat when she visits the horses, I think to have a good moan, knowing it won't ever go any further.

She is a lovely woman and far too good for either of her men, not to mention Mr Andrews' sister who lives with them. Another I have no time for.' Fred wanted to know if he lived local and was told he had a cottage in the village where he lived with his wife and two teenage boys. Fred said how nice it was to talk to him, but thinking he had spent enough time away from the house, he said cheerio, and shaking the blacksmith's hand, walked the rest of the way back to the house.

Getting back, he let himself into the conservatory, and taking his shoes off and leaving them by the door, he made his way back to Henry's study where he knocked the door and was told to go in. James was looking a little flushed when he sat down and wondered why. Had he found his son, Henry wanted to know, and was he able to help you?

'He is a good boy, albeit a little wild at times.' Fred said he had found him with a rifle and what he was doing with it, to which Henry laughed.

'He is a very good shot and can score much higher than me when we get on the range together.'

Turning back to James, he said, 'What were we talking about?' James said,

'Your connection with Anthony Oliver.'

'Oh yes, we do business together. He does a lot of transporting for me and has never let me down, I think he is a great man who has become a good friend.'

It was after three o'clock when James said they must get going, for they had another call to make before getting back to their office. They shook hands and Henry hoped he had been helpful. As he opened the study door for them, Harry was standing outside with Fred's shoes in his hand all nice and clean and polished.

'I thought you might want these,' he said, looking down at Fred's feet. Fred thanked him and said how kind of him it was, to which Henry butted in to say what a good batman he had been in the army and as a butler now. Putting his shoes on, Harry said he would show them to the front door which he did, leaving Henry to go back into his study.

Thanking Harry, they got into the car and started down the drive to the main road. As they approached the gates, they started to open and driving through them without having to stop, making their way back to their office.

The conversation between them on the drive back was rather interesting, for when Fred said he seemed a little bit flushed when he returned from speaking to Edward Andrews, James said he would tell him all that was done and said while he was away. As for being flushed, it might have been due to the gin, but probably more to do with being angry.

'Angry with him,' James said, 'He is one of the most self-opinionated men I have had the misfortune to meet; he thinks so much of himself you would never believe.' He asked Fred how he had found the son. Fred said, he had found him much like his father, from what James had said, and so cruel, he could well imagine what he was like at school with what power being the head prefect gave him, he needs a bloody good hiding, which the blacksmith would give him if he didn't know he would lose his job.

'What's this about a blacksmith?' James wanted to know, to which Fred went over the conversation he had had in the forge. One thing he mentioned was the way the two of them treat Mrs Andrews, in his words 'Like dirt!'

'This might be worth following up if we get a chance and maybe check on Henry's sister who lives with them.'

Getting back to the office, there was just time to think through what they would do tomorrow. James said they would start with the other new members of the board of governors, and that it might be best if they did the rest of them together as two heads were always better than one, starting with a Mr B.W. Keen, who makes his living from pharmaceutical products and hospital equipment. They checked on the address that was at Benfield and, looking up Oxen, found that if they got the time, they could visit both places as they were only thirty-five miles apart. The second member was Mr George Bateman who traded in farm machinery. It was decided they would leave the office at nine o'clock in the morning and see how they got on with their enquiries. James said it might be better to take a chance and go without contacting them, so they would catch them cold.

Chapter 6

After calling around to pick Fred up, James popped into their office to collect the road map that he had forgotten to put in his briefcase the night before. Getting back in the car, he gave it to Fred and asked him to give him the directions to Benfield. It was a shorter distance than James had estimated, and being little traffic, they made good time. They got to the company office at ten-thirty and parked up next to an MG sports car.

'If that is Mr Keen's vehicle, he is doing all right for himself,' Fred said as they passed the almost new-looking car. They walked from the car park to the front door of the office where they rang the bell. They didn't have long to wait for the door to be opened where stood quite an old man. He asked who they wanted, and when told Mr Barry Keen, he said that was his son and he would take them to his office. The old man had difficulty climbing the stairs, but managing it slowly, he got to an office door at the end of a passageway. Knocking it and getting a "Come in", they entered the room. The old man told his son these gentlemen wanted to speak to him and hoped it would be convenient. Putting his pen down and taking his glasses off, Barry got up from his chair and, coming around his desk, shook hands and asked them to take a seat.

The old man asked if he was wanted, and on being told 'No', he left, shutting the door behind him.

'What can I do for you, gentlemen?' he asked. 'And who are you?' James gave him their business card and said he was James Royston and his partner there, looking over to Fred, was Fred Baker. Studying the card, Barry Keen asked what private detectives wanted with him. James said they believed he was a member of the board of governors at the Radcliff Private Boys School in Monkshire.

'Oh!' he said, sitting back down in his chair, 'What about it?'

'We would like you to answer some questions for us, as we are investigating the running of the school and its management.'

'Like what?' Barry asked. James asked how he became a school governor when his business was pharmaceuticals and hospital equipment and how did he get to know Mr Anthony Oliver. Fred spoke for the first time when he enquired if it was anything to do with the Freemasons or if he had a boy at the school. Barry said it was a long story that involved his father who showed them up to his office.

Barry said his father had met Oliver when he was running the business, that he had started from scratch, but he was afraid in the last year and a half, he was making a rather bad job of, before retiring and handing the reigns over to him.

He said, 'Nothing to do with freemasonry, Oliver's used to undertake all their transport commitments. His father had got behind with payments for this service and owed Oliver a great deal of money. That was really why my dad retired, after having a heart attack, and asked me to take over. When I had repaid the debt we owed, I tried to drop Olivers and get another cheaper haulage company in. This he would not let me do, saying my father had agreed and signed a long-term contract, and he wasn't going to release me from it. I threatened to take him to court to get that contract rescinded which is when he turned nasty but in a very subtle way. He invited me to his house for dinner and threatened me with bankruptcy unless I agreed to become a governor of the school he had purchased and that I would have to become a fee-paying member and contribute to its upkeep. I know nothing about running a school and don't want to, but I am afraid I am lumbered with it, for I must protect my father from this man. He doesn't keep good health now, and I am sure having to go through the courts of law would kill him. I don't know exactly what he has got over my father, but it is enough to blackmail us which he is doing.'

James, having sat and listened to all this intently, asked if he was prepared to help them, as they could almost certainly get the situation resolved but only with his and others cooperation. There might have to be a small charge for their services if they were successful, but that would come much later. Fred asked how his business was going and got a positive response. He said trade was good and the profit margin he had created was very satisfactory and could only improve if he could get Oliver off his back. James said they would try to help him with this, but they have other reasons for pursuing Mr Oliver and the school purchase. Barry warned them to be careful as Oliver was a very rich, ruthless and powerful man. James said they would, but that he must not mention a word of there visit to anyone and to tell his father it was two men from a supply firm that had called, so as not to worry him.

James asked him if he could see the contract his father had signed. Barry went to a safe and withdrew a bundle of papers that he passed to James, saying they were copies but his solicitor had the originals. James asked if they could take the contract away with them to study in length.

Barry said he could but asked if he would return them as soon as possible and making James sign for them.

Saying he may not hear from them for a while, for there was a lot more investigation to be undertaken, but to be assured the matter would be ongoing and they would contact him again whenever there was a need. Before leaving, Barry asked how they had found out about him, and James replied that he wasn't the only one that had a grudge against Mr Oliver, and leaving it at that, he shook hands, ready to go. As they went back down the stairs to the front door, James and Fred wished him well and hoped his dad would be unaffected with all that was going on. Barry escorted them to their car, which gave Fred the opportunity to comment on his. Barry said it was a present to himself for that was his interest, rather than to impress the ladies if they understood what he meant. Fred gave him a wink-wink and they all laughed. Shaking hands again before they got in their car and waving as they passed him, they made their way to Oxen.

By this time, the traffic was quite busy, and meeting up with a car crash on the way made them later than they wanted to be getting to see George Bateman. They drove into his yard where there was a car parking area amongst the tractors and other farm machinery on display. Going into the office, they were confronted by a receptionist who politely asked if they had an appointment and with whom. James said they wanted to speak to Mr Bateman. Looking in what was obviously an appointment book, she asked their names. James said they hadn't made an appointment but wondered if Mr Bateman would be kind enough to see them. She said she would see, as he was not over busy that day.

Going away, and returning, she said, Mr Bateman was just going for a late lunch and would be prepared to see them in the local pub, and that he would be out shortly if they were prepared to wait.

Within ten minutes, a very heavily-built man emerged from the same direction that the receptionist had come from, and going over to the receptionist, he asked if those were the two men wishing to see him. On saying they were, she gave him their names. Going over to James and Fred, offering his hand, he introduced himself. He said he was just nipping to his local for a bite to eat if they would like to join him, but adding quickly not at his expense. James and Fred smiled and said it was good of him to see them at such short notice and that they hoped they wouldn't spoil his lunch.

They walked together the two hundred yards or so to the 'Kings Arms' where George was obviously well known. The landlord asked if he was eating, to which he said 'Yes', and asked if he could manage a table for three. Being shown to a table, they sat down and each was given the menu.

After choosing what they wanted and ordering a drink, George asked, 'So what is this all about?' James said who they were and gave him their business card. Studying it, he asked what private investigators wanted with him.

'We are made to understand you are a school governor at the Radcliff private school for boys.' He confirmed that was correct, and a position he never wanted. So why did he take the post on, and how did he come into contact with Mr Anthony Oliver? Once again, it took some explaining.

He said he had got into quite a lot of debt with his business, when there had been a serious fire in his showroom and repair workshop a few years ago, and he had not been adequately insured. He said all his transport requirements were carried out by Olivers who said they would help him out, or at least the owner did.

'I was invited to a meeting with the man himself who said he would bankroll me out of my debts but wanted me to give him sole rights to my haulage requirements and twenty per cent of my company. At that time, I was at my wits end, not knowing which way to turn, so I agreed to his terms.

He had put the price of haulage up which started crippling me, so when he said he had purchased a school, and if I contributed to its funding and become a member of the board of governors, he would reduce the price and cancel the twenty per cent of my company ownership, but only if I agreed with the amount I have to pay to the school.'

Fred asked him if he goes to the board of governor's meetings, and does he know how the school is being managed, and what it's reputation standing is? George said he goes to the meetings but never contributes to them because he has no interest in it, only what he has to pay towards its upkeep. What about the other members of the board, he was asked and answered, to those he had spoken to they felt the same as him, that they knew they were being ripped off but could do nothing about it due to the hold Oliver had over them. Two of the board members David Bright and Barry Keen are under the threat of bankruptcy if they decide to drop out of the school governorship.

'The bloody man is evil, in that he doesn't care about anything other than making money, legally or otherwise.'

Having listened to this, James asked him how much he would like to be rid of the commitments he had to Oliver. He said he would give anything. James said they might be able to help him, but a small charge would have to be made, and that they might seek his assistance at a later date if they were to be successful.

To this, George agreed and said the price of their meal was on him.

James asked if he was married and did he have a family, to which he replied he was married and had two boys, both at boarding school, not Radcliff's, he quickly added. He said that was because he and his wife had gone through a rough patch with their marriage due mainly to the business, but that everything was now fine and the boys liked the boarding school and chose to remain there. Leaving the pub and getting back to their car, rather than going back to George's office when invited, they said their farewells and drove off towards Southampton.

On the way back, Fred wondered if the other board members were in similar situations, that none of them were volunteers, maybe excepting for Henry Andrews, but all being forced into it? James just commented that only time would tell, but Mr Oliver was going to be a hard man to bring down if that was what they were trying to do.

When they got back to the office, they looked up the addresses for Mr David Bright and Joe Mather. David in Deyton and Joe in Botmouth, fifty miles apart.

'Which one first?' Fred asked.

'Whichever is the furthest away, so we have less distance to travel home,' James answered. So it was agreed they start with David Bright, leaving the office at eight-thirty in the morning.

They looked up the distance from the office and got an approximate distance of eighty miles. So, with nothing more they could do and with Susan not there, James said he would see Fred in the morning.

Getting home himself, he asked what sort of day Susan had had and was told she had spent the day with the children. They had supported Joyces' hockey team who were playing in the semi-final of the school's cup and had done very well. Afterwards, they had high tea in the new tea rooms near the recreation ground, and now that they were home the pair of them said they would get on and finish the last bits of their homework. Susan asked how he and Fred had got on and were they able to do two visits or only one. James said they had managed to see the two men, and that the pair of them don't want to be school governors but really have no choice. He said they were going to see the last two tomorrow and hoped to learn more of the pressure being put on these men by Mr Oliver.

Having had a good night's sleep, both James and Fred were ready for the new day.

James once again picking Fred up to go to the office before making the journey to Deyton. Susan said she might go to the office to deal with whatever she could from yesterday's and today's mail and take any phone calls if they came in.

It was after ten o'clock when they pulled up at a very large furniture shop.

It was two buildings knocked into one with very large furniture display windows. They parked in the road as near to the front door as they could, and on locking the car, they went into the shop. A very smartly dressed young man asked them if he could help, to which James said they would like to speak with Mr Bright, the owner. The young man said he would go and see, while they looked around the shop.

They realised, looking around that this was a quality establishment, selling very expensive furniture.

Carpets and all sorts of household fittings where all quality and only for the well-off customers.

The young man came back to them and said he would take them to his father's office in about ten to fifteen minutes when he had finished with a customer. In the meantime, he asked if they would like a cup of coffee. Saying 'Yes', he arranged it with a young lady. He took them to a little room where there were chairs and a rather nice coffee table. Asking them to take a seat, he asked if there was anything he could help them with. James asked him how long the shop had been open and was told the business was started by his great grandfather in the late eighteen hundreds and been handed down from father to son until now. How long has this shop been here, he was asked and said it started as just one building, but over the years, it had become two, and there was another branch about ten miles away that his mother managed with the help of his sister.

It was just as they finished the rather nice cup of coffee that David Bright appeared. He introduced himself and asked if they had been looked after by his son. On saying they had, James asked if they could go to his office. He readily agreed and, on passing the young lady that had made their coffee, asked her to make him one. On getting to the office, David asked his son to manage the shop while he was engaged and left him to do just that.

'Right then, gentlemen, what can I do for you?' James introduced themselves and, as before, gave David their business card. Looking at it, he asked what two private investigators wanted from him, surely not furniture! James smiled and said, 'Do you know Mr Anthony Oliver?' Just mentioning the name made David nearly spill the coffee he had just received. Calming himself down, he said he did, and what was all this about, James asked what his connection with Oliver was?

Once again, it was a bit of a long story. David said he had been employing Olivers to do all his transportation and haulage for a number of years, but recently, he had almost doubled his charges that was making his furniture so expensive, even the well-off customers were staying away from his shops. The other branch being run by his wife was also feeling her customer numbers were reducing. He explained that he could not absorb the increase in costs, and by passing even some of it on to his customers was affecting the business quite badly. So what was he doing about it, James wanted to know. He flushed up a bit, and James couldn't make up his mind whether it was due to anger or embarrassment, but David said a solution had been met.

He said he and his wife were invited to dinner by Anthony Oliver who, during the meal, brought up the fact that he had just purchased a school and had to have a board of governors, and that he wanted David to become one of them. David, with the backing of his wife, said he knew nothing about being a school governor and was not the man for him. This is when the conversation changed and became serious instead of how it had been up-until then quite social. Oliver said he needed a board of governors who had to contribute to the upkeep of the school, and that he considered David ideal for his requirements. David said that he was being bled dry by this man and made that quite plain to him. It was then that Oliver came up with the proposal that he would reduce his haulage costs to what they had been and gave the figure he wanted his board of governors to cough up each year.

'So he was more or less blackmailing you into something you didn't want anything to do with?'

'That's more or less it. My wife was so furious I am sure she could have killed him before we left.'

Fred asked, having sat listening to what David had told them, whether he had been to any of the board of governors meetings. David said that he had, and the only thing all he and the other members could agree with was that they were all being ripped off by a ruthless megalomaniac.

The next question was, and neither James or Fred had thought to ask it before during their enquiries, were the payments they were being made to pay for shares in the school? The answer to that was no, the school and its grounds were ninety-five per cent owned by Oliver and the small number of shares he didn't hold was held by the old retired headmaster. However, there was a question as to whether Henry Andrews, who always has a lot to say and is always in agreements with whatever Oliver puts up for discussion has any or is trying to acquire some. Did he go to parent-teacher meetings, Fred wanted to know. He said he went to the last one, but that was the first and probably the last. Had he met the headmaster and did he come across a teacher by the name of Walter Brent?

He said, as a matter of fact, he had, and what a diverse pair of individuals they were. The headmaster looked like a proper wimp while the master under him came across as such a dominant man, their roles should have been reversed. However, one was a nice man and looked it, while the other I wouldn't give the time of day to. Did he speak to either of them, James wanted to know, to which he answered, to the headmaster briefly, but to Walter Brent for much longer. He really thinks something of himself but didn't impress him one little bit.

'I rather thought he spent more time mentally undressing the mothers than on telling them how their sons were progressing with their school work.

Oliver spent a lot of time speaking to Henry Andrews and his poor wife; I say that because she spent a lot of the evening on her own and looking most uncomfortable. I asked my wife to go and keep her company for a while and later learnt she is a nice woman, totally domineered by her husband. As a member of the board, Andrews pranced about like he owned the school rather than just being a governor of it. His son is rather big-headed too, seems it runs in the male side of the family.'

The question was asked if he realised the reputation of the school was running down, to which he said no, but that if he was a boy, he wouldn't want to go to it and certainly wouldn't send his son to it. It was then that James came clean and said his son goes to it and what he had told him goes on there. He gave him a quick rundown on what they wanted to do and asked David if they could call on his support if it was ever needed. David agreed to help in any way he could and would not mention to a sole that they had spoken to him and what they were doing. He said if he could get out from under the blackmail-type scenario he was suffering, he would do anything he could to help.

On not having anything further they could think to ask David Bright, they said they must take their leave, just mentioning that they were going to try and visit Joe Mather in Botmouth.

'If you manage to see him, will you please give him my regards? For he is another one like me who is under financial blackmail. He is a very nice fellow and the only one of the board members I keep in touch with.' After shaking hands and saying cheerio to David's son, they left and went back to their car.

It took them well over an hour to get to Botmouth from Deyton where they found the road and bridge building offices they were looking for. Once again, they had to put their most persuasive tongues on to get to see Mr Mather. His receptionist asked if they had an appointment and when told no, she shook her head and said it would be impossible to see her boss, but would his partner do. James asked her if Mr Mather was in work today. She said he was but that he would not see them, only if they had an appointment. Taking out their business card from his wallet, James asked if she would be kind enough to take it to her boss, that what they wanted was very important and that time was not available to make an appointment. She looked at it herself before saying she would see what she could do.

She came back to tell them Mr Mather would see them in two hours' time if they could afford to wait that long. James told her they would, and it would give them time to have a late lunch, and asked if she could recommend anywhere they might go to?' She asked what type of lunch they wanted, and when told, she gave them the names of a pub and a restaurant.

They decided to go to a pub and made for the one she had recommended and gave them the directions for.

Although the time was getting on, they were still in good time to order lunch. On entering the establishment and going to the bar, they were escorted to a table for two, given menus and asked if they would like a drink while they waited for their meal. They both ordered a light lunch and a drink, which they made last until the landlord called time just before three o'clock. On leaving the pub, they made their way back to Joe Mather's offices where this time, they were welcomed by the receptionist who said her boss was ready to see them. She escorted them to his office, and on entering in front of them, she introduced them before leaving. Joe Mather was a very intellectual-looking man with longish hair and thick horn-rimmed glasses and was dressed very casually in a checked shirt and corduroy trousers. He asked them to sit down in chairs while he sat on a high bench stool in front of a large drawing board. He said he didn't have many private detectives calling on him, and so he was very intrigued as to what they wanted. James asked him firstly, was he a board of governors member of the Radliff private school for boys at Monkshire. Before answering that, he had a rather quizzical look on his face. James asked how well did he know the owner of the school, Mr Anthony Oliver. He said he used his company to transport all the materials he needed in his work building roads, bridges, and any other structures that came under civil engineering. How did he find him to work with, Fred asked, to which he replied that up until he purchased the school, he had been reasonable, but after inviting himself and his wife to dinner one evening, he became one of the evilest men he had ever met.

'At first, the evening went very well until he dropped a bombshell that was to affect me badly, to a point where I could go out of business.'

James and Fred sat and listened as they were told how Oliver had put the same or similar proposition to him as he had the others he wanted for his board of governors. Pay towards the upkeep of the school and becoming a non-shareholding member of the board of governors, or pay extortionate rates for his companies services, reminding him that he had signed a long-term contract that he would not rescind without going through the courts, that he knew he couldn't afford to take a chance on, due to what it might cost him with more than a good chance he would lose. He said he was in a no-win situation, and so, being the lesser of two evils, he agreed to become a member of the board of governors of the school. What did his wife think of all the treachery, James asked. He said how Oliver had suggested to his wife that she take Mrs Mather to another room in the house where they could have a chat and so leaving him alone with Oliver to continue dropping his bombshell.

'I, at first, was not going to tell her anything about what was discussed, but we have never kept secrets from each other, so when we got home, we sat well into the early hours of the morning, talking it all through.'

'What was her verdict?' James asked, to which Joe just said:

'What do you think?'

Joe said he had been in touch with David Bright on several occasions regarding the situation they were both in but could see no way they could eject themselves from the hold Oliver had over them. James told him they had visited each of the board members and they were all in the same boat, with the exception of Henry Andrews, who, it appeared, thought Oliver was a great man. Nodding, Joe said he wondered if Andrews had anything on Oliver or was in cahoots with him, for he thought and acted differently to the rest of them. James suggested that they had become friends through the army, but they had to find out more.

Again, like the others they had spoken to, James asked Joe to say nothing of their visit to anyone, not even his wife, and asked whether he would help them if they needed him to further down the line. He explained what they were doing or were trying to do, so making Joe realise how serious they were to get Oliver into as much trouble as they could, even perhaps to get him put in prison for what he was up to. Having nothing else to discuss, James said they were pleased to meet him and would stay in touch if there was anything to report that might affect him. He thanked them both for contacting him and hoped they were successful in their endeavours. Seeing them to their car, they shook hands before they got in, and he wished them a safe journey home.

When they got back to the office, Susan must have been in because she had left a note saying that Dr John Mountford had telephoned and asked if Fred or James could ring him at their earliest convenience. Fred said, seeing he had visited them, if it would be better if he rang him, with James listening in on the other phone. James got out his notepad, saying he would write down anything that was necessary while Fred concentrated on whatever conversation went on between them. He said this would have been a good one for Susan as she would do it all in shorthand, but that he would do his best in longhand.

Picking up the phone, Fred dialled the number and waited. It was answered by Hazel who, having met Fred, asked how he was, and that she would get John to the phone. He must have been close at hand for it was almost immediate that he said, 'Hello, John here.' Fred said they had just got back from seeing two of the new school governors, and that they had been left a note, asking them to telephone him. John said he had rung, and that he thought they would like to know Mr Oliver had contacted him, wishing to have a meeting. Where and when, Fred asked and was told at Oliver's house in Gentington. Had he made any firm arrangements, Fred asked and was told it was left to him to set a date and time. Did he know what Oliver wanted him for, to which John said he thought it was going to be on the subject of his shareholding of the school.

Fred, looking over to James, said, 'Put it off for as long as you can, use any excuse you can think of, but don't meet him until we have done more investigating.'

'That is why I have wanted to talk to you, to see if you have made any progress with your enquiries.' Fred suggested Oliver was probably going to try and blackmail him into selling him his shares as he had done to the new shareholders. Fred went on to explain how far they had got and that they had spoken to all the school governors appointed by Oliver, and apart from Sir Henry Andrews, they were all paying towards the school's upkeep but with no shareholding involved.

'He still holds all the shares except yours.'

Fred suggested that it was rather coincidental that Oliver should pick now to contact him when he knows nothing about their enquiries unless Andrews has told him that Education Authority men had visited him.

'Who were they?' John asked and was not surprised when Fred said it was them.

James then spoke, introducing himself and apologising to both of them for butting in, but he asked John if he could think of anything Oliver could use to blackmail him with. John said no, not unless it was something trumped-up that was a pack of lies. Thanking him for that, he left Fred to carry on. Fred then asked the twenty thousand dollar question: 'Would he go back to the school as headmaster if Oliver could be disgraced and made to sell the school as a school rather than anything else?' John wanted to know what Fred meant when he said as anything else. James looked puzzled too, but when Fred said he had a feeling Oliver was hoping to run the school into the ground and sell the school and land for development. It would fetch a great deal of money, far more than Oliver paid for it.

John said, 'But he couldn't do that without him holding all the shares in the school, and he doesn't.'

Fred said, 'Precisely, that is why he is desperate to get your shares.'

Fred then went back and asked him again if he would go back to the school as headmaster. John said, he had been left too long to go back to teaching, albeit as headmaster, but would give whatever support he could to whoever became appointed. He had made a new life for himself and Hazel, that he rather liked, and wasn't going to give that up. Fred explained it was only a thought, that he might be way out with his thinking, but there was a possibility that Oliver wanted to sell the school. He went on to ask of those he had talked to among the Oliver's board of governors, if he held any opinion on any of them. John said he had only met all of them briefly and found them quite nice men but totally uninterested in the school. The one, however, he did take rather an objection to was Sir Henry Andrews.

'He is more than meets the eye.'

Fred asked of all his board of governors, who would be the one to interview to get the most information from when he had said some of them had regretted selling their shares. John said the only one that had shown any real loyalty and was the last one to agree to Oliver's buy-out was Bob Singleton who was an accountant, although he might be retired now. He said he had given Fred his address and phone number but wasn't sure if he had retired and moved home.

Fred thanked him and said they would be in touch and not to have any contact with Oliver if he could help it. He said he wouldn't and, saying goodby, rang off.

Putting the phones down, James asked where the idea of Oliver wanting to sell the school and land for development had come from. Fred said he didn't know, that it was something that had crossed his mind when one of the things that were said about Oliver was that his driving force was to make money. What better way of making a great deal of it without even breaking into a sweat?

Before they left the office, Fred went to the names, addresses and phone numbers John Mountford had given him and suggested to James that they try to get in touch with Bob Singleton before going any further. James rang the phone number as Fred read it out and not getting a disconnected tone hang on for the call to be answered. When it was, the voice said,

'Singleton here.' The voice sounded old and tired, but it was only a voice. James said who he was and what he wanted and got a very cool reception. It was when James went on to explain it was Dr John Mountford that had given him his number and why, he started to soften. James asked if they could come tomorrow and speak to him about his time as a school governor. He said he was only doing a little work now he had retired just enough to give him some holiday money. He said if they could manage tomorrow afternoon, he would agree to speak with them. James said that would be fine and asked, 'Would two o'clock be suitable?' Bob said yes and gave them directions to where they could find him.

Putting the phone down, James said that was enough for one day and, on locking up, left for home. Dropping Fred off, he said they had plenty of time in the morning, and that he would pick him up at nine. On getting home and after being greeted by his two children, he went upstairs to get changed into something more casual. Getting back downstairs and into the kitchen, where Susan was preparing dinner, he asked if she had had a good day. She told him how long she had spent at the office and asked if he had seen her note. She said John Mountford sounded ever such a nice man, and that they had a little chat before he rang off.

James said he had telephoned him and John had given him some idea of what he wanted to speak to him about.

He told her what they were going to do tomorrow and said that would be the last of the board members, old and new, they would question. He told Susan she needn't go to work tomorrow which she said was just as well as she was going into Southampton with Amy and Elizabeth whose closing day it was at the sweet shop.

It was ten o'clock on the dot that he picked Fred up to go to the office before seeing Bob Singleton at two o' clock.

He lived in a semi-detached house near the middle of the village, and on arriving, drove onto the drive behind the car parked there. On pressing the doorbell, they waited for the door to be opened by a very tall man in working clothes.

James said, 'Mr Singleton?' and got a nod, for that was him. James offered his hand and, on being shaken, introduced himself and Fred. He invited them in and showed them into the lounge. Once again, when they had sat down, James took a card from his wallet and gave it to him. Reading it, he asked what they wanted him for.

James gave him a rundown on what they were doing and asked if he would mind helping them with their enquiries. He said after giving his rundown on how he had got his shares and what input he had into running the school, he said it was at the end of the day the amount offered for his shares that tipped the balance of whether he sold out to Oliver or not. He said he felt guilty about leaving John Mountford out on a limb and wished he had never sold his shares. 'It was as I was sacked as a school governor only weeks after the buy-out that it occurred to me just what a mistake I had made.' He said he was a great admirer of John Mounford and the way he ran the school and the reputation he had created. There were not many things he proposed and put into practice that the board disagreed with. He was a good man and very much dedicated to the school.

Fred asked how much he used to get from his shares, to which he replied, it depended on what the fees were and any income that was generated during any school year. It never was enough to live on but was a welcome bonus to one's earnings. He explained how it was the old man of the two brothers that caused the eventual buy-out, one of which committed suicide. No one can blame the old man from passing on, but his greedy sons had a lot to answer for. What had happened to the other governors, he didn't know because he never kept in contact with any of them.

James asked as an accountant, did he have any idea what the financial position was with the school.

He said, 'All that was undertaken by a firm of accountants and not me as a school governor. However, as far as I know, the school was not in debt, in fact, with the value of the building together with the grounds it stands in it was a great asset to own. I can only tell you how things were while I was on the board and would have continued serving on it had I not been sacked by the new owner.

Although I was angry with myself for leaving John Mountford to face the music so to speak, I am glad he didn't sell his shares to Oliver who I found a detestable man. It's easy for me to say all this in hindsight, but it was a great deal of money at the time for me to retire with.'

On leaving Bob Singleton and driving back to their office, Fred said they didn't learn much from that visit, to which James said they had. He said in his opinion it had saved them a lot of time and travelling because none of the old members of the board of governors of the school would be any more helpful than he was, in fact, probably less.

Getting back to the office, James said what they needed to do was learn more about what Anthony Oliver was up to and what was Sir Henry Andrews' part in it all, for he was sure he was more than just a member of the board of governors at Fredricks school.

The army connection between Oliver, Andrews and Brent as well as Harry, being Andrews' Batman, had to be investigated also, there was a need to find out what part freemasonry played in it.

'Whether the latter comes into anything will have to unfold as we go, but the sell-off of the school certainly comes into the equation.'

James emphasised that from now on, they were to be very careful because powerful men don't become powerful by chance or luck. Their homes will be well guarded with the most up-to-date security devices, and in Andrews' case, guard dogs. If there is anything they are doing that is illegal or secret, they are going to keep any records they have in safes, in their offices and homes, in banks and with solicitors or the likes.

'We are going to be put to the test with this case and be on our metal. The people we have so far seen and spoken to have all got reasons to have a grudge against Anthony Oliver except for our Sir Henry Andrews. So now we must concentrate on the big two. The first thing I want to do is try and find out what their army connections are or were, and especially, why Walter Brent was discharged, for I think the reason he left the army was as a result of a court-martial. I intend going to the war office in London to see what we can learn from any records we can get to see. If they say it is all secret and cannot be divulged, we will have to get around it by fair means or foul, but I think starting off with that is going to be our best bet. We will see what we can do.'

Fred asked if he wanted him to go along and was told yes, and that they would go by train when they found out what the address was. He said he would get Susan to check train timings and would ring him at home with a pick-up time. He suggested they take their overnight bags just in case they had to stay in London overnight.

He set about getting the War Office address and on finding what he thought was the address they wanted, wrote it down and rang the telephone number that was with it.

He got through and was told the person he needed to speak to, Captain Ridgeway, had gone home but would be at his desk at eight o'clock in the morning. Telling Fred it was a shame the man they wanted was not available, but it was the correct location he had got through to, he would telephone from home before they left in the morning.

Chapter 7

When the alarm went off at seven o'clock it made Susan jump, but on cancelling it, James got up saying he would make some tea before getting himself ready to start the day. As he went downstairs, Susan went to the bathroom and having washed, dressed and made the bed, she too went downstairs finding James going through the train timetable. She asked what time he wanted to leave and what train he wanted to catch. He said he wanted to get the fast train from Portsmouth to Waterloo as it was better than the slow train from Southampton. After pouring Susan's tea, James went up to get washed, shaved and dressed. Going back downstairs, ready to go, he rang Fred and told him Susan would be taking them to Portsmouth Town Station and that they would pick him up at eight-thirty. He said he would be ready and rang off.

Having had their breakfast and it now being eight o'clock, James telephoned the number he had rung yesterday. It was the same voice that answered and said that Captain Ridgeway was at his desk and said he would put him through to him.

James heard a couple of buzzing noises before a voice said, 'Ridgeway.' James explained who he was and asked if it would be at all possible to see him today. The captain asked him to wait for just a second while he looked at his diary.

Within a very short time, he was back saying James was lucky for he had had a meeting cancelled, so if they could get up to London by eleven o'clock, he could see him for an hour. James said that would be fine and gave him a little background to why he wanted to see him. Captain Ridgeway said he thought he could help but explained there was such a thing as a secrets-act and he could not go against that.

Saying he would see him at eleven, with his partner Fred Baker, he rang off.

Dropping them off at the station, Susan said she would call in on the Mums while she was in Portsmouth to check how they were. As she drove off, James and Fred went to get their tickets and stood amongst the crowd awaiting the train. The station was crowded, but they managed to get a seat, and in ninety minutes, they were in London. They got a taxi to The War Office and, not knowing exactly where they had to go, asked a policeman outside if he could help them. He said he wasn't sure but gave them what help he could. They did what he suggested, and getting into the building, they had to show who they were by showing any document they had to prove it. Asked what department they wanted, James gave Captain Ridgeway's name and said they had an appointment. The gentleman they were talking to, who was a civilian, looked in a book and rang a number on his phone. On putting it down, he told James if he waited, someone would come and fetch them if they would like to take a seat, pointing to them. It seemed like an age that they sat waiting, but it was, in fact, only about ten minutes when an army corporal came over to them, after obviously checking with the gentleman they had been speaking to. He said he would escort them to Captain Ridgeway's office and led the way. It was quite a long walk they made until they got to where they had to go, and on knocking the door which had Captain A. B. Ridgeway…Army Personnel on it, there was a response, 'Come in.' The corporal saluted and said who he was escorting.

Captain Ridgeway, after welcoming them, asked them to sit down. He asked if they wanted tea or coffee but was told they would prefer to get straight down to business. What exactly they wanted to know and how he could help he asked.

James took his notebook out of his briefcase and asked if it would be possible to know anything about two retired officers and a non-commissioned officer, the latter of whom they understood had been dishonourably discharged. Captain Ridgeway said nothing for a moment, then said what was being asked of him was a very difficult request, for even though the gentlemen they were asking after were no longer serving, their records would still be held. However, even though he was a captain, he could not just call on the files to be produced without very good reason. James explained a bit about why they wanted the information, but it seemed he was hitting a brick wall.

Fred asked if they were caught up in a murder, would that help? Ridgeway said if that were the case, he was sure the police would be involved and that they not being the police, would have no leverage at all in getting to see the records they were seeking.

James suggested that the information they required would in no way breach the secrets-act especially as the men in question were now civilians. Captain Ridgeway picked up an internal phone that was on his desk and asked someone to come to his office. Within just a couple of minutes, there was a knock at his door and the same corporal entered, saluting again saying, 'Yes Sir.'

Writing on a notepad and using a rubber stamp over his signature, Captain Ridgeway put the page in an envelope on which was stamped "Urgent" and passed it to the corporal, asking him to take it to the records office and bring back the files he wanted. The corporal took the envelope and left saluting again.

While they waited, the conversation turned to the way the army had changed over the years since the war ended. Captain Ridgeway said that his father had been an army man during the war who had got to the rank of colonel before his retirement. He said when they got together, especially over a drink, the differences in the way the army was run then to how it is run now showed up. It was twenty minutes before there was another knock at the door and the corporal came into the room. He put three substantial files on the desk, and saying the Records Office wanted the files back that day, he took his leave.

'Now, gentlemen, I am about to leave my office for about half an hour, leaving my corporal outside the door and would not expect you to look at anything while I am gone.' Promising not to do so, said they would wait for his return.

On leaving his office with a slight nod of his head towards his desk, he left.

Directly the door closed, James and Fred went to the files. James suggested Fred take the file with "Confidential" on the outer cover (Not Secret) and the name "W. A. Brent" underneath with his service number while he took the one that was a different colour with "H. Andrews" under the confidential together with his service number and rank.

Leaving the one with Oliver on it that they would go through together.

They had to be quick and only take notes of what was necessary and relevant to what they wanted to know.

Fred started from the back, knowing that Brent had been dishonourably discharged working back to when he joined the army. He and James were right in thinking it was by way of a court-martial that he was forced to leave the army, but what for was the information that Fred wanted.

From what he read he was not a very good soldier throughout the time he served but, in one case, very brave. He was transferred to three different regiments in ten years and served several stretches in military confinement. Reading through this service record, Fred wondered why and how he ever became a teacher in civilian life. He was court-martialled for narrowly missing killing a young soldier after being warned by his last station commander for bullying young cadets. There were no reports on how or why the young soldier nearly died, only that he was so badly injured that he had to be discharged from the army on medical grounds. Fred assumed the court-martial report was a separate document. Some details of the young soldier were in the file that Fred wrote down in his notebook in case they wanted to contact him. Working his way to the front of the file, it appeared that Brent had joined the army at seventeen immediately after coming out of prison.

He had been promoted on two occasions and reduced back to private and still became a sergeant before being discharged as a result of the court-martial.

It appeared that his last commanding officer was Colonel H. Andrews and it was him that had signed the dishonourable discharge papers, that indicated he was the chairman of the court-martial panel. There were several entries signed by Captain A. Oliver, one of which down-rated Brent from corporal to private soldier. It was while in the tank regiment that he had been brave, having saved the life and rank of an officer. Noting what he could in the time he had, Fred scribbled down the facts that he thought would be required for the future for them.

They finished their folders at more or less the same time, and on doing so, they started on that of Anthony Oliver. As they did so, James just mentioned to Fred that Andrews was the son of a General and so would be bound to get quick promotion. He said he had resigned from the army, from what he had read, before he was asked to leave. There had been nothing recorded about anything positive, but reading between the lines, he was getting into trouble and that he had taken note of all he could that was relevant to what they wanted to know about him.

Going through Captain Oliver's file, there had been several occasions when he had flown pretty close to the wind but had managed to escape without severe reprimand, although it would seem his promotion had been pegged at captain. There had been a time very early in their army service when Oliver out-ranked Andrews but not for long. Once again, they both put notes, dates and anything else they thought relevant into their notebooks. They had just put the files back on Captain Ridgeway's desk when the door opened and he came in. He apologised for having to leave them for so long and that he had another meeting in ten minutes' time. He asked if there was anything more he could help them with before they left. James asked if he had ever served under any of the men who they wanted to know about, to which he replied all of them when he first joined up, after leaving university. He said Brent had been a drill sergeant and what a bastard of a man he was, and that Captain Oliver was his troop commander, while Colonel Andrews was the company commander. Did he think anything brought the captain and the colonel together, to which he said whenever there was a do in the officers' mess they always seemed to be not far apart.

What about sergeant Brent? He said he had had the opportunity to help get rid of him by being a witness at the court-martial, he had only been a subby at the time, but the young soldier he nearly killed had been a friend of his and that he, Brent, deserved being got rid of. When asked, he said he had no idea what any of them were doing now and wasn't interested, he was only looking to do as well as he could in this man's army now. Both James and Fred thanked him for making the time to see them and were then escorted from the building.

Getting the train back to Portsmouth after ringing Susan to tell her what train they were catching and asking her to pick them up, they found seats and had a good chat on the way home.

Chapter 8

Sitting in the office the next morning, drinking the tea Susan had made, they started separately making more detailed notes of what they had got from the army files while it was still fresh in their minds, for although having taken notes, they both had retained a lot from memory.

It took them quite a time with Susan's help, doing some shorthand for both of them before typing it all out. Then while she did that, they discussed what the collective bond was between them and the probability of why they were all involved in the Radcliff School.

It seemed that the reason the three of them stuck together was to watch each other's backs. Oliver, because he had been left a great deal of money and an already established business.

Andrews, who was also wealthy and a knight of the realm, as a man using his knowledge in armaments and his army rank to make money. Then Brent, who they both knew was a loose cannon that could cause both of them a great deal of trouble if he knew what the pair of them were doing and had done in the army; especially as they had both in their own way been responsible for his dishonourable discharge.

How does Gerald Good fit into the equation, Fred observed, to which James suggested, from what had been learnt from posh Mrs Good, he was Anthony Oliver's brother-in-law.

'How do you make that out?' Fred asked.

'Well,' James replied, 'Don't you think from what we learnt that posh Mrs Good is one of Oliver's sisters? Even though she didn't mention him by name. I am making this assumption from the photographs we have seen in the different houses we have visited. Oliver, Andrews and Brent are connected by the army and Good by relationship. Blood is thicker than water, and that is why Brent can't get the job of the headmaster.

If, what I think is correct, then we must now go to Oliver's house. I don't want to see Oliver as much as his mother if that is possible, for she will be able to confirm quite a lot of what we think but cannot as yet prove if she is prepared or able to speak to us. How we are going to do it, I don't know, but I want him out of the way.' How did he think he was going to do that, Fred wanted to know?

'I am going to ring Oliver's secretary and find out somehow when he will be away from home, especially if out of the country, giving us more time.'

With that, he picked up the phone and rang her number. Answering it, he said who he was, giving his false name, and asked if it would be possible to speak to Mr Oliver. She asked what he wanted him for, just when James thought for a horrible minute that she was going to put him through, but after a pause, she said he was leaving the country on Sunday and would not speak to him even if he wasn't. Did she know how long he was going to be away for?

She let it slip, 'For a week with his wife,' and quickly corrected herself by saying, 'What does it have to do with you?' James said he would contact him by letter when he returned, as it was obvious that he wasn't going to manage to speak to him on the telephone.

Putting his phone down, he said to Fred, 'Bull's-eye.' Fred wanted to know what James was so pleased about, and when told, he just nodded. He asked when was he coming back, to which James said,

'In a week's time, so we must get a move on if he leaves on Sunday.'

'I know we agreed to have this weekend off but will have to work on Sunday.'

They re-checked the address and looked it up and decided to go by car on Sunday morning. Two phone calls came in that had to be dealt with, and after dealing with them, they said that was enough for that day and left for home.

Getting home, James spent a long time in a warm bath. When Susan asked why he had taken so long, he said he had been thinking. He said there was such a lot to think about what they were doing and that he was trying to clear his mind before making his next move. She asked if he was worrying, and getting a "No" in answer, she didn't believe him.

The next day being Saturday, the two partners decided to take the weekend off, that was now to be the Saturday only, and spend it with their families. Fred said he was taking Amy and Elizabeth to a flower show that they wanted to go to and then for a meal in the evening. James decided he would go with Susan and the children to wherever they wanted to go as a family, knowing Sunday was going to be another working day after all. They decided, or at least the children did, where they were going and said they would like their dad to give them a meal out before getting home. With this agreement, preparations were made for the next day's adventure.

James rang Fred and asked him to be ready to leave his house at seven o'clock on Sunday morning to go to Gentlodge, the address in Gentington not too far from Oxford and have his overnight bag ready in case it was required. Fred said he would be ready and hoped he would have a good day with his family.

Each family having had a good day on Saturday, it was a bit of a bind having to get up and go to work so early on Sunday morning, but they had to strike while the iron was hot. James picked Fred up at seven o'clock as arranged, and with their briefcases and overnight bags, they set off for Gentington.

Being that early on a Sunday morning the traffic was very light, on some roads almost non-existent.

They got to the house they wanted to visit, and some house it was. It had the same gate setup as that at the Andrews. Fred was just about to get out of the car when the gates started to open. Knowing the gates had not opened for them, they sat in the car and waited to see what was going to happen. It must have been a couple of minutes before a navy blue Rolls Royce registration number "OLIVER 1" came out through them. It turned left, towards the direction James wasn't facing, so restarting his engine and turning in the road, he started to follow it, making sure he stayed a good distance behind.

Fred asked, 'What are we following the car for?'

James said, 'Oliver and a woman are in the back, being chauffeur-driven, and I want to know where they are going.'

'How did he know it is Oliver?' Fred asked.

'I only got a quick glimpse, but I am sure I have seen him in photographs and looked at the car registration number.' The car drove for about fifteen minutes before it turned into a private airfield, or at least that was what the notice board said.

'What now?' Fred asked. 'We know where he is now, but where is he going?'

They waited in a small lay-by for fifteen minutes when a private plane took off. A few minutes later, the Rolls Royce appeared and headed back the way it had come. As it passed them, they saw the chauffeur clearly, so they would be able to recognise him easily if they ever saw or met him again. He was looking straight ahead, so he didn't seem to see them at all.

Starting up, James drove into the airport and parked in the small car park just a short distance from the reception building. Telling Fred to stay where he was, he got out and walked across to the reception. Going in, he saw a lady behind a desk and asked if that was Mr and Mrs Oliver that had just taken off, for he had a message for him and had got held up by a road accident. The receptionist confirmed that it was them, and that they were on their way to Berlin in Germany.

James thanked her and said he had the address they were going to, so he would contact them after they arrived. Getting back to the car, he drove back to Oliver's house, telling Fred what he had found out at the airport on the way.

Getting back to Oliver's house, they needed to get in through the gates. Fred got out of the car and was getting ready to press the button when a delivery van pulled up beside them. Getting out of the van, the driver asked Fred if he had pressed the button yet. Fred told him he hadn't, and that if he was in a hurry, perhaps it would be better if he did so as it might be quicker with him knowing the routine. The van driver went over and pressed the button on the machine before speaking into it and got back in the van. Fred jumped back in their car. Just as the gates started to open and as the van drove through, so did James.

It was obvious the van was in a hurry for he sped down the drive and was opening the back doors of it by the time James got to the house. A young man came from around the house with the intention of helping the van man.

They both got out of their car and James went over to the young man and asked him how he could get to see Mrs Oliver senior. The young man said he would have to contact the butler whose name was Victor, who was a very large man dressed as butlers do.

James thanked him and, gesturing to Fred to bring their briefcases, started making his way to the front door. Knocking the heavy front door with a rather large brass knocker, they waited. The door was opened by a lady who asked who they were and what did they want. James said they wanted to talk to Mrs Oliver senior about insurances. She said she was the housekeeper and it was her they needed to see, as it was her that could get access to the old lady, who was quite frail but very with- it.

She asked them to wait, saying she wouldn't take long. It was longer than they expected when she finally reappeared, bringing a young nurse with her. She introduced her as Peggy Banks and said she would take them to see Mrs Oliver. Excusing herself, she left them in Peggy's hands. Peggy asked their names and, on being given them, asked them to accompany her to Mrs Oliver's room. She took them right through the house into what seemed to be a private apartment.

It was, in fact, an extension to the main house. On entering the room, Peggy gave Mrs Oliver their names and what they had come for. Mrs Oliver was sitting propped up in a rather large comfortable-looking armchair and looked very bright. She may have been frail but looked fit enough to take on anybody in an argument, but with her legs covered in dressings not physically.

'Right, Peggy', she said, 'Will you find out what these gentlemen want to drink, and I will have my usual with my tablet.' Going away, knowing what James and Fred wanted, they were invited to sit down. The old lady apologised for not getting up but explained her condition. She said she was so pleased someone had come to talk to her for she got so fed up just watching television.

While they waited for their drinks, James asked her how often was she able to get out of the house.

She said, 'Not very often, and only in the summer unless it was something very important that she couldn't deal with at home.' She implied that since her husband had died, she was put aside by her son. Fred asked if she had any other children, that gave him an answer of two. Next question, where do the other ones live? She smiled and said,

'One daughter lives with her husband in Germany, in Berlin.'

'Is that where your son has just gone?' James interrupted, 'To see his sister?'

Mrs Oliver looked surprised and said, 'It would be very unlikely because they don't speak to each other.'

Peggy brought the tray in with the drinks and some biscuits. She put it down on a table before drawing up smaller tables to put what they had asked for on. Mrs Oliver had hers on a tray that fitted over her legs in the chair. Asking if everything was to their liking, she asked Peggy to leave the room. Shutting the door behind her, she left, saying she would be back later.

Taking the pill with the drink that Peggy had brought her, Mrs Oliver said, 'Now, gentlemen, you have not come to see me about insurance, for you must know that I would be well covered for anything I need insurance for, so what is it you want from me?'

James and Fred were shocked and, at first, didn't know what to say. James finally said they had to think of something otherwise they would not have been able to get to see her.

'So what have you come for?' she said, 'And is it anything to do with my son?' James came clean, saying they were private investigators, and it was about her son, on saying they needed information regarding the Radcliff Private School for boys. She looked puzzled before saying, she knew nothing about him being associated with a school.

James explained that his son was a boarder at the school and was being badly ill-treated, and that he and Fred were investigating what was going wrong with a school that had had a very sought-after reputation until it was taken over by her son. In response to this, she became very interested in what they were saying. Firstly, she said, she didn't know why he would have purchased a school but was certain there must have been an alternative reason for doing so, for it had to be for making money and lots of it.

She said he was obsessed with making money by fair means or foul. She went on to give them a rundown on what he had become since his father died.

'He is trying hard to sell this house but can't because I won't let him; the house is mine, and I don't want to live anywhere else.

'It has got to a point where I am beginning to detest him. His father was such a gentleman in every way, both gentle as a man and also a gentleman. Having watched his father build the haulage business up from scratch as a child, and the way he conducted himself whilst doing it, should have been an example to him, but since taking the company over, he has gone power crazy, thinking that money buys power, and he now has far more companies than his father had.'

'He has already tried to buy his sister's shares that their father left them in his will as well as mine. That is the reason one of my daughters moved to Germany as much as because her husband is German and such a lovely man with a very good job. She and Tony had the most terrible row and Tony said things you would never believe. His other sister Judith who lives in Fraisborough only ever sees him if he is at home when she visits me, and that is not very often, I fancy it is all due to him. I am sure that if he would find me in his way, stopping him from making really big sums of money, he would kill me or arrange for me to be killed, he is that ruthless. I am an old lady now but will live on to become a very old lady if I can, just to be a constant thorn in his side.'

'Is Judith married?' James asked.

'Yes, she is.' Mrs Oliver replied. 'But it is now hardly a marriage at all for she rarely sees him due to his work.'

'What is his job?' Fred wanted to know.

'He is a headmaster at a boarding school,' she said, 'So he is only home during holiday times; that's him in that photograph over there with my daughter on their wedding day…not a white wedding, of course, that didn't please my husband or me if I am truthful, but now I understand because he is such a negative type of man that didn't want all the fuss a white wedding creates.' James got up from his chair and looked at the photo she pointed to and was not surprised to see Gerald Good with Judith. Younger than they are now, of course, but still them. While he was looking at that photograph, he also looked at those that were with it, one in particular, the one with all of them together, Tony in uniform, and Gerald and Judith wearing their caps and gowns.

'Where is Tony's wife?' he asked, turning back to his chair and referring to the family group.

'Oh that,' she said, 'Tony wasn't married then, the army was all he thought about, he didn't get married until quite late. She was all right in the beginning, but I think Tony's rank went to her head. Apart from being a terrible snob, she thinks above herself and her station.'

They asked if she could tell them anything about what her son was like when he was in the army, and why he went in it when his father had a business to go into. She started to get upset when she told them how he had told his father he wanted to make something of himself and not just be a removal man. This was a spiteful insult to his father who took it quite badly but still pulled some strings, being well up in the freemasons, to get him into the army as an officer cadet. As it so happened, he became a good officer until a number of years later he met Edward Andrews, a fellow officer slightly below him in rank. It was when he got to captain he could have gone on to become much higher in rank, and probably remained in the army for life, instead, he somehow got into trouble and got himself pegged as a captain with no hope of being promoted further. James asked what had he done to warrant that. Mrs Oliver said she didn't know exactly what it was because Tony was ashamed and only ever mentioned it to his father once. My husband never told me anything about it, only that Henry Andrews had got away with what they were doing by dropping Tony in the shit, excusing herself for her language. It was something to do with the illegal distribution of military equipment. It was within a year that Tony resigned from the army and came back into civilian life, leaving Henry to go on getting further promotions.

But Fred, who had been listening intently, told Mrs Oliver that Tony and Henry Andrews were the greatest of friends and that Henry was singing Tony's praises when they met him only a short while ago. Mrs Oliver shook her head, saying that that just couldn't possibly be true for as far as she knew, he hated Andrews. He had never forgiven him for what he had done to him whilst they were in the army.

Getting off the subject, James wanted to know about Tony's wife. Again, Mrs Oliver started to get agitated.

'I hate the woman, and on the rare occasions that she comes to my rooms, it makes my skin crawl if she comes near me. It is always when Peggy is out of the room that she talks to me like dirt.' Was Peggy a live-in nurse or does she come in daily, Fred asked and was told that she has an attic room and is always on call when she is required.

'I try not to need her when she is not on duty for she is such a dear, adding, she cannot do enough for me. She is the third nurse I have employed since I haven't been able to do for myself, the previous two were only here for the money and only did the absolute minimum they needed to. Peggy is here because she wants to look after me.'

'What did Mrs Tony Oliver do?' the next question came.

'As for work, she doesn't have a job, as such, but she is involved in quite a lot of charities. She is a real social climber, and although it is good to work for charities and make a name for yourself, it is only I am sure, for being able to become chairperson or president of them, she wouldn't be seen dead in old clothes having to do physical or dirty work. She does a lot of entertaining and probably gives money to them. She, of course, accompanies Tony to his company does and spends many hundreds of pounds on clothes. She has come in here on occasions, dolled up to the nines just before going to one of them.

She said she was sorry she could not be of any more help, but since her husband died, she knows nothing much of what Anthony does, only that she is watching her back!'

Thinking there was no more that Mrs Oliver could help them with, James just said, with a smile on his face, 'So there is nothing more we can interest you in with regard to insurance then?'

Mrs Oliver, knowing what the smile was for, said, 'No', but added if there was anything she could help them with in the future, they could contact her. She took a pen and paper from the table beside her chair and wrote on it a phone number. Giving it to James, she said,

'That is Peggy's number. She will take any message, and you can trust her.'

Saying they were sorry they had taken up so much of her time, James and Fred stood up, thanked her for seeing them and said they had a lot more work to do so would bid her goodbye. She said what a nice change it was to have somebody new to talk to before ringing a bell that made a lot of noise for its size but was enough to bring Peggy to the door. Asking her to see them out, she switched on her television.

Before taking them to the front door, Peggy asked them if she could have a word, taking them to a smaller room than they had been in. She didn't ask them to sit down but pulled the door closed behind them. She asked, speaking very quietly what they wanted to see the old lady about. Before James or Fred could tell her to mind her own business, she said the landlady was not to be trusted, everything that goes on in this house is passed on to Mr Oliver.

'I have come to love that old lady and don't want to see anything happen to her.'

'Do you think something might then?' James asked.

'There might be,' she said, 'and I am worried about it.' Giving Peggy their business card, James told her to telephone the number on it or the number on the back that he wrote for her, telling her to give them a ring if she ever wanted help or advice.

Looking on the card, she smiled, saying she thought correctly that they were not insurance men. James, not wanting to spend too much more time in the house, gave her a quick rundown on what they were doing, telling her to keep mum.

She said, 'The housekeeper would want to know what you were here for and what went on…do I keep up the pretence?' They said yes, and that the old lady trusted her, so they were relying on her not to give anything away. She said she wouldn't, and that she would keep her ears and eyes open.

Opening the door, she led them back through the house to the front door, and not seeing anybody on their way, she opened it, saying she would open the gates for them. They shook hands, and Fred and James went to their car. Getting in, they got going, waving as they passed her. As they approached the gates, they were opening, and on driving through they turned to take the same route they had used to get there.

Getting back to the office, Susan was just getting ready to go home. As they came in, she wanted to know if they wanted a cup of tea or coffee after their drive. On saying they would both like coffee, she put the kettle on, making it for the three of them. They sat and drank it, telling Susan what the visit to Oliver's house was all about. When they had finished their coffee and Susan had washed up the mugs, she said she had finished all she had to do for the day and was going home after calling into the shop and saying hello to Elizabeth on her way. Saying she would see James later.

After leaving, Fred asked James where were they going next.

James suggested that having done the rounds, as he called it, having paid the visits they had made, and not yet made any contact with Oliver and Brent of the three men they were after, there was only one more visit to make if they could find him. Fred frowned, not realising who James was thinking of. Going over to one of the filing cabinets, James pulled out the file Susan had made from their visit to the war office. Taking it back to his desk, he opened it and said to Fred,

'Let's find the young soldier who Brent nearly killed and was discharged on medical grounds. I want to know this before we confront Brent in person.'

Fred, after admitting he had forgotten him, asked if his address had been noted. James confirmed it had, but that it was the address and phone number of years ago, but it was a start.

He rang the number in the file and got an engaged tone, so he knew the number was still in existence.

Jotting the name and number down on his notepad, he gave it ten minutes and tried the number again. This time, he got a dialling tone, and soon after, a ladies voice said, 'Hello.'

James asked if he was through to Ian Marks. She said there were no Marks at that address now, but there used to be a while ago. She said as far as she remembered, he was the son of the owners of the house who moved to the south coast somewhere but didn't take the phone number with them. Did she have a forwarding address or phone number, James asked, and after a hesitant pause, she said she thought so, but she would have to look for it. James gave her his number and asked if she would ring him back if she had or hadn't found it. She said she would, and make it as quickly as she could. He asked her name and was told Mrs Ivy Goreman. Putting the phone down, James said he had to wait for her to ring back and hoped she would be quick.

Asked if Fred was in any hurry to get home, and getting a no for an answer, they waited for the callback. In the meantime, they talked of all the people they had visited, what each of them had been of help, and hoped that what they had so far done would eventually bear fruit.

It was half an hour before the phone rang, but when it did, it was good news. Ivy Goreman had found the details they wanted and read them out over the phone as James wrote them down. She said she had also spoken to her neighbour who had lived there for many years and had known the Marks family well before they moved away. She said they had moved in order that their son could recuperate after being discharged from the army. He, apparently, was part of a court-martial that left him mentally affected as well as physically. He liked the army and was getting on well until he had to be discharged on medical grounds. James asked if she knew what the injuries he had suffered were, but she said she didn't know that. He thanked her for ringing back so quickly, and on saying goodbye, he put the phone down, telling Fred they could go home now as they could follow up on Ian Mark's whereabouts tomorrow.

Chapter 9

Getting to the office the next morning, after picking Fred up, they set about following up on locating Ian Mark's whereabouts. James looked out the details he had written down the afternoon before and telephoned the number he had been given. It rang and was answered by a man. James asked if he was speaking to Ian Marks and was told it was his father. He told James Ian wasn't living there any more, that he had moved in with his girlfriend. James asked if he could have his phone number. Mr Marks asked who he was speaking to and what he wanted his son for.

James told him who he was, and that he needed information that only Ian could give him. He explained it was about his army discharge and the cause of it. Mr Marks advised James that to discuss this with his son would be very difficult because he has tried very hard to put the whole incident behind him. James thanked him for the advice and promised he would be very careful not to cause any distress, but that the information he could acquire from Ian would benefit him.

Mr Marks was convinced by what James told him, that to give him Ian's phone number was in order. So given the number, James thanked him and rang off.

On ringing, the number he had been given the phone was answered by a female.

On asking for Ian, James was told he was at work and wouldn't be available until about six o'clock that evening. Explaining who he was and saying what he wanted Ian for, he said he would ring back later, but before ringing off, he asked what Ian's job was. She said he was a train driver and that tomorrow was the first day of two days off. James thanked her and said he might be seeing her soon and rang off.

Rather than do nothing for the day, James decided he would telephone Captain Ridgeway. On getting him, he asked if there had been a file on Ian Marks, the young soldier that had had to be discharged on medical grounds after the court-martial of Sergeant Walter Brent. Captain Ridgeway said there must be, as every court-martial is recorded.

'Would there be any chance of seeing it as well as the record of private Ian Marks?' Captain Ridgeway said he could only get that if the police demanded to see them, and that demand would have to come from a very senior police officer. James thanked him and rang off.

Turning to Fred, he said, 'we are going to have to be very thorough when questioning Ian Marks because we are not going to be able to get his army record or the record of the court-martial.'

Fred said that while James was on the phone, he had written down a list of the questions he would ask as well as what James might ask if they were going to question him together!

Not being able to get any further with their enquiries until they had spoken to Ian Marks, they decided they would look what Susan had put in their diary. There were two investigations they had to look into, one of which could be put on the back burner, and the other they were waiting on the information before they could proceed. Satisfying themselves, there was nothing more they could do that day, they would make it an early one that they could spend the rest of with their families. James said he would take his to the pictures and would see Fred at nine in the morning. Fred asked when he would ring Ian Marks and was told he would telephone him from home before they went to the pictures.

Dropping Fred off, he drove home to find Susan and Joyce unpacking some food shopping they had done. Asking if they wanted to go to the pictures that evening, they jumped at it, knowing they would get fish and chips as they usually did on such occasions before they got to the Odeon.

As James went upstairs to change out of his suit, he passed Fredrick's bedroom with the door open and stood for a moment, watching him playing with his trains. Without disturbing him, he just stood there and tried to imagine how somebody could meaningfully hurt someone as gentle as his son. As he went into his bedroom, the thought had made his blood boil. He must find out what is going on at that school and do something about it within the next five weeks.

He telephoned Ian's number and found he hadn't got home from work yet.

When he asked who he was speaking to, she said it was his partner, and that Ian should be home before seven o'clock, and that she would tell him he had rung.

It was just after six o'clock when he rang again and found Ian Marks in, saying he had got in a bit early. Asking if his girlfriend had told him he had already rung, he said she had and asked, 'What did he want?' James asked if he could come and see him to speak to him face to face as it would be far better than trying to do it all over the phone. He gave him a quick rundown on what it was all about and asked if he and Fred could see him tomorrow. Ian said if what they were doing would get Walter Brent sent to prison, he would certainly see them. He said he had the next two days off, so what time would suit them to visit him. James got his address and some local directions and said they would see him at about ten o'clock. This agreed, he put the phone down, and off they went to get their fish and chips before going to the cinema. The main film was just up their street as a family movie and, being on a big screen, was much better than watching it on the television.

Getting home, they all had a bedtime drink before going up to bed.

At nine in the morning, James picked Fred up and said they didn't have far to go, and that they would be on Hayling Island by ten o'clock. The traffic was although heavy in places but not heavy enough to prevent them from making it to Hayling in good time. It was just after ten when they pulled up outside of a semi-detached house not too far from the seafront. They got to the front door and, ringing the bell, had it opened by a man in his late twenties, they supposed, tall and well built.

He asked if they would like to come in and, closing the door, pointed to the front room. He introduced them to his young lady who said she would leave them to it.

Sitting down, James got straight to the point. He explained how Brent had been ill-treating his son, hiding behind discipline.

'He is now a schoolteacher who is punishing young boys excessively with the cane, my son in particular. The school I chose to put him to had a very good reputation, but since being bought within the last two years, it is going downhill fast. We, Fred and I, are looking into why, for we are sure there is, possibly, criminal activity afoot, and we want to get to the bottom of it! If we can, we will take it to one of the big newspapers, after notifying the police.

'What we want to know is what went on with you in the army and what is your connection with Sergeant Brent, Colonel Henry Andrews and Captain Anthony Oliver.'

Taking a deep breath, Ian started to talk.

He said, 'I wanted to go into the army from when I left school but had to wait until I was eighteen. I worked for the local council until I was eighteen, and as soon as I was, I applied to join the tank regiment. I was getting on very well to start with after doing my basic training. There were eight of us billeted together, and we got on well. We were not getting much money but enjoyed ourselves with what we got. The sergeant we had was a nice guy, and we were happy with what we were learning. Unfortunately, for us, but good for the sergeant, he got a promotion and was moved to bigger things than being in charge of us squaddies. His replacement was Sergeant Brent. Within a week, he had destroyed the friendships we had formed and became the biggest bastard you could ever come across. Being the biggest in stature of the eight of us, he picked on me as though to prove if he could tame the biggest, the rest would be easy to manage.

'I was quite good at sport, rugby, in particular. I had a trial for the battalion team and was thought good enough to play for them. I, much to Brent's dislike, was given time off to train.

It didn't help that Brent had had a trial some time before but had been told he was not good enough.

This, I think, made him pick on me all the more out of jealousy. Cleaning the toilet block as many times as he could arrange, it was something he enjoyed making me do. He would come in while I was doing it and nearly finished and would kick over a bucket of dirty water and make me start all over again. I had to suffer that because I didn't want to get into trouble. He would pick on anything he could think of to goad me into losing my temper and hitting him so that he could get me into jankers (army jail) or even better kicked out of the army. Don't ask me why the man was like he was, but he was evil. He made life for me a misery. The other blokes had sympathy for me but could do nothing to help me. He had one guy that he seemed to favour and who we thought was letting him know what was going on and what we all thought about him. We cottoned on to this and turned on him. It appeared that Brent had found out something about him before he joined up and was sort of blackmailing him into being his informer.'

'How long did this go on for?' Fred wanted to know. Ian thought for a minute before saying, 'About six months. I had to put up with it because I wanted to play rugby, and by getting myself into trouble, Brent would see to it that I would miss training.'

'So what had brought it to a head?' James wanted to know.

'It was after we had just won the inter-battalion cup. I had had a very good game but was tired and half pissed after celebrating our win. When I got back to my billet, I don't know whether Brent went to the match, but he was standing by my crumpled bed when I arrived.

'My kit was strewn all over the floor and was a right mess. He said he was going to put me on a charge for leaving my belongings and bed as it was. I told him I hadn't left it like it, but he said I must have done. I argued with him, and he accused me of calling him a liar and a fool.

With that, he punched me in the guts. That was the last straw for me. I had helped win the Battalion Cup and so didn't care whether I was in trouble or not, but I just let fly at him, I was not going to allow him to hit me and get away with it. He knocked me down with his next punch, and as I was getting up, he ripped a water filled fire extinguisher off the wall and hit me across the head with it. I don't remember anything else until I came around in hospital.'

James wanted to know what happened then.

'On opening my eyes, a nurse asked me if I wanted a sip of water before going to get a doctor. The doctor arrived and, on giving me a check over, said I had been very fortunate not to have died from the injury I had sustained. I had a fractured skull and had been in a coma for two days. He said they had had to remove blood from my brain, and now that I had regained consciousness, they could do tests to see if and what damage there was. The doctor asked what had happened? I told him what I could remember, and he just nodded.

'I couldn't receive visitors for thirty-six hours while tests were carried out. The doctor, who was a captain surgeon, had been at the match and said how well I had played, and it was on his recommendation that I was invalided out of the army and warned to never play rugby or football ever again, and boxing was a definite no-no. It was when I was visited by my mates, with the exception of one, that I learnt more. The lads had done the business on Judas as they were now calling him, and he had been promoted to lance corporal and moved out of the billet. We can only think it was the work of Sergeant Brent as a "thank you" for keeping him informed of what went on in our billet.'

'A charge had been brought against Brent for maliciously injuring me, for apparently two of the lads saw Brent coming out of our billet, and it was them that found me and reported it to the military police after I had been taken to the hospital. Sergeant Brent was court-marshalled and, on being found guilty as charged, was derated. I have left the army for three years now, but still, I miss it. I got a job with British Rail, and driving trains isn't too bad a job. I have taken exams and am waiting to become a guard, so I am not doing bad. When I get a guard's job, I will marry the lady I am living with. I get the occasional headache, but the medication I have to take keeps everything under control.'

Fred asked Ian if he had ever met Brent since leaving the army, and was given a definite "No".

'If I ever see him again, I would want to kill him, so I have purposely not tried to locate him.' James said what they knew of him, he liked hurting people and got an element of pleasure out of it, referring to his son.

Ian said, 'The man should be taken out of society, let alone be able to become a schoolteacher.'

Fred and James went through the paperwork that Ian produced but found nothing more than what they had found at the war office. Discharge papers and other documents signed by Colonel Henry Andrews and Anthony Oliver.

Asking if he had ever met the two officers, Ian said, 'Not personally, but I have seen them often enough on parades and such like.' They asked if they needed his help in the future, would he be prepared to give it, and were assured he would. So, having learnt all they could, they thanked him and said they must get on their way, and apologising for taking up his time when he was a day off, they were escorted out of the house after saying cheerio to his partner.

Getting back in the car, they drove off Hayling Island, but before driving back to the office, James said he would like to call in to see his mum, just to say hello and to introduce Fred to her.

Stopping at the house he had lived in until he married, they got out of the car and walked to the front door. James opened it with the key he had been given when he was twenty-one, an old tradition, and called out, 'Are you in, Mum?'

Calling down the stairs, that she was just coming James shut the front door behind them. His mum appeared at the top of the stairs and coming down and getting to the bottom, put her arms around his neck saying what a surprise it was to see him, but why had he not called as she could have made them some lunch. Going into the lounge, she asked if they wanted a cup of coffee, and after introducing Fred, they said they would. When she brought the coffee in, she said how nice it was to meet Fred after all this time, Fred saying the same. She asked where they had been and what for. James went through what he was able to tell her and knowing her son so well, thought of how he would turn heaven and earth to get his man as they say.

She asked after the family and said she was hoping to see her grandchildren before they went back to school if Susan could find the time to get to see them. He said a visit was anticipated and both the children were looking forward to it. She asked after Fred's wife and sister and how the sweetshop was going. Finishing their coffee, James said they should push off now and get on with what they had to do next. Getting up and going to the door, he told his mum to say hello to his dad for him and that directly the case was concluded, he would come and take him for a pint.

The journey back to the office was trouble-free, and parking up and going in, he found Susan typing a letter.

'What are you doing?' James wanted to know, seeing the look of anger on her face, she said they had been advised not to send Fredrick back to school after the summer holiday.

'When did the letter arrive?' James wanted to know and was told it came with that morning's post just before she was about to leave home.

'Who is it from, and who has signed it? Susan passed the letter to him, and James read it out loud, so Fred knew what the letter contained.

It was on school headed paper but with no signature that was recognisable.

'Who are you writing back to?' James asked Susan, who said:

'To whom it concerns?'

'OK, finish it off, but don't send it. Writing it will get some of the anger out of you, and we will discuss it when I have made a phone call.'

He went over to his desk, while Susan carried on typing, and looking up Stella Boulton's home number, rang it. He was about to put the phone down when she answered, sounding out of breath, saying she was out in the garden when she heard the phone ringing. She was surprised it was James and asked what she could help him with. He asked if she had written a letter expelling Fredrick from the school. He explained that they had had a letter telling them not to send Fredrick back to school after the summer holiday. Who signed it was her first question after telling James she had not had any contact with the school since seeing them, and certainly not written a letter to anyone. James said there was a signature but only a scribble, not followed by a printed name below it. She asked if it was written on official school headed paper, and when told yes, she was even more mystified.

'I am sorry, James,' she said, 'But I can't help you with this in any way, it could be anybody that has accesses to school headed paper.' My advice would be to ignore it unless you can somehow check the handwriting.

'The letter is typewritten,' he said, 'and to find the typewriter it was written on would be impossible to find.'

He asked how she was enjoying her holiday and was told very much, she didn't realise how much she needed it. Telling her Fred sent his regards, he thanked her and apologised for having to ring before saying goodby and putting the phone down. As he did so, he heard Susan pulling the paper out of her typewriter.

'Are you feeling better now, love?' he said and asked to see what she had written. She gave him the letter, and while he read it, she filled the kettle to make coffee for them, going back to James's desk to discuss the contents she had composed. James called Fred over, and they went through what Susan had written.

It was a good letter but to no one in particular. James explained that she could send it to the school but who was going to open it and when? He said it would be a wasted effort, as he thought she would never get a reply. When she had calmed down, she came to her senses and agreed but filed the letter anyway.

While they drank their coffee, Fred came up with what was in the letter they had received, it was not expelling Fredrick, it was advising them not to send him back to the school.

Who would not report what was going on according to Stella because she would lose her job?

James said Fred had something. Susan wanted to know what Fred was talking about. James said it was something Stella had said when questioned about the punishment book. She said the nurse wanted to report Walter Brent for the canings he was dishing out, and that she had had to treat when the boys went to her. Going to one of the files Susan had created, James looked up the list of the addresses they had for the school staff. Under nurse, he got the name, address and phone number.

Picking up the phone, he rang the number of Nurse Margaret Gilbert. On getting through, he asked if he was speaking to Margaret Gilbert and was told he was. After telling her who he was, he got straight to the point and asked if she had sent them a letter advising them not to send their son Fredrick back to school after the holiday? She was very hesitant when James said it was like receiving an anonymous letter with only a signature that was unreadable. She said they were very clever working it out that she had sent it. He said that was the business they were in and asked if she could help them. She explained why she had sent the letter to them, together with two other parents whose boys were being punished too much. She said how it was worrying her and she had to do something to protect these boys without going to the authorities and likely lose her job.

She said she had complained to the headmaster about the punishment Brent was dishing out, and he said he would have a word with him, but if he was keeping discipline in his class then that was part of his job. Asked about Fredrick, in particular, she said he had come to her on several occasions when Brent had caned him on his backside, and it was as if he had been thrashed rather than just caned, and yet the brave little soldier never complained.

'He is a lovely lad, and I just cannot sit back and let this continue. The man is a sadist and a bully, and something has to be done about him.' James said she could rest assured it was going to be and in the not too distant future.

He asked if she would give him the addresses or phone numbers of the other two lots of parents she had sent to, and did she send the letter the same as his. She said she had, and each one was identical in the wording. He asked why she was so frightened of losing her job, she said that like Stella, the secretary, she was a widow with not long to go to pension age and asked, who would employ her now if she got the sack? After giving him the names she had sent the other letters to, James thanked her and asked her not to mention a word about their conversation because if Brent, Oliver or Andrews got to hear of what they were doing, they would be scuppered.

She promised and hoped that they were successful in their quest. Ringing off, James almost threw the phone back into its cradle with anger, saying, 'If only it could be arranged for Brent to be caned by the boys he was caning, justice would be done.' But he was sure they wouldn't do it if given the chance because they are too well brought up.

'What are you going to do now?' Both Fred and Susan wanted to know.

James said he had the phone numbers of the two other sets of parents that the nurse, who it was that sent the letters, and was going to telephone them.

While Susan collected the cups to wash up and Fred continued what he was doing, James picked up the phone again and dialled the first number he looked up. Getting through without much delay, a lady said,

'Hello, who am I speaking to?' James explained who he was and what he was doing and asked whether she had received a letter from the school advising them not to return their son to the school after the holiday. She said she hadn't opened the mail yet but would do it there and then. James waited while she went through it and heard her open an envelope. She obviously read it and came back to James saying yes, they had, but she didn't know who it was from because there was only a scribble as a signature with no printed name below it. The first question he asked was had their son complained about the punishment he was receiving from his class master? She said he had, and that her husband was going to go to the school when it opened and find out why, and that they were going to remove him from the school. James asked them not to do anything while they were working on the case that they hoped would be completed before the new school term began. He explained that it was the school nurse that had sent the letter and why. She said her husband was a solicitor and wasn't going to stand by and see his son punished in the way he was. James said he would like to meet her husband and if he would ring him back at his earliest convenience. He gave her both the office and home phone numbers before saying it was nice speaking to her and rang off.

The second number he rang, he got the father who was, he found out, self-employed and by the sounds of what he had to say was not short of a few bob. They had received the letter from the school but had no idea who to send a reply to due to not knowing who had sent it. He said his son had complained but not until he had got home after breaking up when they could do nothing about it due to the school being closed, but that they were not sending him back anyway after what their son had told them; he added that he knew about James's son and how he was being treated.

After some small talk, James asked that he do nothing as they were on the case as private investigators, and that they were looking into not only the canings but also what else was going on at the school. Asking what his job was, James learnt he owned a large development company. This was music to James' ears, and he asked if he could or would meet up with him. They agreed to meet after James explained what for and settled on the next day at ten o'clock in their office, seeing that they had not worked out where to go next with their enquiries. They decided on their office because he had to come their way on business so that he could kill two birds with one stone.

Fred said he had finished what he was doing and was going to start on the case they had put on the back burner, and perhaps Susan could give him a hand if he needed it. James said that was fine before saying, they had just had some good fortune and how ironic the letter they had received from the nurse was. As well as the advice on Fredrick, we have hit upon a solicitor and a property developer, both of which might be very helpful if they are prepared to work for nothing as we are. The rest of the day, they busied themselves with outstanding ongoing work before packing up earlier than usual. James told Fred he could take the day off tomorrow if he wanted to, but Fred said he would come in and carry on with the new case, but he might come in a bit later than usual.

On getting home, James and Susan spent until late afternoon in the garden, it was a lovely warm sunny day and so relaxing just doing a bit of weeding and sitting in their deckchairs, reading the paper and magazines. When Fredrick came in, his dad asked him about the two boys whose parents he had spoken to where like. He said they were both nice lads and they had become very good friends. He said there were a couple of others he was friendly with, but those two hit it off well with him. Why did they get the cane so much but not as much as him? Fredrick said he didn't know, but it was nearly always one of them when he got canned. He told him about the letter they had received and who it was from, at which Fredrick got quite emotional. When asked why, he explained to his dad what a nice, kind lady the nurse was.

'She told me to tell you what was happening to me, but I told you why I wouldn't. Why are you asking me about the other boys?' James explained that he and they were not going back to that school and that they might all go to another school together if he could arrange it so that they could remain being school friends.

Susan said she would only go to work that day if Fred wanted her, and he could give her a ring if he did. James said that would be fine.

He got ready himself and got to the office at nine o'clock. He called into the sweet shop downstairs and said hello to Elizabeth and bought some mints. As he got into the office, the phone was ringing, and answering it, he found it was Carol Jarvis, Oliver's secretary at his head office. She said he had not followed up on his enquiry about the extra-large load he wanted to be transported. James said he was rather busy right at that moment but would contact them in due course and put the phone down.

It was just after ten when there was a knock at the office door. James got up and answered it to find a very large, smartly-dressed man standing in front of him. He had businessman written all over him. He said he was Joe Harper, offering his hand, who he had spoken to yesterday. James invited him in and asked if he would like a cup of tea or coffee after his journey. Joe took the seat behind Fred's desk while James put the kettle on. While making the coffee, James asked how his journey had been. He said about the same as usual for that time of the day, and that he did a lot of driving with the job.

James passed his coffee with milk and sugar to him to help himself and dragged his chair over to face him.

'Where and who should start?' James asked and was told he could, and was asked what help did he want.

James started from when Fredrick came home and he saw the remains of the bruising on Fredrick's behind. He said how far he had gone with the enquiries they had so far made.

He explained what their thoughts were, his partner and himself, since Dr John Mountford had resigned and how the reputation of the school had gone down since he had, who the purchaser of the school was and who the new staff and board of governors were. He said the board of governors were blackmailed into their posts that none of them wanted, and that the teachers hired were second rate. He went on to say how Walter Brent came into the frame and how it was going after him that they had got as far as they had with their enquiries.

Joe interjected, 'But apart from my son, and my intention to take him away from the school, where do I fit in and how can I help?'

'Well, being the ruthless businessman he is, our feeling is that our Mr Oliver has purchased the school and land to develop it. He no more wants a school than fly in the air but would make a fortune if he sold it for development.'

Joe agreed, saying, 'If he put it on the market to sell as development land, he would indeed make a fortune…I would buy it if I could afford it, and that's for sure.' James asked him if he would go and view the school and grounds and have a guess at what the whole land the school stands in, with the school demolished, would fetch if sold for development. Joe said he had seen the school when he took his son to join it but had not given selling it a thought. The way that he looked at it now he would not demolish the building but would have it converted into apartments for purchase or rent and have other houses built around it for sale. He said he would guess he could build at least fifty properties that would bring in a great deal of capital, far more than he had paid for it. Joe asked if he was the Oliver that owned the haulage business, to which James said, 'Yes, among many other things.' James asked if he could ask around among his fellow developers to find out if there were any rumours afoot. Joe said he would and would keep James informed if he heard anything.

Before Joe left, James asked him where he would send his son if he took him away from Radcliff's. Joe said he would send him to the boarding school his brother had sent his son to, but when he had first tried, there had been no vacancies. James asked him if there were vacancies now? And if there were, he would try and get Fredrick into it too, so that the two boys could continue their friendship.' Joe promised he would do what James asked and would get back to him.

Saying he was now running a little behind time, he said he had to go. As he said it, Fred came in. James introduced him as his partner and showed Joe out. After shaking hands, he watched him get into his Bentley and waving, drive off.

Taking his jacket off, Fred sat in the seat Joe had vacated and asked James what had been said. James said that being a property developer, he would maybe be able to find out if it was Oliver's intention to sell the school and grounds for development if he could get planning permission. He said he had agreed to help and would say nothing to anyone that would cause Oliver and company to have any suspicions that they were being investigated. James now wanted to visit Desmond Cave and see if he would act for them for free if there was a need to get legal advice or assistance. Fred said he would leave him to it as he was finding the case he was working on a bit difficult.

While Fred set about continuing what he had started yesterday, James made the phone call to Desmond Cave, the solicitor, he had obviously given James his office number for when the phone call was answered, a young lady informed him that Mr Cave was not in that day. He asked if she could give him his home number but was told "No", that he kept his work at work and his private life separate. When asked if he would be in tomorrow he was told "Yes". On putting the phone down, he realised he had his home number from the list of the boys' home addresses and phone numbers, but as he was told he kept his work at work, he would respect that and ring tomorrow if he didn't get a call first.

Not to waste time, he asked Fred if there was anything he could do to help him.

Fred said there wasn't, that he had now got it all in hand. James was just going to get a file out when the phone rang. On answering it, he found Henry Andrews' blacksmith on the other end, asking to speak to Mr Fred Baker.

'Who can I tell him is calling?' James asked and was told "Tommy Naylor". Pressing a button on his phone, James asked Fred to pick up his.

Fred said, 'Hello', and that he was surprised to be getting a call from him. Tommy said he thought he would be interested in what he had been required to do and so had looked the card out that Fred had given him before he left to go back to the house. Fred asked what it was he had to tell him. Tommy said Andrews had come down to the forge himself and told him, emphasising told, and not asked him, he wanted him to do some interior alterations on two lorries he was getting in.

He gave him a drawing and said the lorries would be in the next day and would have materials to do the job onboard.

'Getting home and studying the drawing in detail, it looks as if the lorries are going to be used for, not just carrying what they were meant for, so would you be interested?' Fred said they would and thanked him, asking if they came to his home could they see the drawing. He said they could but it would have to be that day. Getting his address and other details, they would require they agreed on a time to meet.

Getting to Tommy's house, the front door was opened by Tommy's wife who asked them in when she found out who they were. She said that her husband was not home from work yet, but he shouldn't be long. She offered them tea or coffee that they accepted and were still drinking when Tommy came in. He gave them the drawing to peruse while he got changed out of his working clothes. James, being a marine engineer before becoming a private investigator, quickly recognised what the drawing was all about. He explained to Fred what he thought the modification was for, and when Tommy came back downstairs, he confirmed it. The dimensions of what Tommy had to work to, showed what he would do, was provide a secret compartment. What it would be used for is what Tommy thought Fred would be interested in.

He said the lorries had arrived and that he had made a start on them. He said they were lorries that normally carried general cargo to and from cargo ships in the docks.

'They are very long vehicles and have "Oliver's Haulage…why go to others?" printed along their sides.' Fred asked him when they had to be completed by and was told by the end of the week.

'Can you give me the registration numbers of the lorries?' Fred asked and was given them. Tommy said there was no way he could get them both done by the end of the week, and that is with a mate of his helping him. How was he doing it, James wanted to know. Tommy told him it was easiest to do them in tandem, doing a bit to one and the same bit to the other.

He said, 'Andrews came to watch how I was doing it and asked why I was doing it that way. I told him he had given me the job, so let him get on with it his way. He left taking his butler with him, the slimy git.'

James said there was no need to go back to the Andrews' house if he could keep them informed each evening how far he had got and when the lorries would be finished and taken away.

They thanked him for letting them know about the lorries and said it would be a good lead to follow up on.

Having met the family, they took leave of Tommy and said they would hope to hear from him tomorrow and, shaking hands, left.

On the drive back to their office they discussed what to do next. It came down to finding out what the lorries would be used for and where they would be going. It was getting quite late when they got to the office, and so checking to see if any phone calls had come in and finding there hadn't, they locked up and drove home.

Driving to work in their own cars and getting to the office within ten minutes of each other, they made a start on what they were going to do that day. James said the first thing he was going to do was to confirm who the vehicles were registered to. He made the call and found out.

They were, he was informed, registered to Oliver's Transport Company and given the age of them.

Putting the phone down and looking over to Fred, he said, 'Here we go.'

Having spent the day together, on what Fred was working on, and making some good progress, they went home a little late. When James got in, Susan said she had received a phone call from a Tommy Naylor, and when told James was not in yet, he asked if James would give him a call when he was. James asked how soon would it be before dinner was ready. Susan told him any time, and that the children had had theirs. Thinking of her and the washing up, he said he would eat first and phone afterwards. They ate their dinner, and while Susan washed up, James phoned Tommy.

When the call was answered, Tommy said they had got on well and that the job would be finished late tomorrow afternoon. Arrangements had been made for the lorries to be collected the following morning at eight o'clock. Thanking him for the information and saying they would be in contact at a later date, they put their phones down.

'What now?'

James gave it some thought and said he would like to know where the lorries would be going and what would they be being used for when they left the Andrews' estate, for they hadn't gone to all this trouble and expense without there being a good reason.

He looked over to Fred and said, 'How would you like to go on a mystery tour the day after tomorrow?' Fred said it sounded as if they would be if they were both thinking the same thing.

James said they must follow the two lorries to see where they go, what they pick up and where they take it to. If they take their cars separately, they could follow them if they split up. If they both remained in convoy together, they would have wasted some petrol. But so what? They will at least be prepared if they go to different places.

They decided they would get into place at 0730 and await the lorries' departure. James went to Fred's house at an unearthly time so in their own cars, they could leave together to get to where Andrews lived in Middleton. They stopped together just before getting to the gates where James got out of his car, and going to Fred's, suggested they park facing each other, as far apart as they could to just be able to see each other so they couldn't miss the lorries when they came out of the gates, and shouldn't be noticed by the lorry drivers if they arrived by car. They would follow at discreet distances as to try and not be seen to be following.

It was ten to eight when they saw a car draw up at the gates and the driver go to the speaker. The driver got back into the car as the gates were opening. James and Fred waited, and at quarter past eight, the gates opened and two lorries came out onto the road. They both turned towards James who was facing towards them, meaning he had to turn around. While he was doing this, Fred went past him, keeping his distance behind the lorries. James, having turned around, was behind Fred by quite a distance, but after a few miles he overtook Fred who drew back. They kept this up for about twenty miles heading in the direction of Southampton. On getting to a place called Templeton, the lorries drove through the main town before turning right. It was a minor dead-end road, and seeing the lorries turn into it, James, who was in front of Fred, let them go without following. He carried on for a couple of hundred yards and stopped. Fred, when he got to him, pulled up behind him. The two of them agreed that now it was fully daylight, they would go down the road on foot and be careful not to be seen.

They didn't know how far they had to walk, but locking their cars they set off in the direction the lorries had gone, knowing the road would come to a dead-end, but they didn't know how far that would be. They walked together for nearly a quarter of an hour when they came across a scrap metal yard. James whispered that they couldn't go through the gates so would have to look for some other way to get in, that was if the lorries had gone in there. The high fence with barbed wire on top looked impregnable, but they would learn nothing where they were; they had to get in.

Walking around the fence, they came to the back of what looked like a row of lockups and an unloading bay with a small portable crane and a larger building. It was behind this that they could just see the tops of the two lorries. They could hear voices but could not see anybody. They were in the undergrowth that went right up to the wire so would not be seen from inside.

'What are they doing, I wonder?' James whispered because they knew the lorries hadn't come here by chance, they had been sent there. They were not picking up scrap metal, they felt sure. So what was being loaded onto these lorries? Fred wondered if there was another entrance, and so, they left where they were and made their way along the fence until they came to a path that led to a gate. Looking along the path but staying out of sight, they could see a building looking like offices as well as a house.

Not seeing any movement anywhere, James said they were going to go through that gate. Getting out his lock-opening tools, that he always carried with him, he got to work on the padlock that was keeping the gate secure. It took him a very short time to see the lock droop down so that he could remove it, which he did. Hoping the gate would not make a noise when it opened, he pushed it open enough for them to get through. Fred, following James, shut the gate and put the lock back on making it look like it was locked.

They moved in the direction they had come but this time on the inside of the fence.

There was scrap metal in great heaps and scrapped cars separated in a huge mountain. Working their way without being seen as near as they could to the lorries, they could once again hear the voices. It was while they were trying to hear what was being said that they saw Sir Henry Andrews. He came around from the front of one of the lorries accompanied by his loyal butler Harry and two other men.

The way they were dressed, they were the lorry drivers who were getting their orders. From what they could hear, and that was not all that easy due to the distance they were away from them, they got the gist they had to load up at Southampton docks and heard "France" mentioned.

Taking his little camera out of his jacket pocket, James took three photographs of the four men and put it back in his pocket. Luckily, the camera made little noise, so there was no disturbance to the men he was photographing. After a few minutes, the men went back the way they had come, and it was time for them to go.

'Let's get going,' James whispered to Fred, 'Those lorries will be leaving soon, and we have a long walk to get back to our cars.' Creeping back to the gate, James removed the lock and letting Fred go through put the lock back as if it was locked when he had got through himself. Still being cautious, they edged their way back and, getting to the road, started walking briskly, talking as they went. James said they had to revisit the scrapyard because he was sure that was a cover for something far more sinister.

Fred asked, 'What about if the lorries go abroad, do we still follow them?'

That was a point that James hadn't thought of. He asked Fred if he had his passport on him and got yes for an answer, he said he always carried it. He said he had his if it was needed.

Getting back to their cars, quite sweaty now after the walk, they decided how they would play things, because, was there any point in now using both cars? Fred suggested they see if they split up before we decide. If they did, they would be ready.

Once again, they moved their cars to opposite sides of the road, facing each other.

It was only five minutes after they were settled that the lorries appeared, both turning left and heading towards Southampton. This time, it was Fred that had to turn around, and they undertook the same routine as before, first one and then the other being behind the lorries, this time, allowing other traffic to get between them but still keeping their quarries in site. It was obvious that they were heading for the docks. Getting to gate ten, they could only follow them so far and had to park up, however, they could see where the lorries had gone. They were about a quarter of a mile away but clearly in view outside of a very large warehouse with a loading platform in front of it. Getting out of their cars again, they decided to split up and head in the directions the lorries took. There was plenty of activity going on, so there was no need to hide on their approach towards the loading and unloading bay. Large crates were already being loaded onto the first lorry. Fred's, with the second one behind, ready to load. They were now close enough, although not next to each other, to see the crates contained farm equipment. The forklifts, two of them, brought the crates of all shapes and sizes from the warehouse to the lorries where two dock workers were putting them into place with their hand-operated loading equipment in the lorry.

When Fred's lorry was finished and secured, it moved off, meaning Fred had to make a hasty retreat to get back to his car, trying to watch over his shoulder where the lorry was going. Getting to his car, he quickly went in the direction the lorry had gone and found it had had to go to a weighbridge. Not too close, he saw the driver receive some paperwork from the bloke at the weighbridge without getting out of his cab and moved off. He drove out of the docks with Fred following.

Where to now? Fred wondered, knowing he was now on his own. He followed the lorry all the way to the Dover car ferry, where, after parking where he was told to, behind a line of other lorries, the driver got down from his cab and went to the booking office while Fred was directed to where he had to go. He had to go to the booking office where he booked a ticket on the next ferry to Calais in France, and showing his passport and with his cheque book, he purchased a return ticket for the next ferry out. The ferry was not due in for another fifty minutes, so he went into the café where the driver he was following had gone.

Having had nothing to eat since leaving home so early, Fred was hungry, and seeing there was an English breakfast available, he got himself one and a mug of tea. He sat next to the table the driver had chosen and had his meal. On finishing it and his table being cleared, he purchased a newspaper. He usually read The Times, but that was delivered at home, so he purchased a Daily Mirror. Going back to his table, a small family had taken possession of it, and when they realised Fred had been sitting at it, they said they would move. Fred told them to stay where they were and he would move to the next table. Now asking the lorry driver if he could sit at his table and getting a 'Yes, of course' as an answer, Fred sat opposite him.

Before opening his paper, he made some small talk, asking if he was going to France. The driver, who was a very pleasant youngish man, said that was his destination and that he would be unloaded and hopefully catch the last ferry back that night. Fred said he was going to France too, so he asked where was he going. He said Dunkirk, a place he had never been to before, but he had a good French map, so it should be all right. Fred asked if he went to France very often, to which he said, yes, but it was usually further north. Excusing himself, he said he was going to get a paper himself and got up and left, but Fred was not on his own for very long. James came up to his table, looking very stressed, saying,

'We didn't reckon on this, did we?' Having now only ten minutes before the ferry from France was due in, he said he would get something to eat on the ferry but was going to make a phone call to Susan to tell her they might be very late home and not to worry even if they don't make it back until tomorrow. He said he would tell her to pass the message to Fred's wife to save him wasting a phone call. He went away to make the call and was back very quickly, getting himself a mug of tea on the way. Getting back to the table, he sat and told Fred what had gone on with him, saying it was furniture on his lorry and was only about half full.

James said, 'With two different loads, the lorries will definitely split up when the ferry gets to France, so we will try and meet back here to catch the last ferry home.' Fred suggested they stay completely independent as he knew where his lorry was going, so he might be back before him and didn't want to sit here for hours, and then James wasn't back in time for the last ferry. James asked how he knew where his lorry was going, to which Fred said, 'I asked the driver.'

When the cars were called to board the ferry, Fred was well ahead of James, not that it mattered, and the heavy goods vehicles were loaded after all the cars and vans were on board. Fred saved a seat for James who found him after only a short time. James said he was going to get something to eat, and so, they both went to where food and drinks were being served. Sitting at a table for two, James got what he wanted and a cup of coffee for Fred. Looking over to one side of where they were sitting, Fred noticed his driver sitting with another man. He was slightly older, being middle-aged, but it was surely the driver of the other lorry. Fred pointed them out and James confirmed it, saying he had seen him at Southampton. There was one problem James had thought of, and that was who would be unloaded first the heavy vehicles or the cars. If it was the lorries they would lose them. Fred said knowing where he was heading for, he might be able to catch up with his, whereas James might not. They would have to see because if the cars were let off first, they could park up somewhere and wait for them to pass.

On getting to Calais, it was sod's law, the lorries were let off first. As they were going off, James got out of his car, and although being shouted at by a crew member, he was able to quickly tell Fred in his car he would follow him when they got off.

Getting off, Fred drove quite slowly so that James could catch him up, and when he saw him behind him, he put on speed. They drove for about half an hour, overtaking lorries as they went before Fred saw his lorry ahead, and as they entered a bend, he could see that the two lorries were together, one behind the other but with another one between them. Fred now slowed down to the lorries speed with now only a few vehicles between them and with James directly behind.

It was less than an hour to get to Dunkirk which they drove through before the front lorry turned off the main road and when the second lorry got to it turned off also. It was quite lucky that other vehicles turned as well to give them cover so to speak. Following at a discreet distance and James allowing cars to pass him, they continued to follow until they came to what looked like an industrial estate, big enough to be a small town. Both lorries went into it, but after a short distance, one carried on while the other one turned off. Keeping to their plan, Fred followed his going straight on while James turned off. The pair, both realising they now had to be careful, kept as far behind as they could but still keeping their lorry in sight.

Not knowing where James had gone, his lorry slowed and pulled into a large building, obviously intending to unload. Fred drove past a little way and was able to park amongst some other cars. Getting out Quickly and locking up, he made his way back to where the lorry had gone, but, how to get in without being seen? As he got to the massive door, it was being closed but not fast enough for him not to be able to see what was inside. The lorry he was following had turned and was backed up alongside a smaller covered lorry, and there were crates stacked up in different parts of the building as if ready to be loaded as the lorries came in to pick them up.

He wondered if there was another door, and going down the side of the building he found one. He tried it and found it wasn't locked, for it opened when Fred pushed it open just a bit, and seeing no one around he stepped in and closed it quickly and noiselessly behind him. He just couldn't believe his luck. Moving quickly behind some crates, he worked his way towards where the lorry was. It was so convenient that when he got adjacent to the lorry he had been following there was a gap between the crates. He was able to see the lorry being unloaded and was sure he couldn't be seen. There must have been at least six men, all in overalls, manhandling the crates from one lorry onto the other. Fred watched for the best part of an hour before the big door opened again and another lorry came in and parked on the other side of his lorry. He could not understand a lot of what was being said, for his French was limited, but he did understand when they had finished, or so he thought.

There was a conversation going on, and the men went back into the lorry, together with a man not in overalls. Fred could see down the lorry and saw the new man go to the back of it.

How he did it Fred could not see, but all of a sudden, there were more crates being unloaded, these he was sure were not the same sort of containers the farm machinery was being carried in.

Straining his eyes to see what was on these boxes, he was sure they were armaments. They didn't have five hundred rifles of five thousand bullets written on them, but Fred was sure they were military items. There was a lot of it in crates and boxes of all shapes and sizes. All that was taken from his lorry was put into the lorry that had just arrived so was obviously not going to the same place as the lorry that was there when he came in. The man not in overalls went back into his lorry, and though Fred tried hard to see, he was unable to see how the secret compartment was closed again. Within ten minutes of the armament lorry being loaded, the main door was opened again and it was driven away. If only Fred could find out where it was going but knew he couldn't. All he had learnt was that illegal gun-running was afoot. However, that was something they could pin their hat on if there was a need later.

The men that had been used to do the loading and unloading went in one direction, while the man not in overalls went to an office that Fred could just see on the other side of the warehouse just to the right of the main door. He, seeing them all go away, decided it was time for him to take his leave. By the same door he had entered, he left. As he got to near the front of the building, he was challenged by a rather large man dressed in overalls the same as those doing the loading inside. He spoke to Fred in French that Fred was able to understand, that being 'What were you doing down there?' Fred tried to explain half by saying and by action that he had been dying for a wee and that he couldn't go in the street. The man seemed satisfied and didn't bother Fred any more.

Getting back to his car, Fred decided he would try and find James, so he drove back to where he turned off, and looking down each turn-off as he passed them, left and right, he covered a good area before giving up. He couldn't see James' car anywhere, or perhaps that was James' intention.

On retracing his journey, passing one of the turnings he had passed, he caught sight of James' lorry coming towards him. He stopped just past the turning and the lorry passed him as it made its way out to the main road. Fred backed up until he could turn around the corner the lorry had come from. He drove slowly down the road and, getting to the bottom, still didn't see James' car. This he found strange, so he pulled into a parking space and, getting out of his car, went on foot to a very large set of doors. He could see lights on under the doors and thought it might be worthwhile investigating. The building was much like the one he had been in whilst following his lorry, so he took a look down the side of this one. He got to the door, as in his, and found it unlocked. Taking a chance, he opened it very slowly and without noise. He only cracked it open a little, not knowing what to expect. As he got it open enough to get his body through, he stepped inside, closing it behind him. Like his building, there were a lot of crates that he could hide behind, which he did. He could hear voices, and going further into the building still hidden, he could see James' car. He worked his way around until he could see who the voices belonged to. He took in a breath when he saw James tied up in a chair with two men getting very agitated, asking him what he was doing there and what did he know. When he would not answer, one of the men punched him in the face. He asked again what was he doing there and what had he seen. Again, James wouldn't answer. This time, the other man hit him. This time, James fell forward in the chair.

Fred couldn't stand by and let this continue, so picking up a length of metal pole that he found, he made a noise with it. The men, who were knocking James about, stopped what they were doing and one said to the other in French,

'What was that? Go and see.' The bigger man that had hit James first, started over to where Fred had made the noise.

163

Fred had moved his position, and as the man came around the wooden cases, without being seen, he brought the metal pole down on the man's head, knocking him sprawling. He fell silently and was out cold. Fred dragged him into a gap in the crates to hide him before deciding to go over to the smaller man, hoping he didn't have a gun. On seeing Fred as he approached at a run, the man made for his pocket, but Fred hit him across the arm with the pole. Giving out a yell of pain, he didn't make his pocket before Fred felled him with a right hook that brought blood spurting from his mouth as he hit the ground, he too out cold. Fred went to his pocket and removed the pistol that it contained, before untying James. Were there any other men around, Fred wanted to know and was happy to learn there wasn't, the rest of them had left the building.

'Right, let's get out of here,' Fred suggested and asked how the doors opened for James to get his car out. James told him how, and getting into his car, Fred opened the doors for him before setting them to close as he left himself. They said they had to get to the ferry before ten o'clock, and so, Fred, going to his car, led the way back to the ferry. Getting on the ferry, they looked for the lorries, but they were not on board; so where were they? They found themselves a seat before James said he wanted to clean himself up a bit and get some of the congealed blood off. On returning from the toilet, they were both hungry and got themselves a meal of sorts.

It was after midnight when they got home, agreeing they would go in James' car to the office in the morning after having a lay in until about eight o'clock. Getting in, the first thing Susan asked James was why did he have blood on his shirt. Saying nothing about the time of night he had got in,

James said he would tell her in the morning, but that he was tired and wanted some sleep.

Shaking his arm, Susan gave James a cup of tea and sat on the side of the bed while he drank it and listened to what he had to say about the trip to France. His face was bruised where the men had hit him, but he assured Susan he was all right.

On finishing his breakfast, he said he was going to pick Fred up and she could follow them when she was ready. This agreed, he went out to his car to pick Fred up. They chatted together on their way to the office and, getting there, sat for the best part of an hour telling each other what each had seen and heard.

It was agreed that gun-running was at least one of the things Andrews, aided by Oliver, were doing, and they wondered how long it had been going on. James said he was going to contact David Bright and George Bateman to find out if Oliver's had transported goods to France for them.

The question came up that where were the arms being sent to, for James had watched similar goings-on in his building as Fred had in his. Both had unloaded from the secret compartments into a smaller lorry that had driven off. This was before James had got caught. He said the side door of the building he was in had been locked, but that he had picked the lock to get it open, and they obviously had not locked it again after they had caught him. Fred wanted to know how they discovered him, and James explained. He said they knew his car because the lorry driver told them he had been following him and was told to go out and find it.

'Going through my pockets, they found the keys before the lorry driver, finding it, drove it into where Fred had seen it.'

'How did he start the car if the lorry driver took your keys?'

'Because he left the key in the ignition after he brought it in.'

'I wonder when the two I hit with that metal pole I found came round, especially the one I hit first, for I didn't half hit him hard. I wonder if I killed him.'

'I don't suppose we will ever know' was all that James could say.

When Susan came in, the first thing she did after taking her little jacket off, was put the kettle on. Making them all a drink, she asked what they were going to do today. James said he was going to make two phone calls before they did anything else.

While she made coffee, James picked up his phone and dialled George Bateman's number. It didn't take long before the call was answered by George himself who asked who wanted him. On saying who it was that was calling, George said, 'Hello.'

James asked, had he had any of his farm machinery transported abroad lately. George said he had, and that the company he had sold to had been asking where it was. James informed him that it had been unloaded in Dunkirk yesterday. George said it was picked up from his warehouse over a week ago, and it was bound for Germany and not France, so he wondered what was going on. James gave him a rundown on what they had done yesterday but without mentioning the armament part. George thanked him for letting him know and said he would get onto Oliver's to find out what the delay was and when was his machinery going to get to Germany, where it was expected and well overdue. Saying goodbye, James put the phone down and drank the coffee Susan had made.

He then phoned David Bright and asked if he had exported furniture of late and was told he had, and that Oliver's transport had collected it eight days ago. James had to ask what its destination was. David wanted to know why this was being asked because his client had telephoned asking when it was due to arrive. He said he had been onto Oliver's and was told the lorry they used had broken down and a replacement lorry was being sent to replace it. James told him where it had been unloaded and was told it should have been taken to Southern France, not Dunkirk.

It was then that James came up with the suggestion that maybe it was stated somewhere in his contract, that Oliver was holding them to, that on-time delivery was guaranteed, for if it was, could that not be reason enough to break the contract? David's reply came that if he tried to enforce that, it would have to be done through the courts and would cost a great deal of money, plus the fact that excuses Oliver would make could mean he wouldn't win the case and would have to pay court fees. James apologised and said he hadn't thought of that.

Saying goodbye and that he might be in touch at a later date, he put the phone down.

Fred, not wanting to go through their French escapade again, put it to James that Oliver's also transported what Barry Keen and Joe Mather deal with, and were they having anything transported abroad in the near future? James said it was worth thinking about and would contact them to maybe open another can of worms. He would telephone them in due course.

They knew what Andrews and Oliver were up to, but it was far too early to go to the police, plus they had no actual proof other than what they had witnessed themselves.

It was still a mystery how the connections were with Andrew, Oliver, Brent and Good came together; it surely couldn't still be the army or through marriage…or could it?

Chapter 10

It had been over a week since the two of them had seen Oliver and his wife fly off to Germany and taken the opportunity to visit his mother. They had made progress with other detective work that had come into the office, plus the case that Fred had now completed.

James had phoned both Barry Keen and Joe Mather about any transport arrangements they had made with Oliver's and found out theirs were in the UK only, nothing at this time for abroad.

James was sitting at his desk when the phone rang. It was Joe Harper, the developer and the father of Fredrick's school friend, who wished James well and said he had some news for him. He said he had made some quite extensive enquiries about the school and Oliver in particular. He and Fred had been correct in assuming Oliver was making inroads to sell the school and the land that it stood on. He said he had had to call in a favour to get the information he had acquired, but that was of no consequence. As far as he understood, Oliver was not fussy who he sold to but was likely to make a lot of money out of whoever it was. He said he wondered how Oliver had not contacted him, but perhaps he thought he was not rich enough. He said he had very recently been to Germany on business, and it was thought part of the visit was to do with selling the school. James thanked him profusely and asked him to keep his ear to the ground and let him know if there was any way he could be prevented from selling or at least be held up. Joe said that was not all, but that it had been mentioned that he was also fishing around in the market for selling the property he lived in, but apparently, he was having problems with that. After saying he would be in touch again later, the conversation was ended and James rang off.

Fred, after finishing the case he had been working on alone, asked James if it would be all right if he took a few days off to take Amy his wife away for a break, to celebrate their wedding anniversary. James found this no trouble, especially as things on the Oliver front had gone a bit cold.

He asked if he knew where they were going and was told the Lake District, as Amy loved the scenery and had always wanted to go there. Asking if Elizabeth, her sister, was going with them, Fred said she had told them to go off on their own and enjoy the time together.

It was the afternoon after Fred had left that morning for the lakes, that James received a phone call from Peggy Banks, Mrs Oliver senior's nurse. She said she was telephoning to let James know Mrs Oliver was ill, and that it was being considered whether she should be taken to hospital.

Mr Oliver was against it, but the nurse was all for it. James asked what was the matter with her and how long she had been unwell. Peggy said she had started vomiting the day after Mr Oliver and his wife got home from Germany. She said she had consulted with Mr Oliver over his mother's condition and he agreed to call his doctor in to see her.

'The doctor came and, on examining her, said it was a bug and that if she took the medicine he prescribed, she would be better in a couple of days. Well, she isn't, and I am worried about her.'

James asked if she was still being sick and was told she was and quite often.

'Who cooks her meals?' James asked, and was told the cook with the housekeeper overseeing them. The reason, James explained, he was asking such questions was because he was wondering if she was being fed food that was causing her to be sick. Peggy said she had asked if she could take over the preparation and cooking of her employers' meals but was told not under any circumstances, that she was employed to nurse her, not cook for her. James put it to Peggy if she could do food shopping without being found out when she bought food for herself or did she have to have meals supplied.

It was after Peggy had said she had to feed herself that James suggested that if it was possible to ditch what the kitchen was supplying and giving her what she could feed her with, that would determine if she was being poisoned or the likes. Peggy said it was a good idea, and that she could at least give it a go.

'Do you know what the medication the doctor has prescribed is ?' he asked and was told it was some medicine that had to be taken with meals or after being sick that she had never come across before. James's mind started to race, and he was sure Tony Oliver was not wanting the hospital to find out what he was doing to his mother, but he was sure he was trying to kill her.

He put his thoughts to Peggy who said it was possible and the blame could be put on her as the old lady's nurse. James asked when her next day off was, and was told the day after tomorrow. He asked if he could meet her if she was prepared to give up some of that day to see him.

She said she would willingly if he thought anything could be gained by it. He said it might make a break for her, and that she might be able to bring him up to date with the situation. They decided on a time and place to meet, and just before putting the phone down, James asked if she knew who the doctor was, who Oliver had employed, and who stood in for her when she had a day off.

She said she didn't know who the doctor was by name, but she could try and find out, and as for her relief, a nurse was employed each week from a private source and not always the same one.

Eventually, putting the phone down, he asked Susan if she would like a trip out the day after tomorrow. She asked why, and when told, she said it would make a nice change.

While Fred was away, James got two calls asking for help, one as a new case and one from Mrs Brent who said her husband had returned home from his fishing trip, and because things hadn't gone well and the weather had not been very good in Scotland, he wasn't in the best of moods and had done his best to take it out on her and her son; they were both treading on eggshells. She said her son was back from his summer camp with the ATC and was spending most of his time either out during the day or in his locked bedroom. James asked if he had hit her, to which she said not badly but it wasn't to say he wouldn't. He advised her to go to the police before he injured her badly. She said she wouldn't or couldn't because she thought he would kill her.

The phone call from Mrs Brent was a wake-up call for more investigation to be made into Brent and his connection between the army and the school, and part of this would have to be observing what he did while he was not at the school. So he thought he would follow him wherever he went while on his own until something occurred that might throw some light on what the connection was. But how was he going to know when he was going and what he was going for? He was going to have to stay in digs near to where Brent's family lived. Thinking back, he still had the card Mrs Moore (Trixie) had given him, and so, looking it out, he gave her a phone call. On answering, she remembered him and told him a room was available for the dates he quoted. He asked her to keep the single room free and he would be seeing her soon before ringing off.

James spent the next day going through all the information he and Fred had so far accumulated and that Susan had made files for. He pondered on what he was going to do about Gerald Good and his two wives, for that was going to be exposed at some time or another before this case was closed. They had enough already to go to the police with, but nothing so far was bringing everything together to achieve what they were looking to do.

James and Susan were ready to leave home by eight o'clock to go and meet up with Peggy Banks. They drove to their destination and talked about Mrs Oliver and what would happen if she died. Where they had agreed to meet was a tea room in a small village much nearer to Peggy than them, and when they arrived and went inside, Peggy was already there. She got up from the table she was sat at and looked at Susan with some trepidation, which James relieved when he introduced Susan as his wife and secretary. They all sat at a table for four, and James ordered coffee from the counter. On looking over to the table, he asked by action if they wanted anything to eat.

They wagged their heads indicating no and carried on talking ten to the dozen. Susan was a good conversationalist and had obviously hit on a subject they were both very passionate about. After paying for the coffees and being told they would be served at the table, he went back and joined the two ladies.

He asked what they were talking about and was told it was woman's talk.

As they drank their coffee, James asked what had happened since they spoke on the phone. Peggy said she had spoken to Mrs Oliver and she seemed to be unsurprised at what Peggy had told her and was willing to go along with what James had suggested. The meals came, including beverages, and directly Peggy had got them to give to her she disposed of them and took into her what she had prepared.

'What about what the doctor had prescribed?'

She said she had stopped giving it to her, and she was keeping what Peggy was giving her down and not being sick. So it was clear someone was putting something in her food that was making her ill. James wanted to know if Peggy had any suspicions who it might be and was told the housekeeper rather than the cook, for the rest of the household, including the staff, ate what was coming out of the kitchen except for her, and none of them was ill. Whatever was added to Mrs Oliver's food must have been added after the meals had been prepared and delivered to Peggy to give her.

James asked if it could be possible in her capacity as a private nurse to have the meals being given to Mrs Oliver tested for poison. Peggy doubted it but said she could see if it was possible through an acquaintance she has that works in a laboratory. Susan suggested it would be risky and could put Peggy's job in jeopardy if it was found out what she was doing, plus the fact how was she going to get the food to the person she knew. James had to admit perhaps he was being too ambitious with someone else's job at stake and told Peggy not to do it even though it would be good to do so. They were together for well over two hours and got through a copious amount of cups of coffee. Before she forgot, she had to pass on Mrs Oliver's best regards and to thank him for what he was doing. She was very impressed with him and Fred and hoped between them they could prevent her son from killing her.

On leaving the tea room, they said their goodbyes, and Peggy said she would pass on to James anything she thought he should know about. On leaving the car park, they drove off in opposite directions. Susan said how nice Peggy was to talk to and how dedicated she was to the old lady, she almost looked upon her as her own grandmother. They got home in good time and found both their children busy getting a meal for their mum and dad which they thought was wonderful and very thoughtful.

Chapter 11

James got to Mrs Moore's by eleven o'clock and on being welcomed and shown to the room she had allocated him, he sorted himself out before going downstairs. She excused herself for asking, but she asked if he was back to see Mr Brent. James said he had received a phone call from Mrs Brent that had caused him some concern, and that he needed to get to know much more about her husband. Once again, Trixie warned him to be careful of this man, as he could be, as she put it, a very dangerous individual.

He explained to Trixie what his intention was, and that his comings and goings could become very erratic and asked if he could have a key to be able to get in during the day or night without disturbing her and any other people using her B and B. She went and got him a key and thanked him for being so considerate. He also asked if he could use her phone and was told yes, but he would have to pay something towards the bill if he did. All this agreed, James made a call to Brent's house, and on it being answered by Mrs Brent, he asked if her husband was home. She said he wasn't so she could talk. James asked where he was and what was he doing at that moment in time.

She said he was out with one of his mates but would be home for a meal before going out again at seven o'clock. Thanking her, he said he would try and get the opportunity to get to see her before he went home.

He went back to the pub where the landlord remembered him and asked if he was back for another one of his chef's pies. He said he would be around for a couple of days so would be seeing more of him. After finishing his meal, he left the pub in plenty of time to be in sight of Brent's house by seven o'clock.

Right on the dot of seven, a car drew up, and getting out of the car, the driver went and knocked on the front door. James couldn't see if there was anybody else in the car, but Brent got into the front passenger seat. James was parked in such a way that he could follow the car without having to turn to do so. This was now to be the start of 'The Brent hunt and the unknown.'

The driver got back into the driving seat and took off at some speed. James was not quite prepared for such haste, but he didn't lose the car he intended to follow. He stayed well behind it as it worked its way through the next village out into the countryside. It took about half an hour before they came across a farm and its outbuildings. It was at one of these that the car pulled up and parked among a lot of others. James stopped well behind it, letting other cars pass him to also park.

He saw three men get out of the car, Brent being one of them, and go into the building. When he thought it was safe, he also went and parked in amongst the parked cars, well away from Brent's car. When he got out, he locked it and made his way to the building all the other men were going into. He didn't know what he was going to find when he got in there but got behind several men as he got to the entrance.

He guessed he would have to pay to get in and was surprised it was ten pounds.

Getting in, he found it was very noisy. There were a few women among all the men who were all standing around a sectioned off square in the middle of what was a large barn. Amongst the hubbub of the people, James heard the sound of barking dogs, which he thought was out of place. He looked around among the crowd to see if he could see Brent. He walked around three of the sides of the square before he spotted him with the other two men in the car. They seemed to be part of a group of other men who they had met up with. A right lot of scruffy and hard nut individuals they appeared to be. James stood near enough to hear what they were saying, for they had to almost shout due to the noise around them. He was glad he had put on very casual clothes, for he didn't stand out from the crowd.

It was well over half an hour before a lovely, sexily-dressed young woman together with a man well into his fifties, James estimated, entered the square. The young woman was holding a board on a pole with two names on it. The man who was the MC welcomed everybody and asked for some quiet. He said if anyone else wanted to place a bet, they should do so now as the first fight would start in ten minutes. There would be six fights and a surprise event at the end. The young woman holding the pole paraded around all four sides of the square with the two names displayed on the board. After ten minutes, a bell sounded and the MC said betting was now closed. Brent had been one of those who had made a bet together with most of his mates if that is what they were.

It was then that James realised what the barking was that he had heard, for two handlers appeared with a bull mastiff each on leads. Both had muzzles covering their noses and mouths and were very hyped up. They got into the square in opposite corners where the muzzles were removed but still kept on their leads. Both animals were badly scarred from previous meetings so obviously knew what they had to do.

When the bell sounded, the two dogs were let off their leads and they set about each other. The whole thing made James feel sick. He loved animals, and to witness what he was seeing was more than he could stomach. However, he watched the fight to its conclusion when one dog was pulled off the other having done terrible damage to it. James hoped one of the dogs would set on its handler but it didn't, the loser couldn't have anyway it was too badly injured.

Brent had obviously, with a couple of his mates, backed the winner, for they made their way to the betting table to pick up their winnings. The barn was being well used in between fights, so there was obviously going to be trouble of some sort by closing time.

It was more than James could handle, and leaving the barn, he sat in his car for a while just thinking. He could hear the cheers coming from the barn as the crowd witnessed the dog fights. There was no point in him following them back to Brent's house, for what would that achieve? The thing that he realised was that Brent just enjoyed either hurting things himself or witnessing others being hurt. This was the sadist the boys spoke of coming out in him.

Organised dogfighting would be something he would report to the police when Brent had been dealt with, not that he knew at that moment how or what that was going to be.

Knowing where Brent was, he decided to go back to the digs and phone Brents wife to arrange a meeting with her. This he did, and although it was quite late, he wondered what time what he had been to see would be over, and what time Brent would be home. He also telephoned Susan to let her know he had arrived safely and had settled in, also that he didn't know how long he would be away.

On phoning Mrs Brent, she didn't seem to be very responsive to his call. She said she didn't want to see anybody and certainly not for the next few days. James prompted her by asking if her husband had knocked her about since he had been home from his week away with his mates, but she just went quiet before saying sorry and putting the phone down.

Slowly putting his phone down, James wondered just what this man was really like for he was sure he had beaten his wife again. He went to bed with this on his mind and laid awake for quite a while, thinking of what he alone, or with Fred, could do to this man and how they could get him sent to prison.

He woke up with a start, and looking at his watch, he saw it was half-past seven. He got up, washed and dressed, and going down to breakfast, he had a good one. After finishing it and with the other boarders gone, he asked his landlady if she belonged to anything where she met up with Mrs Brent. She said only the bookclub she belonged to, and that was only on the very rare occasions that Mrs Brent attended. She asked James if he had seen her, to which he said he had and was worried about her because he was sure her husband had given her another beating.

He left the digs and decided to try and learn something from Brent's neighbours. He realised this had an element of danger attached to it, but he had to find out if there was any way he could get something pinned on this man. He got near to where Brent lived and parked in the road well away from their house. He walked to the house next door and, ringing the doorbell, waited. It was after a short time he heard a woman shout out she would only be a minute.

It was while he was waiting for her to come to the door he saw Brent come out of his house and go to the car. He knew it was Brent because of seeing so many photographs of him in uniform in some of the different houses he had visited. Brent didn't look in his direction, but James could now see him in real life, and he could understand how the boys he had under him felt about him. He didn't look to be a nice man in any way, and what James could see of him, he had bully written all over him.

Brent had driven off by the time the door was opened, and a lady was standing in front of him in what looked like an old dress, slippers and a towel wrapped around her head. She apologised to James, saying she had been soaking and reading in the bath and hadn't realised what the time was. James said who he was and asked if he could go in to speak to her. She said her husband was at work, but she supposed so. Going in and being asked to sit down in a very tidy lounge, James broke the ice by asking if the book she was reading was a good one. She said it was and that she loved reading crime and mystery stories. He explained what he was doing and asked if she could help him? To which she replied she would if she could.

She said, when asked, that she and her husband had lived in the house since it was built, and that the house next door had been built later when the developer had acquired the land from a different owner.

James started from when Brent moved in. She said when they moved in, it was only Mrs Brent and her son. She said the previous owners were lovely people and they had become good friends, and that she had been sorry to see them leave. She said Mrs Brent was a very nice and reserved lady who kept herself to herself and that her son was a lovely boy. She had said when they first met that her husband was in the army and wasn't home very much. As it happens, she went on, it was the lull before the storm.

It must have been nearly a year before Brent came out of the army and what a difference that made. Everything changed, especially with the boy. We think Brent finally got a job as a teacher at a private boarding school where he still works, but he was out of work for a good six months before he got the job. How did things change, James wanted to know. Margaret Davis, who had introduced herself, said it wasn't long after leaving the army that arguments started and a lot of shouting about. Men arrived and booze nights used to and, still do, go on until the early hours of the morning. We only ever saw Mrs Brent occasionally and her son even less mainly going to and coming home from school. James then asked, although even he thought it a stupid question, what is he like as a neighbour. She said, funnily enough, when properly sober, he is quite good, especially when he first came out of the army.

He helped my husband build the shed in the garden and also with other projects he undertook. I think he was probably influenced by some of the men he hangs out with. The one thing about him I don't like is he is very cruel; we often wonder if he knocks his wife about because after a lot of shouting, we don't see her for days, and when we do, she is heavily made up.

'Have you ever notified the police?' James wanted to know, and when told no, he asked why not.'

He asked if Brent goes out at regular times on regular nights, to which she said she wouldn't know as they now have nothing to do with them.

'While he is away at the school, things are fine, it's when he comes home we get trouble.' He asked why they now have nothing to do with them. She said about a year ago, her husband was invited to go out for a drink with him, and whilst in the pub, a fight started and he got caught up in it. He has avoided him ever since.

James realised he was not going to get anything worthwhile from this visit, so he made to go. However, as he got up to leave, he saw, through the window, the car next door arrive back. He was this time able to see Brent properly and didn't like the man from the way he seemed to be self-important with an attitude. He thanked Margaret for seeing him and asked her to let him know if there was any more trouble before the school term started, giving her his card and asking her not to mention to anyone that he had been there.

He drove back to the digs to collect his things and square up with Trixie, including some money for the phone. He told her he could learn no more from staying on any longer so was going to go back to his office, then home. She thanked him for the phone money as well as his rent and wished him well in his endeavours for the future.

Getting back to the office, Susan had been in and left him a note saying Peggy Banks had telephoned and asked if he could ring her back at his convenience.

He rang her there and then on her private number, and he was lucky enough to get her. She told him she had discovered that Mrs Oliver senior was being slowly poisoned, and that she had taken a sample of one of the drinks she was given to her friend at the lab, who was going to find out what the substance was. She also said it was the housekeeper that was administering the poison, whatever it was, as she was always in the kitchen when the old lady's meals were ready for taking to her. She said she had learned this from the cook by stealth. She asked if they could meet and assured him Mrs Oliver senior was safe as she was making the tea she drank herself, throwing the tea away that was being provided by the kitchen. She also told him, whenever her meals came, the old lady was in a deep sleep and had to be woken up and never knew where she was. She might be old but is a very good actress for she was sure they thought whatever they were giving her was working, although quite slowly. They arranged a day and time to meet at the same place as before. She said she could only make it on her day off so it would have to be the day after tomorrow; she added she had told the old lady to not drink the tea while she was not there and drink water if she could manage it.

It was as he was sitting, wondering where to go and what to do next that the phone rang, and it was Fred who said his wife had had a fall and broken her arm and that they would be back later than what he had said, owing to her having to attend the hospital and her arm put in plaster and all that goes with it. James said how sorry he was to learn of Amy's accident and told him to take as long as it took to get back. Fred asked how things were going and sounded disappointed when told they were at the moment at a standstill, other than his meeting with Peggy Banks. Sending their love to Amy, he rang off.

He looked in the diary to see what he could do with what Susan had put in it.

He found there had been another call from Oliver's transport, so he decided to ring them. There was no indication who the caller had been, so he decided to call Oliver's private secretary Ann Fingles. He put the call through and was told she was not available, but if he rang the number he was given he could get Carol Jarvis at the head office. He rang the number he was given and got Carol who must have been having a good day, as she was charming. James said it was Edward Miles calling (his false name) and he wanted to know what the call was for. She said it wasn't her that rang, so she didn't know what the call was about, but she would make enquiries and telephone him back. She asked him about the large, wide and heavy load he wanted to be transported and he told her that he had arranged with another company to do the job. To this, she said he had done the wrong thing for whatever the price he had been charged they would have undercut it. Asking if Mr Oliver was in his office, she said he was, but that he was very busy and wouldn't take any calls. This being the case, he wished her a good day and rang off.

He took two calls from customers wanting the services of Royston and Baker, both of which he took on but only on the understanding they could not be undertaken immediately.

He telephoned Joe Harper who when he got through said he was going to ring him for he was sure Oliver was making loud noises about selling what was presently the school. But

James said he could not sell it because he didn't own it all. Joe said that maybe so, but he certainly was testing the market.

James thanked him and said he would do some research.

He rang John Mountford's number and got Hazel who said he was out, but he shouldn't be long and she would get him to ring him. Knowing she knew what there was to know about the school, he asked her if Oliver had made any contact with John. She said he had, and that John was going to ring him and tell him all about it. She said, 'He should be back within the hour, and he will tell you what the contact was all about.' James said he would be in his office if John would like to ring him on that number.

It was less than an hour before John rang back, apologising for not being in when James called. He said Hazel had told him what James wanted and went about telling him.

He said it was only a couple of days ago that Oliver had come on the phone, as nice as pie, before getting around to the shares John owned. He said he had offered him an exceptional amount of money for them, half of the total amount he had paid the other shareholders for theirs.

James asked, 'What was his reply?'

John said he told him he could offer him all the money in the world, but he would not sell his shares to him, and that he still wouldn't get them if and when he dies. James told him why Oliver wanted his shares so desperately and he was not surprised and added, he could not, as far as he knew, sell the school without one hundred per cent ownership.

Thanking him and mentioning that Fred's wife had broken her arm while on a short holiday in the Lake District, he was sure Fred would send his regards to them both and rang off.

He was sure John was right but rang Desmond Cave to make sure. When he got through to him, he confirmed that until Mountford sold his shares to him or gave his permission in writing for him to sell the building and land with John retaining his five per cent of the value of what the sale accumulated, he could not sell. He added it was a good thing Mountford told him he would not get the shares even if he died has probably saved his life. James thanked him for the information and just smiled when Desmond said he would receive his bill through the post.

With Oliver trying to kill his mother and selling the school, he wondered what Andrews was up to. He knew he was smuggling armaments illegally because of what they had witnessed in France, but he must be doing something else to make money, so what was it?

Knowing that both he and the son treated his wife and mother like dirt, he wondered if she might be able to tell them if she was willing and able to do so. This might also be an opportunity to get to learn what the connection was between them.

He would be able to bring this up with Peggy when they met, or at least get her to pump Mrs Oliver senior for any information she had.

It was well into the afternoon when he got home and found the family relaxing in the garden. He said hello to them and went upstairs to change into something more casual than a suit. On returning to the garden, he asked what they were having for their dinner. Susan said it was going to be a surprise because Joyce was making it and wasn't saying what she was going to do.

Fredrick asked his dad if he would play chess with him if he got it out? While they played chess, Joyce went indoors to prepare what she was doing for a meal, leaving her mother to just relax.

After letting Fredrick beat him, or so he said, he asked if they wanted a drink before their meal.

Getting up, he got them what they asked for. Elisabeth telephoned, asking if they would like to go over for a meal tomorrow, as with Fred and her sister away longer than she expected, she would like the company.

The next morning, James had a light breakfast after having such a big meal the evening before, where Joyce did herself proud with a little help from her mum. He said he didn't know how long he would be seeing Peggy, but he would certainly not be too late home.

He set off in good time and, getting to the tea room, sat and waited. Peggy got there within ten minutes of the arranged time and excused herself for being caught up in traffic. James ordered coffee for them both and a tea cake. Peggy got right down to why she was there, saying she was getting worried about Mrs Oliver senior. She said Mrs Oliver (Tony's wife) had been in to visit when the old lady really put on an act. I was told to leave the room so wasn't able to listen to what the conversation was about, but when my bell rang and I went back to the room, the old lady was in a bit of a state. She told me her daughter-in-law would probably not visit again because she had read her the riot act, but she had admitted among other things that she knew they wanted her dead, so hopes she hadn't inadvertently told them she knew she was being poisoned.

James asked if she had had contact with her friend that worked at the laboratory and she said she had. She was correct in her assumption that Mrs Oliver senior was being poisoned. She said the poison found in the sample she had given her friend contained paraquat, but it was only a very minuscule amount.

Whoever was administering it knew what they were doing for the amount was so small that it would take quite a long time to kill her. James wondered where it was acquired from and was told by Peggy, probably the greenhouse, as weed killer contained it. She said she had read up about it to see how it worked as a poison to humans. Large amounts would kill quickly and do great damage to the internal organs. She first picked it up when the old lady started vomiting for no apparent reason. She said as a precaution, she had stopped her drinking the coffee she was having and was making that herself as well as the tea and not letting her drink that that came when she asked for it.

James asked how she ordered what food she wanted. Peggy said the cook asks each afternoon what she wants to eat for the next day, together with beverages, and if she wants anything in between, she rings for it or gets me to fetch it. The cook writes it down and is very good and complies with Mrs Oliver's wishes.

How does the housekeeper come into all this, James wanted to know, and was told she and the butler ran the house between them. Whatever went on within the house, they knew about it, especially the butler, for the housekeeper came under him as well…he is the top dog.

Peggy went on to say, 'Mr Anthony Oliver had come to see his mother yesterday early evening who I pretended to wake up so that he could talk to her. He, like his wife had done, told me to leave the room. This I did but, not shutting the door completely, listened at it to what was being said. I knew if I was spotted I would probably be sacked. However, I wasn't, and as the voices were being raised, I got most of what was being said. The main reason he had come to visit his mother was to tell her off for the way she had spoken to his wife the evening before. He started by saying how upset his wife was but didn't get very far before his mother told him to shut up and proceeded to read him the riot act as well. She really went for him. She told him what she thought of his wife in no uncertain way and followed this up by telling him what she thought of him, and what his father would think of him.

'He started to argue with her, but she would have none of it. He said he was a good businessman and was keeping her in a fashion she was used to. She answered this by telling him he was not a good businessman but a crook. She laid it on the line of what she thought of him and added on to this what was he doing buying a school?

'This opened a can of worms, for he wanted to know how she knew about it. It then went quiet, and I could not hear what she was saying. When the voices were raised again, she was talking about him wanting to sell the house. She told him she would die in her house, and there was no way he would sell it while she was still alive. She said although she was not feeling well and was sleepy a lot of the time, since she had stopped being sick, she wondered if she should see a doctor. He answered her by saying he didn't think a doctor was necessary for it was more than likely due to an upset tummy and her age. She started to cry, I could hear her. She said she was getting no respect from anybody and wanted the housekeeper sacked.

'Anthony went mad at this point, saying the housekeeper would not be sacked, and that he would employ anyone he thought suitable for any post he saw fit to fill in or out of the house. She reminded him again it was her house, and although she was no longer mobile, she would have who she wanted to be employed and not him. He told her there was going to be no sackings and she could do what she liked. Thinking this would end his visit, I got away from the door and quickly went to my room. It must have been about ten minutes before she rang for me, and when I got back to her room, she had a smile on her face and told me what she had told him and put him in his place.

'She asked me to sit down and pour them both a brandy. Using the decanter and two of the crystal-cut goblets that were on a tray on her drinks table, I sat with her while she talked about her son and what a horrible man he had become. She told me she wanted the housekeeper sacked, and he would not hear of it, and that she could not overrule him.

Peggy went on to say she had spoken to the gardener to ask if he had lost any weed killer. He said he had ordered and was using new stuff that had been recommended but still had some of the old stuff left. He went and checked there and then and came back and said there was some of it missing.

He, of course, wanted to know why I was asking about weed killer. I told him I needed some for my house, as I was living in and only visiting my own home on the odd occasion, it was becoming overgrown with weeds, and that I wondered if he could let me have some.

He asked me how big my garden was, and when told, he gave me three little packs, warning me to be very careful with it, to wear gloves and old clothes when I used it, as it was deadly stuff and to be handled with care. He said he could not understand why some had gone missing, but perhaps there wasn't as much left as he thought.

James thanked Peggy for meeting him and telling her about Fred's wife and her fall, she said it would take some time for her to recover, for broken limbs in older people take longer to mend. Telling her to keep the protection of Mrs Oliver as a priority and keeping up the acting and making sure she is kept away from paraquat for a while longer, he said his cheerios at Peggy's car, giving her a peck on the cheek, they shook hands, saying they would stay in touch. James then went to his car to drive back to his office.

Getting back to the office, he found it quite strange being on his own. He had got so used to Fred being there, he felt that something was missing. He sat pondering, wondering how he could best get to lock Oliver, Andrews, Good and Walter Brent together. There must be something, but what, surely not just the army?

Chapter 12

It was now time to speak to Gerald Good. He rang the number he had for his on school holiday home, and getting Mrs Good, Oliver's sister, he asked if he was available. She said he was but not at that very moment in time, if James would leave his number, she would get him to let him know when he was available. James asked after her and she said she had been very busy with her charity work, and that Gerald had taken some of the time he was on holiday to visit some old friends. She said she didn't know exactly where he was because she wasn't interested but reassured James he would be home soon.

He wondered if Gerald had taken it into his head to visit his other wife, so he dialled her number. The phone was answered by a man who said, 'Good here.'

James was a little taken aback, expecting it to be Mrs Good. He asked to speak to Mrs Good, and when she came on the line, he heard her husband say he was going out into the garden. She said hello and asked what James wanted when she realised who she was speaking to. She said Gerald had finished his course but had to go to another one next week. James asked if he could visit them and was told yes. He asked if tomorrow morning would be convenient and was told yes.

This being confirmed, he put down the phone and looked at all he had written about the man so that he could try and get some sense out of him as to his connection to the others, apart from being Oliver's brother-in-law.

The following morning, he got to the Good's house in Fraisborough, and on being invited in, he found the place a lot cleaner and tidier than it was on his first visit. It still had the smell of stale cigarette smoke, but that he thought natural for someone living in the house that was a heavy smoker. He asked if he could talk to Mr Good in private, to which Judith said she had shopping to do and would take this opportunity to do it. So getting herself ready to go out left them to it.

When she had gone out, James explained to Gerald Good who he was and hoped this would not blow what he and Fred were trying to do. He explained that his son Fredrick Royston was in his school and that he was being badly treated by one of his masters, Mr Walter Brent. Gerald looked guilty and said he had been made aware of this by the school nurse, and that he had spoken to Mr Brent about it but was told he only punished pupils if they deserved it. So James wanted to know what did he do about it when the nurse came to him a second time, saying the punishment was still happening and was too severe. He said he had spoken to Anthony Oliver who had employed him. He had said he was the headmaster, and it was up to him what he did about it, but he could not sack him.

James now put it to him as to why did he have two phone numbers. And why was it so important that they were never to be mixed up. Gerald now started to squirm, and his attitude went on the defensive. Rather than go into all the details, James told him he knew he was a bigamist, and that he was breaking the law. Gerald said he had married Judith because he loved her, and that he intended to divorce Oliver's sister.

'So why haven't you?'

Gerald said he had made the mistake of not divorcing his first wife before marrying Judith, the reason being, although she had first agreed, she had changed her mind and said she prefered staying married as it was better for her image and reputation.

He went on to explain how difficult it was keeping bigamy secret, and it was very unfair on Judith in particular.

The question James next asked was how did he get the job at the school and why he cannot get rid of Walter Brent. Gerald said he thought it was due to when Oliver and Brent were in the army together. It was as if Brent had some hold over Oliver that was so strong that Oliver was frightened of him. James asked if he had any idea at all what it was. Good said, 'It has something to do with why he was chucked out of the army, but I have no idea what it is.'

James now used a kind of blackmail of his own by telling Good that he would not let it be known that he had two wives if he didn't let on to the others what he was doing.

This he promised and wanted to know what James was actually doing and why.

James stated it was Brent he was after, but he had uncovered things during investigations they had made that were breaking the law. He asked why the standard of the school was doing a nosedive, from the standard it was when John Mountford was the headmaster. To this, Gerald said it was mainly due to the teachers that were being recruited by the board of governors.

He said he had no control over who was appointed and had to do the best he could with them. He said he had never seen any of their qualifications and wondered if some of them had any. During the last year, half of those that had left to be replaced were what was left from the staff that was at the school when Dr Mountford was in charge. James then asked if there was any reason for this, and Gerald said if there was, he didn't know about it.

'Could it be anything to do with running the school down in order to sell it?'

Once again, Gerald claimed he knew nothing of it if that was what Oliver had in mind.

'What about Mr Henry Andrews, what do you know about him?'

Gerald said he had influence over Oliver because, although he was only a board member, he always had a lot to say at the board meetings whenever he attended one.

'What about the other board members?'

'If the truth were known, I don't think they are interested in what happens to the school; they just have to keep paying their fees.'

'Now that leaves Mr Brent. What do you think about him?'

'I detest the man, he is a permanent thorn in my side. He does and says what he wants, and he is maybe the cause of so many of the old masters leaving, and I know my secretary can't stand him. She says he is a pest and is always insinuating sex with her. I have been to Mr Oliver as the chairman of the board of governors, and he has deaf ears when it comes to complaints about Brent. I know he is cruel, especially to your son, but I can do nothing more about it.'

James butted in and said, 'You could have written or phoned me and suggested I remove Fredrick and to the other parents of the boys he is beating. You have a punishment book, don't you ever look at it?'

Gerald, when asked, said he hated the job he was in, especially as a headmaster that had no real control over running the school as he should have been allowed to. He said when he first worked there under Dr Mountford, he enjoyed what he did. He got on well with the staff and wanted to turn the promotion down when John Mountford left. James asked if he knew why he had resigned and was told he thought it was on principle. James asked, why didn't he do the same.

'How can I, when Oliver knows I am a bigamist?'

'If he knows that, why doesn't he tell his sister?'

'I cannot answer either of those questions,' Gerald said, 'but I don't want to go to prison.'

James then told him he was looked upon as a wimp and asked him if that is what he felt. He said he did, and that was why he hated the job and situation he was in. Before he finished with the school, James asked why Andrews' son Edward had been made head prefect? This again was taken out of his hands, and that if he could, he would expel him together with the prefects he had chosen.

The question was now, what would he do if he and Fred, his partner, could get Oliver removed, save the school from being sold, give him the control that he should have as headmaster and get Brent sent to prison.

Gerald just said,' Pigs might fly.'

He went on, 'If you can achieve that, I will get a divorce and live happily ever after. I would do anything to remove my brother-in-law from my life. He is such a horrible man even his sister has no time for him.'

Before thanking him for being so frank and answering his questions, James said that if they were to be successful in what they were trying to do, he was not to mention to anyone the conversation they had had. As he got up to go, Gerald asked James how he had got so much information, and James just smiled and said, 'It was his job, and that he and his partner had been on the case since the school broke up, and they had been very busy, and that if they could get success, it would be just before the new school term started.'

They shook hands, and as James was about to leave the house, Mrs Good drove up having finished her shopping. Getting out of the car, she walked over to them and asked if they had had a good chat. Gerald said they had, and that he would help her unload her shopping.

James just winked at Gerald and made his way to his car to make the drive back to the office.

As he got to the office, he was surprised to see both Susan's and Fred's cars parked outside. Getting inside, he said hello to Elizabeth in the shop before going upstairs. Opening the office door, James wanted to know what Fred was doing back after saying he would be delayed.

Fred said the hospital was happy with Amy's condition and was happy to release her, telling her to report to her local hospital in two weeks' time for a check-up. So here he was and raring to go. Susan said she had had a phone call at home, so she had come in to follow it up.

Saying how pleased he was to have Fred back, they sat and talked about James' visit to the Good's. He said how he had got Gerald Good on side and that they could forget about him now and just concentrate on the other three. He said he had met up with Peggy Banks who was worried about Mrs Oliver senior being slowly poisoned. Fred was all ears and could only say what a busy boy James had been while he was away.

After Susan had left, having finished what she had come in for, the pair of them started talking about what to do next. James said he had been in touch very recently with Joe Harper, and that Oliver was indeed making inroads to sell the school to a developer together with the house he lives in but at this moment without success, due to John Mountford's five per cent ownership of the school and his mother's ownership of the house.

'So what are we going to do next?' Fred wanted to know.

'I think we had better try and sort out Mr Brent,' James suggested. 'I have seen him now but not met him.'

Fred asked how, and James explained he had visited a neighbour and Brent had gone out and come back while he was there.

'I first saw him when he went to the dog fights but couldn't get close to him. He doesn't look a very nice man, and I am glad you are back so we can tackle him together.'

'But how are we going to do it?' Fred Questioned.

'Full-on,' James said. 'I will make sure he is at home so that I can see the state of his wife who, I think, he has knocked about again, for the neighbour said she had not seen her for a few days. It must have been after he came home from the week's trip he had with his mates. I will try and make arrangements tomorrow to go to his house if he will see us, of course.'

They spent the rest of the day with Fred explaining how Amy broke her arm and the follow up in the hospital.

He said, 'The way she fell, it could have been worse, for she could have done far more damage to herself had he not partially prevented her from falling. She is bruised quite badly, but that will go away in time. She is in good hands if I have to go anywhere with you because her sister Elizabeth will look after her.' It was still quite early, but they decided they would make it a short working day and went home.

The next morning, on getting to the office with James, he made a telephone call to Brent's house. The phone was answered by 'Hello, Brent'.

Not a very good start, James thought. He said who it was calling, giving his false name, and asked to come to see him. Brent wanted to know what for, and James said it was about the school being sold. It was tempting enough bate to lure him into agreeing to see him, having said he knew nothing about the school being sold. He agreed to see him that afternoon when he got home from the pub. This was very good news as it would give them the opportunity to do the journey and see Mrs Brent before he came home if they timed it right.

They got near Brent's house just before twelve o'clock and saw Brent drive away, obviously, on his way to the pub. James remembered the local pub landlord telling him he had banned him and his mates, so making it necessary to drive to wherever he did his drinking now. They parked up outside of the house and, getting to the door, rang the bell. It was ages and three rings before the door was opened by Mrs Brent. On recognising James, she asked them in. Once again, she was heavily made-up which James put the delay in answering the door to. She ushered them into the sitting room and asked if they would like a cup of tea or coffee. They said they would and both went for tea. They asked how long Walter would be, and she said she didn't know but he should be back by three o'clock for his dinner. James apologised for asking but asked how long ago did she have her last beating. She said she would go and make the tea. Before sitting down, James told Fred to look at the photographs closely that were on view, so they would have both seen them, and if he asked to go to the toilet, he would see more going up the stairs.

On bringing in the tea on a tray and putting it on the coffee table, she asked if they took sugar. She gave them their tea and sat opposite them. She explained to them that when he came home from the trip away he had made, he wasn't very happy for some reason. He was only home a couple of days when her son returned from his ATC camp. He had been to the pub soon after the boy had got home. She couldn't remember exactly what the argument was about, but he got physical and they started to fight. Getting between them and telling her son to go to his room, he started on me. Her boy was now staying with her sister and was looking forward to going back to school.

She said, 'My husband is very remorseful when he sobers up and pleads with me not to leave him, but I can't put up with it any longer and am going to a solicitor when he goes back to school, to start divorce proceedings. He seems to get some sort of pleasure out of hurting people and animals and can be very cruel.' James asked what she thought it was that made him lose his temper.

'This is the funny thing about him, it is not only when he loses his temper, for when he canes your son, I think he is caning mine and he hasn't lost his temper then.'

'You might well be right, but we might see when he comes home.'

Walter Brent got home early mid-afternoon, and it could be seen that he had had a pint or two. He had let himself in and told his wife that he didn't want dinner because he had had something to eat in the pub. Coming into the sitting room, he offered his hand to James and Fred and introduced himself as Walter. Fred declined the handshake and just sat back down. He told Mrs Brent she needn't stay and to get on with the housework.

Now flopped in the chair his wife had occupied, he wanted to know what all this was about, the school being sold. James started off by asking how he didn't know about it, seeing he was so close to Mr Oliver. This brought a response, 'Who says I am close to Oliver?'

James just said quietly, 'You were in the army together, and since being at his school you seem to be untouchable.'

'Why is it that everyone at the school detests you? And you don't have any friends other than those you go around with, who are not very nice people either?' He wanted to know where James had got all this bullshit from, and he said that it was not true. James went on to say he couldn't stay in the army without being dishonourably discharged which in itself is a disgrace. That was the statement that triggered the outburst. Brent started to get agitated, and the booze took over.

Getting up out of his chair, very unsteadily, he said he was a good soldier and sergeant major was a good rank to reach as a non-commissioned officer.

James added, 'Twice, after being reduced to private for misconduct.' Brent went on to say that on that occasion, he took the can to save an officer from getting court-marshalled.

'Was that officer Oliver or Andrews?'

Brent said, 'Oliver, who was pegged as captain but was not discharged.'

'What was the can you took for?'

Brent, trying to control his temper said, 'Oliver was his platoon commander whilst Andrews was a major and company commander. Oliver didn't get on with Andrews but always threatened to get even with him.'

'As he?' Fred wanted to know, speaking for the first time.

'I don't know,' Brent said, 'For it appears they are as thick as thieves.'

'Perhaps they are,' James suggested, 'for they are still working together.'

'In what way?' Brent wanted to know.

James just said, 'What we know is that they are partners in crime, and that is all you need to know.'

'How did you become a teacher at Oliver's school?'

'He telephoned me one day and, knowing I was out of work, asked if I would become a schoolmaster at the school he had purchased because he wanted someone he could trust. I told him I was not a qualified teacher and, therefore, I couldn't. He said I could run and control grown men, so boys under eighteen would be a doddle.

'He said it was a private school, so whether I had qualifications or not was immaterial, for he owned the school and the board of governors would do what they were told or else. He said he wanted me to bring discipline not only to a class but to the school in general.'

'So why didn't he make you the headmaster?'

'Because he had appointed his brother-in-law as the headmaster, and he was qualified.'

'What do you think of Mr Good?' Fred asked, and was told he was a wimp, and that he was one of the easiest to control.

'He is one of life's softies, and I can walk all over him.'

James now came onto how he controls the boys. Brent wanted to know at this stage what were all these questions for, and how were they associated with the selling of the school.

It was now that James came clean when Brent said that he punishes the boys that step out of line, and they are frightened of him, and fear is a means of control.

This now brought the blood up both in James and Fred. Fred could see how James was controlling himself by the way he was clenching his fists.

'I believe you have a son,' James went on, to which Brent quickly said,

'A stepson.'

How did he get on with him, James wanted to know.

'To be truthful, I don't see much of him when I am home, he stays in his room.'

'Is that because he is frightened of you?'

'I dislike the boy and think a bloody good hiding would do him the world of good.' James now asked, was it because he couldn't give him one that he took it out on his wife. Brent was now furious and made a threatening move. However, Fred got up far quicker than James would have imagined and pushed him back into his chair without ceremony.

Fred said, 'We have some more questions to ask yet so sit where you are and listen, because at this moment in time, you are not in charge or in control.'

The questioning went on, and Brent was getting angrier and angrier. James now told him who he really was as Fredricks father.

'You have beaten my son who is only twelve years old, but you are not beating him into submission, you are beating your stepson because they are look-a-likes, and you cannot beat your stepson because your wife won't let you, so you beat mine and her instead. Are you doing all the canning to get the boys' parents to take their sons away from the school, and get the school a bad name so that it will get a bad reputation and become rundown due to the reputation it is getting? You are a cruel and spiteful man and should not be in charge of any human beings, especially children. You get pleasure out of hurting people especially with the cane on young boys and are spiteful when on the rugby field. My son is a very gentle boy and properly brought up, so to do what you have done to him is criminal, and you are going to pay for it.'

Brent said, 'Are you going to beat me up?'

James said, 'No, however, as much as we would like to, but we are certainly going to see you get your comeuppance. Bullies are usually cowards, and that suits you down to the ground.

'If the school is sold as a school, that I don't think will happen, you will have done your bit to make it come about. I hope it makes you feel proud. Once again, you will be taking the can for Mr Oliver who would walk away with a lot of money and leave you to stew.'

Once again, Brent said, 'No, he won't because I have too much on him.'

'Well, that might have to come out in court if that is where all this is going, for at the moment, you are the guilty party and your actions within the school and with your wife are not looking very rosy.'

Fred picked up the bit about what Brent had on Oliver and asked what it was. Brent just screwed up his face and said that was his business. What he had had to drink and not having a nap was telling on Brent, and he was now getting ratty. He said he was not going to answer any more questions, and that they could get out of his house and stay out. He started to rise from his chair as did James and Fred. Although unsteady on his feet, he made to have a swipe at Fred who took pleasure in punching him first in the stomach, and then on the jaw. The force of the punches sent him back in his chair where he stayed without moving.

Turning to James, he said, 'You witnessed that, and it was self-defence, he went for me first.' Having made a noise falling into the chair, Mrs Brent came in to see what made the noise. Seeing her husband in a crumpled heap in the armchair, she wanted to know what had happened. Fred explained that he had attacked him but had come off worse and would be asleep for some time. James asked how far away her sister lived, and when told about seventy miles, he suggested if she wanted to not be there when he comes around, they would take her to her sister's house to be with her son. She thought for a minute or two, and then said if they would be so kind it might save her getting another hiding.

She went upstairs and was not long before she came down with a packed suitcase. She picked up a set of keys and her handbag before saying she was ready to leave with them to go to her sister.

'Will he come and find you when he wakes up?' James asked, and was told, 'No, for he doesn't know where she lives, that is why I sent my son to her. She moved recently and he hasn't got a clue where to.'

'But if he goes to where she lived, won't the current occupier tell him where she has gone?'

'I don't think so because the reason for her moving was so that the council could pull all the houses down in the area and build flats, she was one of the last to leave, so there will be no one to ask for her forwarding address.' She said leaving was the quickest decision she had ever made, but she couldn't stand another beating for not only was it facial but her whole body was covered in bruises, and she was lucky he hadn't broken bones or put her in hospital. He could, on one occasion, have killed her.

James drove in the direction she gave them as they went, which was quite a bit more than seventy miles, almost a hundred, and they learnt more about Brent as they drove. She said she was looking forward to seeing her son who was about to start his last year at school. They would have to find a way of getting him a new one as Brent would make contact with the school he was at to try and locate her. However, she was sure he would manage at a new school for he was very adaptable and was a clever boy.

Getting to her sister's house, which was still council, the time was getting on.

James got her case out from the boot while Fred escorted her to the front door. Her sister opened the door when they rang the bell and called over her shoulder who it was that had just arrived. She invited them all in, with James putting her case down in the hall, before joining them in the lounge. Mrs Brent introduced them and said how kind they had been to her. James said they could not stop as it would already be late when they got home, but before they left, could the sister write down her address and telephone number so they would have a contact number. This she did and suggested James telephone home to let their wives know they would be late. While she wrote down what James wanted, he rang Susan to tell her they would be late home and if she would let Amy know. Giving Mrs Brent his card James put what her sister had written in his wallet and they made their departure with James saying if there was any follow up to please let him and Fred know. This she promised to do, and on leaving, James wished her son all the best for the future and hoped he would be able to join the airforce when he left school.

They got in the car, and Fred got the road map out to work out the quickest way to get home. As they travelled, they chatted about how the day had gone and how alike the son was to Fredrick. Fred said his hand was hurting and swelling up a bit after it met Brent's jaw, but what pleasure it had given him hitting him. He knew he wouldn't go to the police accusing him of assault because it would open the biggest can of worms he could imagine. James said he was surprised Fred had done what he did, but as Fred said, he was only defending himself.

It was nearly ten o'clock when they arrived at Fred's house, and letting him out, James said he would pick him up in the morning at about nine. He then drove to his own house and parked in front of his garage. Going indoors, Susan asked if he was hungry, but he said it was too late to eat then, but he could do with a drink. They sat up talking and drinking a nightcap, while James told her what they had been up to all day.

Chapter 13

True to his word, James got to Fred's house and, going in, asked Amy how her arm was. She said it was fine, but that the plaster cast was heavy, and it was making her shoulder ache. She said she was over the shock of doing it and how silly she was falling.

Getting to the office, they went through what had happened the day before and decided they would leave Brent, that there was no more they could do about or with him other than go to the police. It was agreed between them that they wouldn't get the police involved until they absolutely had to. James said he wouldn't contact their old friend Joyce at The Times Newspaper until they were ready to contact the police.

'So, what next?'

James said he would love to know what it is that Brent has on Oliver, for the way he spoke, it must be something a bit special, for he mentioned Oliver being frightened.

'Oliver doesn't seem to be the type to be frightened of anybody, but not knowing what it is we cannot make a judgement. But Oliver is the next one we have got to concentrate on. His mother says how ruthless he is and his obsession with money. I think that is the way we must approach this man, as well as his association with Andrews.

We know the pair of them are into illegally selling armaments, but both are rich men and must make their money in other ways apart from that. Let's go for it and find out.'

James rang Peggy Banks but could not get her on her private line, so he thought he would try again later, maybe after lunch when perhaps the old lady would be having a nap.

He wondered if he used his false name that he had used when dealing with head office in Oxford, he could entice his secretary to put him through to him at work. Fred suggested they get to him by bating him at home with an anonymous phone call. James thought about this and thought it to be a good idea, but what to use as bate?

Fred said, 'Why not say there is a way of him being able to sell the school, and that you could arrange it if he would see you?' Speak through a hanky so that he wouldn't recognise your voice and see what happens. We have to get into the house, and I can't see myself climbing over eight-foot walls with broken glass on the top or being eaten alive by guard dogs.

James thought Fred had a good idea, and that it was worth a try.

He did as Fred suggested and, putting a hanky over the phone's mouthpiece, dialled the number for the house. The call was answered by the butler who said Mr Oliver was not available and asked who wanted him and what was his business. James, not liking the way he was being spoken to, just said the reason for the call was a matter for Mr Oliver and not one of his servants, but he gave his phone number and told the butler that if Mr Oliver wanted to sell his school, he should ring it, and then he put the phone down.

The butler must have contacted Oliver whether at home or at work, for within the hour, Oliver telephoned the number James had left. Realizing it was him, James put his hanky over the phone and indicated to Fred to pick his phone up to listen into the conversation they were about to have.

Oliver said, 'What is this about me selling a school?' James just said there was a way of doing it, and he knew what was holding him up from being able to do so. Oliver asked what it was. James said he would only talk to him face-to-face and not over the telephone. Oliver said he was a busy man and could only do it by phone. James told him it had to be face-to-face or to forget it.

Knowing Oliver wanted to sell the school so badly, he added, 'If you don't see me by tomorrow, you won't be able to see me at all.' Oliver made a coughing noise as though he was smoking a cigar and the smoke had gone down the wrong way. He said he would meet him at his home that evening and went on to give James the address, which James, of course, knew.

'I will see you at eight o'clock,' he said and rang off.

Putting their phones down, James just smiled and said, 'He is a man that is now clutching at straws.' They worked out roughly how long it would take them to make the journey to Gentington at that time of day and decided what time to set off. It was going to be another late night.

The journey was trouble-free, and they got to the gates of Gentlodge a little early, but on getting out of the car, Fred went to the wall and did the necessary to contact the house.

A voice from the wall told them to come up to the house and park where it indicated "Visitors". As Fred got back in the car, the gates started to open, and so they drove up to the house and parked where they were told. There were already four other very expensive cars parked, and so James drove up and parked beside the furthest one. They walked to the front door that was opened by the butler or one of the servants and shown into a room that was comfortably furnished and told to wait for Mr Oliver's arrival.

There was a large painting on the wall that James supposed was Mr Oliver senior and another, with him and Mrs Oliver together. Mrs Oliver was a very attractive woman when she was young, with the twinkle in her eye that the artist had highlighted, that she still had to this day. There were also two aerial photographs, side by side, of what could be seen of the company buildings in the old man's days and a recent one of what it is now. This one James studied with some interest and commented on what a difference time makes.

Right on the dot of eight o'clock, the door opened and Anthony Oliver was standing in the doorway, resplendent in a dinner suit and miniature medals, with a cigar in his mouth and brandy in his hand. He went over to James and Fred and asked which one was Mr Edward Miles. James said he was, and that he had brought his partner with him. Not shaking hands, Oliver sat down in a chair facing them and said he was hosting a dinner party and could only spare them half an hour of his time.

Starting off, James said what a difficult man he was to get to speak to, and how hard it was to get past his two secretaries, works and personal. This brought a slight smile to his face and he just said that was what he employed them for. He asked them to explain how they knew he was trying to sell the school, for it was not common knowledge. He asked them who they were and how could they know how he could sell the building and grounds without owning one hundred per cent of it. James said, lying through his teeth, that he and Fred were part of a consortium, and that they had heard through the grapevine that he wanted to sell a school for either demolition or conversion together with the land it stood in. Oliver said he didn't know where they had got this information from, but they were accurate in what they were saying, but he asked how did they know he didn't own the school in its entirety.

'One of the members of the syndicate found out about you, and so we have been sent to speak to you.'

'Well, what is your solution?'

James said how they understood his hold up is the previous headmaster of the school, and that he will not sell his shares to him, and therefore, he cannot sell as the outright owner because he doesn't want the school sold. Oliver was beginning to get impatient now because he wanted to get back to his dinner party and up until then, James hadn't told him how he could sell the school with the previous headmaster still holding his shares. James suggested why doesn't he arrange to have him killed.

Oliver just said, 'Don't you think I have thought about that, but even if I did that, he would still not get the shares because his wife gets them, he has told me all that, and if I arranged to have her killed, I still wouldn't get them because they then go to their children, neither of which will sell to me.

Getting them killed, would be no problem, they could both be killed in an arranged car crash, but that is no solution.

As yet I cannot see a way around my problem and wondered if you had some legal way I could make the sale.'

Fred spoke up for the first time and asked him if he had offered enough money for the shares, to which Oliver said he had offered him as much money as he had paid the rest of the shareholders for theirs together, but the man wouldn't budge.

'What about going in as partners? You will become a very rich man if you can sell the school to a developer and with Mountford getting five per cent, he would have a big payday also.'

Oliver said he had tried that also, but he is adamant that the school will not be sold over his dead body.

'In that case, we will have to go back to the members of our consortium and tell them there is no way we can do business with you. We apologise for wasting your time.'

They said they would see themselves out if that was all right with him so that he could go back to his guests. He was in such a rush to get back with them that he just agreed and went off.

'Right,' James said to Fred, 'Come with me.' He led him through the house and up some stairs and knocked on Peggy's door. On opening it, she quickly ushered them in.

What on earth were they doing in the house and how did they get in, she asked. James explained what they had done and asked how the old lady was. Peggy said she had put her to bed and wouldn't want to wake her. She said she was still play-acting with the effects of the poison she was not taking and is so convincing I have a job to tell myself that she is only acting. She really is an astonishing old lady. James explained they couldn't stay for long as they didn't want to get caught after asking to be able to let themselves out. James asked how the meals were brought to Mrs Oliver.

Peggy said, 'The maid usually brings what she has ordered on a tray, but not before the housekeeper has checked it.'

'Could it be arranged that you fetch her meals direct from the kitchen?'

She said, 'To change the normal routine would arouse suspicion because I would have to give an explanation of why it should be changed, plus the fact it would not always be convenient.'

Knowing she was right, James said they must go, and saying good night, they left Peggy's room. It was very quiet as they were leaving the house except for just before they got to the front door when they heard from somewhere in the house three cheers. It was coming from a room way back in the house and then went quiet again.

They left the house and, getting to the car, James said, 'How do we get out? The bloody gates will be shut. Oliver was in such a bloody hurry to get back to his guests that he said we could make our own way out and forgot the gates, and so did we.' Once again, Fred came up with the solution,

'Wait until the first of the guest leave, and the gates will be opened for them. If we are down at the gates as they open, we can drive out and no one will see us.' But they could be stuck there for hours. Fred said that Andrews' car was one of those that were parked two away from where they had parked, he had recognised it. So, they wondered who the rest of the visitors were. However, whoever they were, it was not going to get them through the locked gates before the first of them left. Starting the car, James drove down to the gates and stopped. He switched off the engine and turned out the lights, and the pair of them just sat there.

They must have been there a good half hour, with Fred nearly going to sleep, when there was a tap on the window. James lowered the window down, and standing there with one of the guard dogs on a lead was a man. He asked James what he was doing there. James explained that they had been to see Mr Oliver, but the gates were shut when they got to them to leave. He suggested it was just as well he had come along as he would let them out. They saw him write down the car registration number before going over to a little metal box on the wall beside the gates, and with a key, he opened it and pressed a button, and the gates started to open. Starting the car and putting the headlights on, James drove out, thanking the man as he went.

Knowing what a stroke of luck they had had because they knew they could have been stuck there for hours, they drove back home, getting there before it got too late. Once again, James dropped Fred off, saying he would pick him up at nine o'clock, before driving home himself.

When he got indoors himself, Susan was in her dressing gown, ready for bed.

She asked James if he wanted anything to eat, but he said a good night's sleep might do him more good, and so they both went up to bed.

Getting to the office, what they had talked about on their way home the night before, James started getting on with. He phoned all four of the board of governors who had been forced into it and asked them if they were having any shipments undertaken by Oliver's transport in the very near future, with only one saying yes. He had pleasant conversations with each of them, all wanting to know how they were getting on with their enquiries. It was David Bright who said he had more furniture to go to the continent, who said he had a delivery to make. He said the last lot that went sold so well that the buyer had asked for a repeat order, and asked if he could get it to him as soon as possible. He had contacted Oliver's in Oxford, and they said he would have to speak to Oliver direct and put him through to him. He had asked to wait for him to make a phone call and he would get back to him.

He got back to him within two hours and said, 'Yes, that would be fine.' But he had to check that a suitable vehicle was available, and it was, and so he could do it.

James, putting his thinking cap on, asked when the pick-up was to be made.

David said, 'Tomorrow.'

James asked him if he could leave the running of the shop to his son for a couple of days. He said he could leave Michael to it without any worries, but he asked why?

James said they would like him to join them on a trip they would like to make, and it might be to his advantage. If he could take an overnight bag with him containing his shaving gear, toothbrush, change of shirt and underwear and anything in that line he might want for an overnight stay somewhere, his passport and some cash, they could make arrangements. David said it all sounded very adventurous, and it would make a nice change from being in the shop. James asked him if he could come to them and he would put him up for the night. Checking that David still had the business card he had given him, he gave him some directions and said they would see him later that day.

'What are you thinking of?' Fred wanted to know when James put the phone down.

'I have just thought about it, and I apologise to you for not discussing it with you, but wouldn't it be good to have an independent witness when and if we go to the police and the case goes to court?'

All Fred could say was, 'Good thinking.'

'I have arranged for him to come to the office where he can leave his car and he can sleep at my house tonight.' Susan hadn't come in that day, so he rang her and asked if Fredrick could sleep on the camp bed in the dining room after the evening meal was cleared away and make dinner for David Bright who he had invited to stay the night.

It was unusual for Susan, for she seemed a bit put out, without saying so. She said 'OK' but with a little reluctance in her tone and asked what time he would be home. He said he didn't know, but it would be soon after David arrived at the office. He told Fred where David had told him the pick-up would be from, and the time, and that it was going to be another following job, so they must be near the pick-up early enough to see the furniture loaded, with whatever else was going to accompany it.

It was nearly five o'clock when David arrived and parked up. It was a big car he was driving and James had to move to let him in. He said hello to Fred, and getting his overnight bag out of the boot, together with a briefcase, he transferred it to James' boot. On seeing him arrive, they had gone down to meet him, locking up as they went.

On the drive home, David said it had been very busy on the road, plus an accident that had held him up. He said the journey to the loading warehouse, from where the furniture was going to be picked up, was about a two-hour journey, and that it was due to leave to catch the one o'clock ferry from Dover. He said he had studied the road map before he left and they would have to be up and away by four o'clock. Fred commented that they should be paid for this and laughed when James said it was for a good cause.

Dropping Fred off, James drove to his house with a comment from David that they lived quite close to each other. James explained how it had all come about, and that it was a sweet shop below the office that Fred's sister-in-law ran. Getting indoors, James introduced David to Susan, Joyce and Fredrick before asking him to sit down and make himself at home and asked if he would like something to drink. James asked what he would like, giving him some alternatives, to which he informed him he would love a cup of tea as he was a reformed alcoholic.

Making the tea, which the two children said they would like as well, they made small talk. Susan said she hoped David liked toad-in-the-hole, to which he said he would love it as he hadn't had one for years. She asked what time they would be leaving, and when told four o'clock, she asked if they would want breakfast at that time in the morning. James suggested if Susan could make some sandwiches and a flask of coffee, they could take that and have it whenever they could fit it in.

They watched a bit of telly, including the news, before going to bed early.

On being shown Fredrick's room, David remarked on the electric train set layout, and how much he would like to play with it. Fredrick asked him not to touch it as he had set it up for the next time he would play with it. David said he was only joking and would not touch it.

They left to pick Fred up at ten to four and, taking the directions David gave them, got underway to do some investigating.

It was a good run, and they got to the warehouse that contained the furniture that had been ordered before the lorry arrived to pick it up. They parked the car where there were others parked which left them a little walk. Although still quite early, it was light enough to see what was going on at most of the buildings. There were lorries of varying sizes being loaded or unloaded, excluding the one they had come to see. There was nobody in the car park that they could see, so James took out the sandwiches and coffee. They had eaten their breakfast by the time the lorry came and parked up outside their warehouse and the driver jumped down from his cab and went in.

Fred said aloud, 'That was one of the lorries they had followed to France, with the same driver.' James agreed and said it was time to go. They got out of the car together, David with his briefcase, and separated as they had planned with James and Fred going to a side door they found and David going to the main door.

The side door was open when they got there, and there was nobody around.

They hid behind some crates and watched what was going on until the lorry came in.

David had gone into the office and came out with another man and the driver. The driver went outside to bring the lorry in while David and the man with him went over to a very large collection of wooden crates. He saw David with some papers in his hand going around them and speaking and nodding to the man from the office. The lorry they were going to follow came in and stopped beside the crates.

Four of the men, who had loaded the lorry that had just left, came out from what was obviously their canteen or restroom, after having a cup of tea and a rest presumably. One climbing onto a forklift truck that moved over to where the other men were standing. They saw the driver indicating what crate was to go where and David checking each one as they loaded it. It took an hour to load up, and when they had, they saw David shake hands with both the office man and the driver before leaving.

The driver went with the loaders to the canteen, while the office man went back to his office. James and Fred had no trouble getting back to the car where David was waiting for them. They all got in and sat and talked while they waited for the driver to come out with his lorry.

When the lorry came out, James let it go well ahead but keeping it in sight, he started to follow it. He asked David if everything was all right with what he had seen loaded and was told yes, including some bits that he had had to add to the list at quite short notice. When they had gone so far, James said he knew where the lorry was going, as did Fred. David, who was not aware, wanted to know where they thought he was headed. They followed the lorry up to where it turned down the lane they had walked when it loaded the armaments before. James turned the car on entering the lane and stopped by a set-back farm gate. Explaining to David what was now going to happen, unless he was very much mistaken, was that the lorry was going to load up with military equipment that was being illegally sent out of the country. So we just wait for the lorry to come back and head for Dover and the ferry. It seemed an age before the lorry appeared, but before it came in sight, a car that they recognised came before it. Both Fred and James knew it was Andrews but could not be positive if it was him driving, but just assumed so.

It was as the lorry came down that James started the car and, letting it go ahead, followed it until he was sure it was heading to the Dover Ferry. Looking at his watch, he was sure the lorry would be catching the one o'clock ferry, and hoping he was right, he overtook it and headed for Dover.

Getting to the port and having to get into a designated line of cars, they had to get ferry tickets, show their passports and wait to be called forward to board. Having plenty of time, they decided to have a meal and keep an eye open for their driver. The restaurant, if that was what it was called, was being very well used, and so, they were lucky that a table near the entrance was just being vacated. Not knowing when they would be eating next, they each decided they would have a proper lunch. They were halfway through it when they saw the driver walk in. James uttered a sigh of relief, saying history was repeating itself. The difference being, this time they would follow the small lorry to find out where the armaments were being delivered to rather than the furniture.

Once again, James took a chance and, staying well behind the lorry, hoped it would go to the same warehouse as before. When he was certain, he got amongst about half a dozen cars and passed the lorry. They got to the warehouse and once again parked up where James had parked before he was caught.

David asked, 'Is this where they unloaded my furniture? For this is not where it is to be delivered.'

James explained, 'This is where it was dumped last time and so must have been taken to where it had to go later. This time, we don't know, but it is a smaller lorry we are going to follow this time.'

The lorry drove into the same warehouse James had been in before being caught, and Fred volunteered to see if the smaller lorry was inside or had it not arrived yet. Fred got out of the car and went on a snooping trip. He wasn't very long

223

before he said the smaller lorry was already in there, and by the look of it, the furniture was not being unloaded. James said that was good and asked Fred if he had taken note of the registration number. Fred said he had, and so they waited to follow it.

While they waited, James told David what their last trip had been like and how he was rescued by Fred, 'I am sure if he hadn't got to me when he did, by now I could be dead meat.'

Fred was a bit embarrassed saying that he would have done the same for him. One thing he did say was, 'One of the men in there is walking with a terrible limp. I think he is one of the men that was giving you a hiding that I hit with the iron bar.'

It was only half an hour before the lorry Fred had observed came out from the warehouse and turned in the direction James was facing. So starting up, the chase was on. Fred said he had taken a few photographs and would try and take some more when they got to where the arms were going to be delivered. James found it difficult to follow at too much of a distance as the lorry driver was not hanging about. He drove over the border into Germany where they were stopped to show their passports. The lorry went to a different checkout point but luckily went through like them with no holdup, so the trailing could continue. David was trying to follow the road map James kept in the backseat of the car as they went through different villages. They had been driving for nearly two hours before the lorry stopped at a roadside café, locking up and going in. It was rather fortunate that there was a petrol station next to it that James was able to fill up at. Just as well he had brought some French and German currency with him.

Fred said he had to spend a penny, and so, he went into the café to have a pee. Coming out, he said, 'It was lucky he had gone in, for their man was in deep discussion with another man and not just having something to eat or drink.'

When their driver came out, he was accompanied by the other man. They both got into the lorry, and James followed. They got to the city, and James had a job to follow but just manage it until they got to the outskirts. He then went into some side roads before coming to a halt outside of a building that had no name on it but was obviously where the load being carried was to be unloaded. James drove past and turned down the next turning he came to. They had to get into this building, but how? James said he couldn't speak German or French and nor could Fred.

'It is lucky that I came along with you,' David piped up, 'for I speak fluent French and very good German. But we have to get you in there if we are to find out anything, let alone any photographs.'

As the main doors were opened, they saw the lorry driving in, and the doors shut behind it.

The three of them walked over to the building and, along the side of it, looking for another door. There wasn't one, so they went around to the back. At the back was another small building looking like an office of some sort, but there was no one around. There was a door at the back of the main building, but on trying it, they found it locked. James looked at the lock and winked at Fred, who knew what he was about to do. Getting out his little tool kit, James set about the lock. After a very short time, there was the sound of a click and James gently tried the handle. It moved down as he pushed it, and making sure the door did not squeak or make any noise, he pushed it open just a little bit. He got his head in and could see there was enough cover for them to get in without being seen. So, beckoning the other two to come in and shut the door behind them, he moved behind the crates and other equipment so they could get within hearing distance of the men around the lorry.

James whispered to David, 'Can you understand what they are saying?'

Knowing the camera he was using wouldn't flash, Fred took photos of all the men there, including the men who had started unloading. He used the zoom option to get closeups and was sure they were in focus.

It took them over half an hour to unload with different crates going to different places. Fred was able to get shots of the bigger uncrated pieces of equipment while David carried on listening to the conversations and passing what they were talking about to James. On completion of the unloading, the driver went into what must have been an office and came out with several sheets of paper. He shook hands with the man that came out of the office with him and got back into his lorry, leaving the man he had picked up at the roadside café still there. It was time for them to go. So leaving the building as quickly and quietly as they had got in, they got back to the car.

Fred asked if James was going to follow him, he assured them that he was, and he was going to try and stop him.

As the lorry started off, James got behind him, but he was not too close. He was going back the way he had come and, once again, stopped at the roadside café. Parking the lorry, without locking it up, he went in. Fred followed while James went to the cab door and, finding it unlocked, went through his papers. There were lots of them in a big envelope, and he took the lot. Taking them back to the car, he gave them to David and said he was going into the café to look for Fred. When he found him, he asked where the driver was, and Fred said he had gone through those curtains, pointing in that direction. James said he wondered why he had gone there and was told by Fred that he had accompanied a young lady who had been sitting over there with that one, looking in the direction Fred was looking, it was obvious what she was.

James just said, 'Good luck to him.'

Getting back to the car, they made their way back to the ferry. They had a meal, that David insisted on paying for, while they waited for the next ferry to leave for Dover. It was nearly eleven o'clock when they arrived back at their office and David took his leave of them. He said he had had an exciting day, and thanking James for putting him up, he went to his car boot and took out a bunch of flowers which he said he had got for Susan and had forgotten to get them out when he got to the office. Also, taking two ten-shilling notes out of his wallet, he asked him to give them to his children and thank Fredrick for allowing him to have his bed, adding, he would still love to play with his train set one day. James thanked him on Susan and the kids' behalf for the flowers and money and him and Fred for the meal. Getting into his car, he drove off, waving as he went.

Fred and James got back into the car and drove home.

Chapter 14

Having now had an opportunity to visit and speak to all those associated with the school, it was now up to them to find out how Oliver and Andrews made money legally or otherwise.

Having studied the aerial photograph on Oliver's room wall, he knew what had been added on, over the years since Oliver had taken the business over from his father. It was time for them both to go back to Oxford. James, with Susan's help, went to the phone book and looked up all the numbers they could find that had any association with either Oliver's Haulage or anything else associated with Oliver. They got quite a long list with the intention of ringing them all, to find out if it was the Oliver they wanted. Anyone associated with Anthony Oliver in any way. It took all the morning, and after Susan had got them some lunch, they got on with phoning them all. Fred, meanwhile, had busied himself, trying to locate the places they had called at in France and Germany and trying to find out who the warehouses and the building in Germany belonged to.

After lunch, James and Susan set about making the calls, knowing the area the phone book covered.

Between them, they made over thirty calls and had success with seven of them. Each one they found had a connection with Anthony Oliver, mainly distant relatives down the male line. One, however, was not a particular friend of Anthony. He was the son of Mr Oliver Senior's brother who had died during the war. Apparently, when his father was killed in action, he was more or less forgotten and certainly neglected after his mother sought help from the Oliver dynasty. She had gone to them for financial help after losing her husband and got turned away. He had a sister in his mother's arms when they were evicted from the home they lived in and spent the rest of the war going from one home to another before she met and married a rich man who was suffering from poor health. Although he thought a lot of his stepfather, he never called him dad. He lived in the house his stepfather had provided together with his mother and sister and took over the business his stepfather had left them in his will before he died.

James said he would like to meet him, and after explaining who he was and what he was doing, a meeting was arranged. The address he gave James was very close to Southampton, and so it wouldn't take long to get to him. James told Fred who he had been talking to, and that he had agreed to meet him the next afternoon. Fred asked if it was a one or two-man job, to which James answered, 'One.' What had made him go for this meeting, Fred wanted to know after James suggested it might lead to something big.

Of the six other numbers rung, they were people who knew Oliver through business of one sort or another, rather than a distant relative. All the others were just coincidentally named Oliver.

Before leaving for home, Fred said that he had all the details they may want of the warehouses, who owned them and what they were usually used for. He said that Andrews' name had been mentioned on the one in France and the one in Germany. He didn't own any of them but paid a heavy price for using them. James wanted to know how he had found out about Andrews' input and involvement, and Fred just said he had asked the right questions to the right people. He said he would ask Susan to type up all that he had got for his efforts, so they looked sensible and would go with all the rest of what they held that was becoming quite a large file.

It was just after one o'clock the next day when James left the office to meet Mr Malcolm Oliver. It turned out to be only three-quarters of an hour's drive, and when he got to the address he had been given, he realised it was where Malcolm worked and not his home. He parked up alongside two other cars and went to the front door of the building. He asked the lady sitting at a desk if he could see Mr Malcolm Oliver, giving his own name. She said he could see her husband, as he was expected. Getting up from her desk, she led the way to an office, and knocking the door, she was asked to enter.

Going in, she said, 'This is Mr Royston, darling, who you have been expecting.'

Getting up from his desk, he came around and, shaking James' hand, said he was pleased to meet him.

Being asked if he minded his wife staying while they talked, James said he didn't. He introduced her as Miriam who was his secretary, bookkeeper and receptionist. He was asked if he would care for a drink and was offered tea or coffee. He accepted the coffee, and as his wife went out to make it, Malcolm then added,

'And tea lady.'

It broke the ice as they both smiled, and Miriam scoffed as she left the room. James asked what business he was running, and being told he was a flour merchant, James asked how he had got into that. He said it was the business the man who married his mother owned, and that he left everything to her. He said she knew nothing about flour, other than cooking with it, so she asked him, her son, to run it for her. Although by then, still a young man, he agreed to do it for her. He said it was very hard work to start with, as he also knew nothing about flour. His stepfather was not a miller but a flour distributor. He purchased flour from most of the large flour companies in bulk and, bagging it, supplied it in bags of all sizes, from half a pound to hundred-weight sacks, to shops and companies all over the world. He said it was hard work because his stepfather died quite suddenly. He said he had a lot to learn in a very short time and his step father's manager was his lifeline as far as the business was concerned. To keep him on his side and to make sure he kept the business flowing smoothly, he offered him twenty five per cent of it. This was, by nature of where they were now, a very good decision. We have added other raw materials that compliment flour over the years and have a very flourishing business now. Still retaining his status as general manager, we have become very good friends.

Miriam returned with the coffee on a tray together with milk, cream, brown sugar and biscuits. She put them on the corner of Malcolm's desk, and asking how James wanted his, she poured them out. As they sat drinking the coffee, James asked what sort of thing they did when they were not working. Malcolm went through the things he did without Miriam, and

Miriam went through the things they did together and with their children.

One of their hobbies was genealogy, and this became the subject that James wanted to stick with. He asked who started it, to which Miriam said it was her. She said she was interested with the past and had gone back to the seventeen hundreds. Malcolm had caught the bug from her but had gone into much more detail and wrote up on most of his past family history.

This was of very great interest to James, who said so.

He asked if that was why he didn't like Anthony Oliver. He said it was because of the way the Olivers had treated his mother when she was at her lowest ebb. He said he had only met Anthony Oliver once that he could remember, and that was years ago when he was quite a young boy. James now asked if he could make the time and be agreeable to go through the Oliver's family tree with him. He said he had most of what he had written about them at home and asked if James would be prepared to go home with them to go through it. On readily agreeing to this, Malcolm picked up his telephone and asked his general manager to take over while he was away with Miriam for the rest of the day. This being arranged, they set about leaving the office for home.

Getting outside, James realised he had parked alongside Malcolm's car, an almost new Austin, the latest model they had produced. Malcolm said to follow him and the journey would only take about half an hour. Getting to the large detached house in a rather posh suburb on the outskirts of Southampton, towards the New Forest, they parked up in the large drive. As they alighted from their vehicles, Malcolm acknowledged the gardener who doffed his old hat and said hello to Miriam.

Malcolm opened the front door, and the three of them went inside. Putting down what they had brought with them in the hall, Malcolm led the way to his snug-come-office. On their way, they heard an old voice asking if that was Malcolm.

He said, 'Yes, Mum, it is only us.' He explained to James that his mum lived with them in a granny annexe he had had built on to the house with an adjoining door.

Making themselves comfortable in the snug, Malcolm went to a safe in the corner of the room and removed quite a sizeable box file. Putting it on the desk, he opened it and, taking out about a dozen or so files, asked where James would like to start. Not to feel left out, Miriam asked if James would be interested in her family tree. James said perhaps another time, but he really wanted to get into Malcolm's family.

Telling them both in as much detail as he could, he explained why they were doing what they were, starting with Fredrick and his caning. This led to where some of the money came from to furnish the haulage business and the purchase of the school.

In the 1880s, there were three Oliver brothers and three sisters, and in those days, it was usual for the oldest son to inherit everything from a father's will, which is what happened when their father died. However, the eldest son of that family, that was very rich, decided he would share out the money between his siblings. His mother was already dead, so all of the old man's estates went to the eldest son. Oliver's father was one of those sons and used his share of the inheritance to start a business. He worked hard and for very long hours to get a haulage business started. It was explained by Malcolm what the other brothers and sisters did with their share, but James was not too interested in them except for one,

George Oliver. James did comment on the fact that the sisters got less than the brothers, but as Malcolm explained, in those days they were lucky to get anything.

George Oliver, one of the brothers, became a loose cannon as far as the family were concerned, and unlike the rest of his siblings, the money went to his head. He lived a life that gained him nothing other than trouble. It was he who was the father of Henry Andrews. He apparently raped a well-to-do woman after a drunken night out, and to keep it secret because the woman was well-to-do, it cost him a great deal of money. The woman died two months after Henry was born, and her family made George pay dearly for the child's welfare and upkeep. He was taken on by one of the sisters who although married was without child, although she had been married to a wealthy man for five years. He was a banker in London and knew his way around money. His name was Andrews, and that is what the child's surname became after he was taken on by the sister.

It was after the business was started that Anthony's father married his mother Agatha. Working so hard and long hours apart, the marriage was put under severe strain until Tony was born, followed by his two sisters within the next five years.

So, James wanted to know how had he found out about all this. Malcolm explained how he had got all this information. He said what he had not got from his mother, it had taken a long time and quite a lot of money to acquire. Recapping on what Malcolm had told him, he said, 'So Henry Andrews is Anthony Oliver's cousin; do they know?'

'Anthony's mother must know.'

'Is George Oliver still alive?' James wanted to know.

Malcolm assured him he wasn't. He was sent to prison for embezzlement and died there. His passing was kept hush-hush due to bringing disgrace to the family.

Apparently, it was when they went into the army that all this came to light when birth certificates were required, and it became known that the two of them were related, albeit not by traditional descents but through Tony Oliver's mother's side of the family.

Mentioning the army, James asked if Malcolm had ever heard of a man by the name of Brent, Walter Brent.

'Oh dear,' Malcolm replied, 'you are now opening another can of worms.'

'How so?' James wanted to know.

'It started at a party thrown by Henry Andrews, at that time a young army officer, to celebrate his wife's twenty-first birthday. It was a party not only for officers but also for friends and families. Corporal Brent had been invited as one of the guests because he was one of Andrews' men and a friend. It is said that Andrews became so drunk that he passed out and had to be put to bed. Brent was also quite well-oiled but sober enough to make a pass at Mrs Andrews. She liked the attention Brent gave her and went to bed with him before going back to her husband's bed. This resulted in another cover-up, for when it was later obvious that she was pregnant, it was naturally assumed the baby was Andrews' baby.'

"Bloody hell" was all James could say when he heard this and asked, 'How did you acquire all this intimate information?'

Malcolm said it was all part of the genealogy process and his mother.

James just asked if it could all be substantiated.

Malcolm smiled and said, 'Genealogy becomes an obsession and makes you become nosey; ask my wife? What she has found out about her family going back in time, is unbelievable. The things that can be uncovered if you delve deep enough just cannot be believed, but, of course, it takes enormous amounts of time, patients and money.'

They went through the lives of the remaining siblings of the Oliver family, and apart from George, the rest had all done well. The money that came down from the oldest Oliver son was well used, and their offsprings had done well with what they had inherited. That led them back to Anthoney Oliver's father who had married Agatha.

James explained that he had met and spoken to Agatha, (Mrs Oliver senior) and found her to be a charming old lady.

'You would say the same about my mother if you got to know her. She is becoming very frail now but is still a wonderful lady. It is her I have to thank for a lot of what I have told you, but she holds no grudges against anybody including her family of the past. I think her and Agatha are the only ones still alive, for all their other siblings are now dead.'

They had been looking through all that Malcolm had brought out from the safe, as if time had stood still, and it was past five o'clock when Miriam asked if they would like a cup of tea and if they could offer James a meal with them. James said yes to the tea but said his wife was preparing dinner for when he got home, so he thanked her for the offer but said 'no thank you' to the meal.

While Miriam went to get the tea, James asked if a court case arose from all that he and Fred were doing, would he be prepared to be a witness. He said he would, and that it would be his way of getting some retribution for the way the Olivers treated his mother.

He suggested that if James could speak to Mrs Oliver senior, he might learn more, for he was sure she might still have skeletons in her cupboard.

Having drunk the tea that Miriam had brought, James made to go.

He thanked Malcolm for giving him so much help, and that he now knew what the connection was between the three men that he was after, but not knowing what each knew of the others part in the connection.

The short drive home was uneventful although the traffic was heavy at that time of the day. Arriving home, Susan asked the usual question about how he had got on.

James said he had learned a lot and felt that he had saved himself days, if not weeks, of work by making the visit. He said he was sure Fred would appreciate what he had found out, and they would make a start on working at it tomorrow. She said dinner was nearly ready, and that Joyce had laid the table, so if he went into the sitting-room, he could spend a little time with his children.

They both welcomed him when he went in, and Joyce got up and gave him a hug. They sat and talked, and Fredrick asked how much longer the case he was on was going to take.

James said he still hoped that it would end before he had to go back to school, for he only had two more weeks before the new term started. He asked if he had to go back to Radcliff's.

His dad told him what he had learnt today was going to shorten the time it would take to close the case, but, of course, that depended on unforeseen things they may come across that could slow things down.

He said he had to ring uncle Fred and, on getting through, told Fred he would pick him up at eight-thirty the next morning.

Chapter 15

It was eight-thirty on the dot when he rang the doorbell and Fred opened it immediately, having seen James arrive. Going the short way to work, they arrived in fifteen minutes, and on getting into the office, James relayed to Fred what yesterday was all about. Fred sat and listened very intently and was amazed at what James had found out. James said while he phoned Peggy Banks, could Fred get out every bit of paper and anything else they had on the Radcliff case.

Getting Peggy on her private extension, he asked her if she could arrange for them to speak to Mrs Oliver senior, preferably when Oliver and his wife were both away from the house. She said Oliver had already left for Oxford, and his wife was due to chair a church social committee meeting at eleven o'clock, and that would be followed by lunch, and that she was never home before four at the earliest. She said she would arrange to let him through the gates if he could get there by noon. She added that it appeared that the old lady was now being affected by what she was eating and drinking because she was genuinely sleeping a lot more the last couple of days.

James assured her that they would get there by twelve o'clock and rang off. Putting the phone down and turning to Fred, he said they would have to leave what Fred had got out of the filing cabinet, for they had to leave right away to make it to Gentington by noon.

They got themselves ready, and with a briefcase in hand, they left for Oliver's house, stopping to call into the shop to let Elizabeth know where they were going, to be able to tell Susan when she arrived and to pick up a packet of boiled sweets to suck during their journey.

They talked during the drive and James mentioned what Fredrick had asked about when they were going to finish the case they were on.

James drove up to Gentington Lodge just before noon and waited. The gates opened after only a short while, and they drove in. They saw or heard nothing from any dogs and wondered why, but only wondered but didn't ask. Peggy came out through a side door near the back of the house and indicated to come quickly as they got out of the car. They hurried to meet her and were soon in Mrs Oliver's bedroom. She was awake but looked very dozy. She welcomed them saying how pleased she was to see them and asked what they wanted to see her for.

Peggy went to get another chair while James dragged one over nearer to the bed. He sat while Peggy was gone and asked Mrs Oliver if she knew of Malcolm Oliver. She immediately showed signs of recall and said she did. Peggy brought the chair for Fred and sat with him further back from the bed. Mrs Oliver was now attentive and asked why she was asked about Malcolm. James told her all about his visit to see him and what he had told him. Mrs Oliver said his mother was her sister and how the Olivers had treated her during the war after her brother-in-law got killed. She said she had never seen her sister and felt ashamed to think none of the family helped her when she needed it, including herself. She asked if she was still alive and showed compassion in her old eyes when told yes.

James asked what she knew about the rape by her brother of the well-to-do lady and the illegitimate son that her barren sister took on before marrying Henry Andrews.

She said the whole business was swept under the carpet because of pride and snobbery. She said it was true that Henry was Tony's cousin by default, and that they really didn't like each other although they made out they did in public. She admitted that things had not been good between the families, and yes, Andrews' son (Flashman) was likely to be fathered by Walter Brent. So, was there anything else she might tell him. She said that the members of both families were good and bad. Those that were good were very good, but those that were bad were very bad. She said that while she was young, she was a part of a good family but fell out with them after she was accused of having Anthony by another man, that wasn't true.

James explained what the connection was between the three men and what they were doing. When he told her about the gun-running, she said she was not surprised, and that she supposed Tony supplied the transport because he was threatened by Andrews that he would expose him for things he was doing illegally.

'As I told you the last time you were here, I have grown more and more to dislike my son after my husband died. I am now an old lady with not much time left to live, so it doesn't matter to me who knows what, but I still have a skeleton in my cupboard that I was going to take to my grave, but with

241

all that is going on, I will let you know Anthony might be the son of George, my brother.

'As I said, my marriage didn't run smoothly early on and I wanted children. My husband was working all hours, so I only saw him late in the day when he was very tired. I left him and went home for a few weeks as a trial separation. I stayed for three weeks before deciding I must try to make my marriage work. Before I left to return to my husband, we had a bit of a get together with what family there was and a few friends. The party went well, but I decided as I had a long journey the next day, I would go to bed early. It must have been the early hours of the morning that I was woken up by someone in my bed. I started to try to loosen the hand over my mouth, but the man was too strong for me. I could see enough to know it was my brother George who was laying on me. I tried to move away from him, but he was having none of it. He said I had said I wanted a baby, and if my husband wouldn't give me one, he would, and he raped me. There was no point screaming as he withdrew from me, as the deed had been done. He had obviously had too much to drink, but not enough to prevent him from having his way with me. He lay back on the bed and said no more.

'I got up and went to the bathroom to clean myself. I tried to clean up inside of me and just hoped I wouldn't become pregnant. I know how wrong it is to have relations with someone as close as a brother, but what could I do? When George woke up, he wondered where he was, and realising where he was, he asked what he had done. When I told him, he nearly went mental, and he was so sorry for what he had done. He asked what I was going to do about it, could I get rid of the baby if I became pregnant? I said I didn't know but knew of illegal abortions going wrong. It was five o'clock in the morning when he left my room and went back to his.

'I left the house that morning to return home to my husband. He was at work as usual when I got there, but he was so happy when he got home and found I had returned. As usual, he was tired, but we made love that night. He said he was sorry for causing me to leave but would change the way he was, and the following few months were bliss, especially when I told him I was pregnant. I don't know to this day which of them is Tony's father, but by the way he is going, I would guess it might be George. He is becoming more like him every day. However, they say that too close interbreeding can cause problems with the child, but there is nothing wrong with Anthony, or at least not that I know of.'

James asked her again about the house. She said what she got from her eldest brother, who was one of the kindest and fairest men she had ever met, she kept invested, and when they had grown out of the house they bought, soon after they were married, while their children were growing up, she said she called on that investment and bought the house she now lives in.

'Because it is mine, I will not leave it until I die. The reason I bought it with my money was because what money my husband made from the business, he could plough back into it.'

'Both my girls dislike their brother, and other than for the haulage business, I have left everything else to them in my will. That includes one-quarter of the shares in the business, meaning that with my quarter and their quarter each that their father left them, Anthony only owns a quarter of his haulage business. I am not sure if Tony understands or realises how much he is going to lose when I die. So if he is trying to kill me, he is shooting himself in the foot. But, of course, he doesn't know what is in my will, unless he has bribed my solicitor to let him see it, which I am sure he wouldn't have, for he is a great friend of mine as well as being my solicitor.'

Agatha was now just about all in and was falling to sleep. She was trying hard to stay awake when Peggy tapped James on the arm and whispered to him that that was enough. He clasped her hand and said, 'Thank you, you are a wonderful lady.' Whether she heard him or not, James will never know, but he meant what he said.

As they left the room, Peggy said enough was enough, and that she was going to call an ambulance and get her to hospital. As a qualified nurse, she was able to do such a thing and not bother to call the doctor to do it. She said she would inform the doctor what she had done and would see what happened. She admitted she should have done it before but hoped by what she was doing by preventing her from drinking what she was being given by the kitchen was enough, but it obviously wasn't, and she couldn't let her starve. As they got to the car, she said she would get the gates open and let them know what the outcome was from the hospital.

Thanking her, and getting in the car, they left her to get the gates open.

They drove down the drive very slowly, and within a very short time, the gates started to open to let them out. Glancing over at James, Fred could see a tear running down his cheek. He said nothing to him for ages other than did he want a sweet. Not having had any lunch, they stopped on the way home to have some, and it was then that James said he was very sad for he didn't think they would see the old lady again.

It was two days later that they got a call from Peggy, saying she had been sacked the same day as the old lady went to the hospital, and that the Olivers were running scared. Anthony's mother was still alive in hospital but wasn't expected to live for very much longer. She said the housekeeper, the cook and the butler had left, and the doctor who had come when she told him Mrs Oliver was in the hospital, was shitting himself. She said Mr Oliver went mad when he returned from Oxford and found out his mother was in the hospital and he wasn't allowed to see her because of her condition. The first thing he did was sack me, although I was ready to go anyway. As I was driving out, it was the gardener that told me the housekeeper, the butler and the cook had already gone, and that the police were on their way. Fred had listened in on Peggy's phone call and said to James when they had put their phones down, 'Talk about deserting a sinking ship?'

James rang the hospital to ask after Mrs Agatha Oliver and was told she was stable and comfortable and allowed no visitors other than direct family.

The pair of them didn't know what to do next.

Now the police were involved, all the money in the world would not get them off Oliver's back, and the pressure would increase more when his mother died.

Was now the time to contact the police themselves? They thought not, as the police would only be interested if they could prove that Mrs Oliver senior was dead due to poisoning.

James suggested Fred to get out all the files they had amassed and go through every piece of paper they contained.

Starting from the visit to the school and meeting Stella Boulton and calling on John Mountford and the information they got from them. The notes they had made from all the other people they had visited and spoken to. There was a considerable amount of it, and apart from refreshing their past enquiries, they also picked up on what questions they might have asked but didn't. They made fresh notes of them.

Their main priority was now making sure the school could not be sold for development. If it remained as a school, how could they persuade John Mountford to try and put the school back into a college of learning that had a superior reputation, even in an advisory capacity?

They were sure he would take on the challenge if he knew it was for a limited time.

Stella, of course, would retain her job as would the school nurse.

What would have to be John Mountford's first priority was getting rid of the unqualified, non-effective staff Oliver had employed, and get quality teachers back.

Fred asked would Oliver sell the school as a school. James said he thought he was going to have to struggle for money when his mother died, and he found out that everything apart from the one quarter of the haulage business went to his sisters. But who would buy the school, Fred persisted.

'That is where we go from here.' James suggested.

'I am going to contact John Mountford separately and then call a meeting for all the school governors that have been blackmailed into it by Oliver.' 'Not,' he quickly added, Andrews. 'If we can do this before we go to the police and The Times newspaper through Joyce Sheen, then we will save the school and get it back on a steady high standard footing.'

'We have to make sure Walter Brent is got rid of, which we can do through his wife if we can persuade her to take him out of society for wife-beating, if nothing else.

'Whatever happens, he must go. Don't forget, we have built up enough against those we are after to get them into lots of trouble and can produce witnesses to back up in court what the prosecution would require to prosecute these men.'

'When do we start? Fred asked. James said that day.

Asking Susan to put all the files back in the cabinet as she wanted them, James asked her to make them some coffee. While she was doing that, he telephoned John Mountford's number.

It was him who answered and was surprised to receive a call. James asked if he and Fred could pay a visit, as things had moved on with their enquiries and they would like to speak to him about the school. He said he was willing to see them as long as they came to him. James asked when would be a good time to come and was told that day or tomorrow would be convenient. James said if they left early the next morning, they could get to the West Country and back in a day. A time was set for the next day, and John added, before ringing off, that they were invited to lunch and he would get Hazel to bake a cake, as he knew Fred liked his wife's homemade fruit cake. James thanked him and put the phone down. Telling Fred what he had arranged, they sat and drank their coffee.

They both realised it was going to be well after the school was due to open before court cases were dealt with. If they could use Desmond Cave to start with, they could bring Oliver, Andrews and Brent to court themselves. Cave would have to get a barrister organised, but they were sure he would know a good one. But this was in the future, old Mrs Oliver would have to die before anything they wanted to happen would happen.

The drive to Merymarch was quite uneventful except for having to go through Torquay, that was very busy with holidaymakers when they reached it. It was eleven-thirty when they arrived on a lovely summer day. John opened the door when they arrived, welcoming Fred like an old friend. Fred introduced James to John and Hazel, who by then had come to greet them. They ushered them into the front room, and Hazel said she had the kettle on, for they must want a drink after such a long drive. Fred said he would like a long cold drink if that was possible and James asked for the same. Asking John, he said he would have coffee. As she went off to meet their requests, John told them to make themselves comfortable.

Before they got started, Hazel was back with some homemade lemonade with ice cubes and a slice of lemon and coffee for John and herself. She asked if she was to sit in or did they wish to talk privately. James said they wanted her to remain, as what they were going to talk about very much concerned her.

John said, with concern on his face, 'You haven't driven all this way if what you want to talk to me about isn't important or is controversial and couldn't be said over the phone.' James smiled and said that Fred had told him what a shrewd man he was, and that he was quite right to think what he did.

He and Fred between them said what they had accomplished and who they had spoken to since Fred visited them. John was very impressed and said so before asking where they were going to go from there. James explained what they had in mind before going to the police, and they wanted to get some answers from them before they went any further.

'Right,' John said, 'Fire away.'

Before James could put what they had in mind to them, Hazel, looking at the clock, asked if they would like to have lunch now and talk while they ate their salad that she had laid out in the dining room. They all agreed what a good idea that was, and getting up, they went to the dining room. She said she had to warm the potatoes through, but it would only take a few minutes if they would like to start helping themselves to the cold meat and salad. Getting back with a steaming dish, she asked them to help themselves to those too, before sitting down herself.

John asked at this juncture if there was any way that Oliver could sell the school over his head. James said he had made enquiries about that from a pupil's father, who is a solicitor, and who, on going into the matter very thoroughly, assured him he couldn't.

It was now that James put their proposition to both Hazel and John. He said if they could persuade the enforced board of governers to buy Oliver's shares, not including Andrews, who by then might be in prison, would he advise on what should be done to bring the school back to what it used to be. At this point, Hazel took in an audible deep breath, not actually a gasp. She immediately asked if this would mean moving home or having John away for long periods.

James said this wouldn't be necessary. He said with Brent out of the way, Gerald Good might make a good headmaster, and between John and him, they could make the school perhaps even better than it was. All this would mean that a few days here and there would have to be taken up at the school, but the rest of the time, things could be done by letter and telephone. If it wasn't for long periods, John could take Hazel with him, and she could occupy herself in Monkshire, or perhaps visit one of their children for a few days. He would only be expected to advise and not get involved in running the school.

John asked about the school governors Oliver had coerced into being board members. James said in his opinion, all of them would take an interest in the school if they part-owned it, and they would get a return on their shares, as he would. They are all businessmen and wouldn't miss the opportunity to make money. It really depended if Oliver would sell the shares.

Fred said Oliver would be in so much trouble he didn't think he would take much persuading to sell.

John looked at Hazel long and hard without saying a word.

'All this could be pie in the sky,' Hazel said at last, 'for there are so many things that can go wrong!'

James had to agree, but he said that all they wanted to know was if John would cooperate for a year and then go back into retirement, to the life they were living now. We know he loves the school because he said so, and this is the way he can prove it. Fred butted in by saying a lot would be put on Gerald Good, but he was sure he would respond to any guidance John would give him.

John now said, it wasn't a decision he or Hazel could make just like that, they would have to be given time to think about all the implications involved. He said when they moved to the West Country, that was where they were going to retire and nothing would alter that. He said that even on a temporary basis, his retirement was being sabotaged. However, if they gave him a week to think it over and would let him know what the men James spoke of agreeing to buy Oliver's shares if he would sell them, he would let them know what he would do. Hazel nodded in agreement, and when they had finished their lunch, they went back to the sitting room where Hazel said she would make a pot of tea to have with a slice of cake, looking over at Fred. They agreed on this, and after Hazel had given Fred and James almost all of the remaining cake to take home, they got ready to leave; knowing they had at least a four-hour drive ahead of them.

As they drove home, Fred said what a hard decision they were asking John and Hazel to make, but it really was essential if the school was to return to its previous glory.

It was early evening when James dropped Fred off, telling him what time in the morning he would pick him up.

They got to the office by eight o'clock, and James started ringing the people they wanted to see. As it happened, they were all at work. What he said to each of them was virtually the same thing, that they wanted to speak to them and made a time and date to visit.

They had worked out a route that would see the first one, the farthest away, working their way home as they visited the others. They worked out they would go to Benfield first, then Oxen, Dayton and Botmouth. They didn't imagine they would get an immediate answer but would be as persuasive as they could and hoped all of them would have enough money between them to buy all of Oliver's shares without making themselves bankrupt.

They decided they would do all the visits together, so each of the men they wanted on board could be persuaded by both of them rather than one. There were no other cases that needed their full attention, so it wasn't going to be detrimental to the agency to be together.

It was ten o'clock when they set off for Benfield and took about two hours to get there to see Joe Mather. Joe was dressed as they saw him before in a check shirt, corduroy trousers and heavy leather boots. He was out in his yard, when they arrived, with a customer. He said he would not take long if they would like to go into his workroom/office. It was only ten minutes before he joined them, and sitting together, James asked how business was and was told very good. He said the chap he had been talking to had put twenty thousand pounds his way for road work on a new building estate, which in the nineteen seventies was a good amount.

They eventually got around to what they had come for. It took James a while to explain how far they had got in Oliver's affair and what they were trying to do to reclaim the school. He asked Joe straight out if rather than paying Oliver the fee he required each year for no financial gain, would he be prepared to buy a portion of his school shares, from which he would get a dividend each year. Joe thought about it for a while, whilst Fred added his bit to what the benefits would be over the long term. He asked how much the shares would cost. James said that as one of the school governors, he would have to pay what portion of the total equally divided between them all. If they all agreed, he would call a meeting with a solicitor in attendance and an accountant to see what his investment would cost.

Joe said at the moment what he has to pay is giving him nothing in return, so if Oliver does agree to sell, then yes, he would be prepared to invest in the school. However, was there not a doubt that Oliver would not sell. James explained what Oliver's position was and said,

'When his mother dies, which is imminent, and then knowing he is getting nothing from his mothers will, and not owning all the haulage business, his sisters own some shares in that, and going to prison most probably, I think he will be prepared to sell his shares of the school even at less than he paid for them. Wave a few thousand banknotes in front of him, and I think he will take them.' He said it would be a gamble, but he would be prepared to speculate if the other people Oliver had under the same threat as him agreed to buy the school between them, that way he would not be gambling on his own.

They left Joe, after about an hour, and after getting a bit of lunch on the way, they went on to visit George Bateman who said his farm machinery company was doing very well, and after listening to what James and Fred told him, he too agreed to buy Oliver out if he got the chance.

It was an all-driving day, but with Fred sharing it, neither of them were as tired as they would have been on their own, and were company for each other. Without going into any more detail, their visits to the other two, David Bright and Barry Keen, were also in favour of buying a portion of the school if they got the chance. David Bright said he would buy his share of the school and put the shares in his son's name, as he thought Michael, as a younger man, would be able to add more to the board of governors than him, and that it could be put in his will.

Before they left, he told them he had another shipment to the continent coming up, and asked if they would like to know what the arrangements were when they were settled on.

James and Fred said yes together, and so it was agreed.

They stopped for a meal on their way home from Botmouth and arrived at Fred's house at eleven o'clock. James drove off as he saw the light go on and made his way to his own house.

Susan had waited up and asked James if he wanted a nightcap before he went to bed. He said he would like a hot milk drink, and they both sat and drank it while he told her how his day had gone. She said that she had gone into the office and that a call had come in from Cunard asking for their assistance for the Queen Mary's next voyage to New York. James asked what did she tell them. She said she told them he would ring them in the morning. Looking at the local newspaper, he found the sailing days and times for the ships sailing from Southampton and told Susan the Mary was due to sail tomorrow, so they had twelve days to try and reach a conclusion to what they were doing, for they couldn't afford to start losing business due to what they were doing.

She asked why didn't he go to the police now. But he said they had a little way to go yet, and he wouldn't go to them until Mrs Oliver died, for that was when the shit was going to hit the fan.

They went to bed well after midnight, and though James was tired, he couldn't get to sleep with so much on his mind. He wondered what they were required for on the Queen Mary, as well as what next to do about closing the case on Fredrick's school and whether he would be going back there. He looked at the clock at three o'clock and must have gone off to sleep after that because when Susan woke him with a cup of tea, it was half-past seven. By the time he had washed, dressed and had his breakfast, it was half-past eight. Before he went out to his car, Fred arrived, asking sarcastically if he was going to work today. James answered just as sarcastically couldn't he sleep? They both laughed, which set the mood for another good day's work.

Getting to the office in Fred's car, James told him of the Cunard call and said he would ring them directly he got in. Saying good morning to Elizabeth in the sweet shop, they went up to their office to get started. James telephoned the Cunard offices in Liverpool and asked to speak to their security officer. Getting through to him, he asked what they were wanted for, and he was told it was a hush-hush job, and that he or they were needing to go to Liverpool. James agreed and said his partner Fred Baker would be there because at the moment, he was unavailable. This agreed, a time was set and who Fred had to report to and the office he could find him in. He said Fred was in the office, did he want to speak to him. He was told yes and handed the phone over to Fred.

When Fred had ended the call, James telephoned Desmond Cave, the solicitor, and getting him, told him what they had been doing and asked if he would help them if they called a meeting with the school governors and would he be able to have a barrister on call. Desmond said he would, and yes, he could have a very good barrister ready if one was required. Thanking him, James said he would get back to him in due course. Getting an accountant would not be difficult, but to get a really good one might be.

Ringing the hospital, they would tell him nothing other than Mrs Oliver was comfortable. He rang Peggy at her home and asked if she had had any news of her. She said she had, using her nursing position and influence to get to see her, and that she was a very sick lady, and from what the doctor treating her had said, they didn't hold out much hope of her surviving for very much longer. He said they would be doing a postmortem on her as soon as she passed away; that wasn't far off. They were keeping her sedated so she was out of pain, so she could not speak to anyone, not even family. She said she had asked the nurses if she had many visitors and was told her son and daughters had been in, but only once each. James told her what the hospital had told him, and she said that was the normal procedure in response to calls from non-family. He asked her if it was possible, to let him know when she did die as it would help him a great deal, as time was not now on their side. She said she would, and that she hoped it would be soon, for the poor old soul has nothing to live for now. She said she would keep in touch and rang off.

James was getting worried regarding their timing in getting in touch with the police, and which station to contact when they did. He was certain it couldn't be before Mrs Oliver died, and before he knew the shipping movement of David's furniture; he had to be patient.

Fred went off to Liverpool early the next morning and decided to go by train.

Susan had done the usual and found out train times and purchased the tickets return first class as Cunard would be paying the afternoon before. He went from Portsmouth Town Station, as getting to London was quicker than from Southampton. Susan gave him a lift and said she would visit the parents on the way back. It was late afternoon when he received a phone call from Peggy telling him Mrs Oliver has passed away an hour ago. She had got a call from the hospital that she had arranged with one of the nurses she had worked with when she was working in the hospital, and she said that after being sedated, she had never woken again. Peggy asked before she rang off what James was going to do now. He said he was going to ring the local police station, the number of which he had found out yesterday, and would try and get to see them. He said that it depended on what the postmortem showed up, he supposed, where they would take it, or if they would contain it in house.

He asked if she would accompany him to the police station, and she agreed. He said he would pick her up on the way.

James left a message for Susan, and getting his briefcase, he put in it all he thought was necessary to tell the police about when he got there. He was on his way within the hour after ringing the police station to tell them he was coming. He picked Peggy up, and they got to the police station in good time. They parked up in the station car park and, going in, said who they were, and asked if they could speak to the officer in charge. The desk sergeant said his boss was busy, but when he was told they wanted to speak to him about a murder, he changed his attitude and picked up his phone. After speaking to whoever he had rung and putting the phone down, he said his chief superintendent Charles Ormrod would be coming himself in a few minutes.

When he came, introductions were made and he asked them to follow him. It was quite a large police station hence the rank of the senior officer. He escorted them to his office and asked them to take a seat.

'Well,' he said, 'what is it that is so important that you have to speak to me personally, and not one of my junior officers.?'

James just said, 'Murder.'

He told him what they suspected, and that as a private investigator, what he was going to tell the chief superintendent was facts and not a fairytale.

Ormrod listened intently as James related all he knew about Mrs Oliver and how Peggy had realised she was being poisoned. Peggy told him about her suspicions and what she had done about it. The chief superintendent, when he spoke, asked, why weren't the police informed of her suspicions and notified before this? She said they had no proof until they got a sample of the beverages she was being sent analysed, that they were sure poisoning was being attempted. How did she get the samples tested, he asked, and Peggy had to admit how she had managed to get it done. The chief superintendent didn't waste any time and picked the phone up to telephone the hospital they had told him she was in. He asked to speak to the doctor that Peggy had said was Mrs Oliver's doctor at the hospital. They said that Doctor Snelling was not available at that moment in time, but that they would get a message to him that he was wanted by the police to speak to him, and they would get him to ring the police station when they had located him. The chief superintendant gave them the number for him to ring.

James now confronted Ormrod on the other subject. He explained that Oliver's lorries were being employed in gun-running. He told him it was Oliver's haulage that was being used to transport armaments from England to countries on the continent. The chief superintendent sat up and his eyes opened as if he had been shot.

'Do you have any proof of this?' He demanded to know. James explained how they had followed the lorries that were carrying the loads and how they had been modified with the secret compartments. He explained who had the modifications made and where it all took place and who carried out the work.

It was Andrews that was selling illegal armaments to foreign countries and Oliver providing the modified lorries. He went on to say there was going to be another shipment shortly, that he was awaiting the shipment details for.

The chief superintendent picked up his phone again, and this time, it was an internal call. He said he wanted Chief Inspector Meadows and Inspector Richardson to come to his office right away, no matter what they were working on.

Chief Inspector Meadows arrived first, closely followed by Inspector David Richardson, who both had notepads with them. The chief superintendent introduced them as they came in, and getting his secretary to bring in two more chairs, they sat around in a semi-circle formation in front of the chief superintendent's desk. Addressing James, he recapped on what he had told him so far to bring his other officers up to date. He then handed the floor over to James. He started from the beginning and the excessive canning of his son at Radcliff's Private School for boys. He went on to tell them all the investigations he and his partner had made, and what they had done to follow up on the gun-running. He then went on to tell them about Mrs Oliver senior who had just died. He handed over to Peggy who told the assembled group how she was Mrs Oliver's nurse chosen from the interview and who had worked very closely with the old lady. She said she suspected that something was wrong when she started being sick for no apparent reason. She knew relations were not good with her son, and that he was trying to sell the house from under her feet, but she was going to have none of it.

'So,' chief superintendent Ormrod said, 'Where do the police come in?' James said they think, in fact, they are sure, Mrs Oliver was being slowly poisoned.

'With what?' the chief superintendent wanted to know. They both said together, Paraquat. It destroys the internal organs such as kidneys, liver, etc. If given in large doses, it will kill almost immediately, but in tiny doses, it will kill humans slowly.'

What is she being poisoned for, he wondered and wasn't surprised when they said to get the house on her death. But he was wrong because in her will, she had cut him out, so he wouldn't get it anyway. The chief superintendent wanted to know how James knew this, and he had to explain how and why she told him, Peggy said this was true and that she had witnessed the signing and had signed to say she had. The poisoning wasn't being done by Oliver himself, but by, we think, the housekeeper carrying out Oliver's orders. The housekeeper, butler and cook have done a runner, so they must be frightened that the police will catch up with them. They did this directly the old lady was taken to hospital.

The chief superintendent asked who her home doctor was, and Peggy gave him his name, adding it was the doctor that acted for all the family.

James said he didn't want to go into every nook and cranny of what they had found out at this time, but he wanted assurance that a police pathologist was present when the postmortem was carried out, as the hospital doctor said it would. Although she had been in the hospital for a few days, if signs of paraquat was in her body, it was murder. The chief superintendent said that would be the case and he would follow it up.

Returning to the gun-running, as it was now being referred to all around, James said with what they had done and where they had been, the police should have enough information to act on, to confirm and convict the perpetrators. He gave them the registration numbers of the lorries that had been modified and said he would let them know locations and times of pick up. If the police did what they had done, they could surely get the police, in whatever country they were delivering to, to make arrests if not able to do so themselves. The chief superintendent said that was to be left to them and they would deal with it as they saw fit. James gave them the addresses of Oliver and Andrews and copies of photos they had taken.

With all the verbal and written information James had given to the chief superintendent, Ormrod took immediate action. He, looking at his chief inspector, ordered him to take up the gun-running case and his inspector to deal with the death of Mrs Oliver.

'Drop or delegate what you are doing and get on with this right away. I don't want either of these cases to be transferred to anywhere else. This is on our patch, and that is where it is going to stay. So, gentlemen, get to it.'

Both Chief Inspector Meadows and Inspector Richardson, said they wanted to speak to them before they left, especially James, for they said they wanted more detail to work on. They both agreed but not before the chief superintendent asked them to join them in the officer's dining room for lunch.

Getting there, the chief superintendent arranged for a table for five to be set-up instead of the usual table he used. They were asked if they wanted a cup of coffee while they waited for the table to be laid up. All present went into a question-and-answer session. It seemed to James as if more emphasis was being put on the gun-running than the possible murder, which, when it was thought about, was more serious as many lives could be lost with the ammunition being supplied than one lady perhaps being murdered, not to say they were both very serious cases to follow up.

They enjoyed a nice lunch that lasted for some time before James went with Meadows and Peggy with Richardson to their respective offices.

Chapter 16

It was well into the afternoon before Peggy and James left the police station, with the chief superintendent seeing them off the premises himself and thanking them for what they had brought to them. It would be being dealt with at this very moment he assured them both, and telling James, on his request, they would keep him in the loop as things went along, as long as it was possible to do so and not to have to be kept police restricted.

James dropped Peggy back home and thanked her for accompanying him.

She said it was very interesting and she found out that Inspector Richardson wasn't married and was a very nice man.

James smiled and wished her luck.

Getting back to the office, Fred hadn't got back yet from Liverpool, so James waited until he did. He knew Susan had arranged to pick him up at Portsmouth when he got in, so he wondered if she knew yet what train he was catching from Waterloo. He was tempted to ring her to find out but thought better of it. Instead, he sat and, going through his diary, tried to work out how many hours they had spent on the case so far, to give him some idea how much it would have cost if they were paying for their services, since he told Fred what they were going to do about Fredricks school, he knew how many days they had spent but wondered how many hours.

When Susan drove up with Fred, she had the two children with her as well, and she told James she had spent the whole day with his mum, and called in to see hers just before she got the call from Fred saying what train he was catching. She said she thought they had not seen their grandmothers for such a long time that taking Fred to Portsmouth was a good opportunity for them. She said she had given Fred the numbers to ring, so there was no problem and that they had had a very enjoyable day. Saying she was now going home to get a meal and taking the children with her, letting him take Fred home when they had finished.

When she had gone, having left Fredrick and Joyce with auntie Elizabeth in the sweet shop below on their request, Fred sat and told James what it was all about in Liverpool. He said who he had met, and what the job was going to be. It sounded interesting and one they shouldn't let slip through their fingers. It was indeed hush-hush and it could do their reputation the world of good if everything went according to plan. It was a very important person, and their entourage travelling to New York on the Queen Mary, and they were wanted to be not only detectives but part of their security team under cover from them. No one was to know what they were doing. It was Cunard's way of looking after their important passengers safety without them knowing it. James became as excited as Fred at the prospect and said if only we can get what we are working on sorted out in a week, or at least have all the groundwork done, we can give what we have to do for Cunard our best-uncompromised effort. After telling Fred what his day had been all about, and that he thought they had picked exactly the right time to get the police involved, he drove him home, collecting the children from the sweet shop on his way.

It was getting quite late in the afternoon the next day when a phone call came into the office that James answered. It was Chief Superintendent Ormrod who said his pathologist had reported that the postmortem had been carried out on Mrs Oliver and that she had been poisoned, adding, Anthony Oliver had been arrested. James said he had had a call from David Bright, only an hour ago, with the details of the furniture pick-up going to the continent. Ormrod asked if it would be possible for one of them to accompany the police officers that had been assigned to follow the pick-up of the furniture and armaments the lorry was going to carry. James said it would be him, and that he was standing by for further instructions.

Coming off the phone, James told Fred who the call was from and what arrangements he had made, and that Oliver had been arrested. Fred just said, 'The police are not hanging about, are they?'

James rang Peggy to let her know the autopsy had been carried out on Mrs Oliver and that traces of paraquat was found in her body and it was that that was responsible for her eventual death. Peggy said she was sorry to hear that but felt satisfied that she had done her best to prevent it.

James could hear her filling up, so he cut the call short and said he would contact her later if there was anything she should know about. She thanked him and said goodbye.

Oliver, now being in police custody, made it possible for him, James, to maybe get permission from the chief superintendent to speak to him, knowing he couldn't do anything about the forthcoming trip to the continent being stopped, and to maybe get him to agree to sell his shares for the school. He would leave that until tomorrow when Oliver might have had a little taste of being in a police cell. He was going to want to get out of it at any length and wouldn't worry what he had to do, to do it, or how, money certainly wouldn't help as he would then be charged with attempted bribery as well.

It was the next morning that he asked Chief Superintendent Ormrod if he could speak to Oliver and was asked what for. James went through what he wanted to find out and what a successful chat could achieve. Ormrod must have given it a lot of thought in a very short time because it was a few seconds before he said he could, but he would have to be in attendance.

James said that would be fine and arranged a time later that day to visit the police station.

Being together again, James and Fred went to the police station where James introduced Fred to the chief superintendent. He thanked him for getting things underway so quickly and for being able to speak to Oliver. He explained that the gun-running had come out of enquiries they were making on the school his son went to, but it was surprising what one can come across when you least expect it.

Getting Oliver brought to an interview room under escort, James and Fred started talking to him with the chief superintendent listening in. James got straight to the point and asked Oliver if now he was in custody, with a good chance it would be for a lot longer, what was he going to do with the school he owned or at least nearly owned. He said he was a businessman and saw an opportunity to make a lot of money quite quickly. He bought the school with no intention of keeping it going as a school but that the building and the surrounding land would make a lot of money if sold to a developer.

James said, 'But you found that you had an unmovable obstacle stopping you. The same with your mother's house, you wanted to sell that too but she would not let you. What you don't know is that you won't get your hands on it now she is dead, unless your sisters both agree to sell it to you and that is very unlikely.'

Oliver said he wished he hadn't bought the school, but the opportunity came up and he took it. James asked him why he had got rid of experienced teachers and put poor quality teachers in their place. He said he didn't have to pay them so much in wages. He said if only Mountford would have sold him his five per cent shares, he could have sold the school ages ago.

'What are you going to do now that you are not such a rich man anymore, are you wanting this financial burden around your neck?'

Oliver said he was a rich man that owned numerous companies that were not all haulage. James pointed out that his sisters had shares in the haulage business that their father had left them and also his mother.

'Do you know what is in her will? and that she made a new one only a few months ago? I put it to you, do you want to sell the school if someone is willing to buy it?'

Oliver thought about this and on the spur of the moment said yes, he would.

He said he wasn't guilty of what he had been arrested for, but James said he wasn't interested in that, that was a police matter. All he wanted to know was whether he was prepared to sell the school.

'When your mother's will is read out to your sisters, as you will probably not be there, it will show you are missing out on a lot of assets you thought were going to be yours.'

Oliver wanted to know how they knew all this, so James told him he and Fred were private investigators and that detective work was part of their business. He said he had had long talks with his mother and learnt a lot about him.

Asking the chief superintendent if it was possible to set up a meeting in prison if he wasn't allowed bail, he said yes, it could, but it was a very irregular thing to do. However, if it was going to help close his case quicker, he would allow it under strict supervision. What about him being brought to us, James asked. Thinking about it, the chief superintendent said that might be easier, and that he could arrange for a police van to bring him to their office under escort. This was agreed to with James giving them a day's notice.

Oliver was not a happy man and protested all the time, saying he had nothing to do with his mother's death. The chief superintendent just said quite quietly that they will find out soon enough when they had made further enquiries.

'I will get my solicitor to arrange for me to get bail, and we will see,' Oliver replied to that.

'You will certainly stay in custody until your housekeeper, butler and cook are found, and your doctor spoken to,' the chief superintendent answered. 'We are sure they will all say that anything they did was under your orders to save their bacon, but they will be judged on what they have done on your behalf. If it is proven that you ordered them to do anything unlawful, you will become an accessory to the fact, that will certainly mean a prison sentence.'

Before leaving the police station, James asked what time the policemen assigned to follow the lorry were due to leave the next morning. The chief superintendent said he would contact Chief Inspector Meadows and find out how he was handling things. He contacted him and told James they would be leaving the station in two cars, of which James would be in the one containing a sergeant. James said he would be there.

Knowing that Oliver would sell his shares of the school, on leaving the police station and thanking the chief superintendent, he and Fred went back to the office to make some phone calls.

Although only just over an hour's drive, it seemed to take longer than that to get back to the office, probably due to their eagerness to try and get the meeting set up to get Oliver's shares sold.

Susan was in the office, typing when they arrived back, and he immediately stopped what she was doing when they came in.

'Coffee?' she said and left her desk to make it. They got straight onto the four governors, John Mountford and the solicitor to find out if they could make a meeting in their office in two days' time at eleven o'clock. They didn't think it would happen, but all six could make it. James gave them all a quick rundown on what had been going on and said he thought a lower bid for the shares was on the cards from what Oliver had paid. On contacting John Mountford, he stated what Oliver had paid each of the old shareholders, and when ringing, Desmond Cave asked if he could draw up four identical contracts, giving him the names of who they were for.

Speaking to Fred, he said if they could pull this off, they might not get it all settled until after the school term would start, so they asked what they would do about it. Fred's response to this was, he had been thinking about this too, and in his opinion, they should do nothing and let school term resume as if nothing was going to happen. What about the canings, they asked. James said to leave that to him.

The new board of governors would have a meeting directly the school term started, and under John Mountford's guidance, they would sack Walter Brent if he wasn't in prison already if his wife was divorcing him on the grounds of cruelty, in way of wife-beating. Which reminded him that he must contact her.

He telephoned Mrs Brent on the number her sister had given him when she went to live with her. She was still there, her sister said, when she knew who was speaking to her and said she would pass the phone to her. Coming on the line and saying hello, Mrs Brent said the divorce papers were going through, and that she had complained to the local police who said they would look into it. James asked if she had any dates of when her case was being dealt with, to which she said not yet, but she would let him know when she heard. He asked after her son and she said he was much happier staying with his auntie, without the threat of a hiding or being beaten up every time Walter came home drunk. He thanked her and said things were going well with what they were doing. Ringing off, he put the phone down and just sat back in his chair. Fred asked if there was anything more he could do, and James apologised for seeming to be going it alone, but that he could not manage without Fred's support and loyalty, and smiling, he said he would be in total charge of the office tomorrow when he would be chasing gun-runners with the police. Fred laughed and just said, 'Big deal.'

It was very early the next morning when James left for the police station, leaving plenty of spare time to meet up with the sergeant and his crew when he got there. On arrival, he first met Chief Inspector Meadows who said he had briefed his sergeant and the policemen he was taking with him. He said they all had passports and some foreign currency if any was needed, and they hoped he had covered any eventuality. They were all in plain clothes and left the station with two cars, with the one James was in leading. It was sort of old hat for James, but he didn't know what this event was going to lead to. He had to leave everything to the sergeant who only had to ask for advice.

The lorry, with one of the registration numbers that James had given them, arrived at the furniture depot on time and after loading took off to load up the hidden compartment in the vehicle. They went to the weighbridge in the docks in Dover and went to the lane as directed by the ferry controller. In the lane they were directed to, they could see the lorry clearly. The sergeant told his crew they could have breakfast on the ferry rather than at the Dover terminal café. Loading the vehicles onto the ferry and leaving them, James saw the driver he had followed and pointed him out to the sergeant. The trip was carried out exactly the same as before, and by using two cars that were in contact with one another they had no trouble in following it.

They followed it to unload in the same buildings as used before, and the same routine was adopted. The smaller lorry picked up the unloaded armaments, and the second police car followed it.

The car James was in stayed with the lorry they had followed back to the ferry and Dover. The lorry driver drove back to its depot where he was arrested by the sergeant. The two lorries with the secret compartment were parked alongside each other, and the other policemen in the car searched both vehicles thoroughly, including the secret compartments. The sergeant impounded them both for forensic checks to be made on them.

The driver arrested was not going to go down alone and told the police the name and address of the driver of the other lorry, and to perhaps help his case, he told how many other trips he and the other driver had made. He said he only agreed to do the trips because Oliver offered to pay them more money to what they were normally paid.

Taking James back to the police station, and debriefing with Chief Inspector Meadows, late as it was, he got home in the early hours of the morning and went straight to bed.

It was after seven when Susan once again had to wake him up with a cup of tea and sat on the side of the bed while he told her what his day was like yesterday. She said she and Fred had received phone calls, that they had dealt with, and finished by two o'clock. It was nice spending the rest of the day with their families. James told her they were going to arrest Andrews for questioning that morning and getting a warrant to search his house. He said they were not hanging about and were catching them cold. Although Oliver had called his solicitor, he was not given enough time to prepare himself for Oliver being questioned or what he was being questioned about. It might be the same with Andrews.

Doctor Snelling was questioned by the police at the hospital, who said Mrs Oliver was a very sick lady when she entered the hospital and that from what he learnt from her personal nurse, she had been given poison and what she thought it was. The housekeeper and the butler, it seems, were an item and were caught trying to leave the country; they were actually on the ferry to France when they were arrested and taken to the police station. Being questioned separately, they sang their little heads off, one blaming the other for a lot that went on in the house. The housekeeper said she was given the substance by the butler, and he said he had been given it by Oliver. They both said they did not know what it was, but the housekeeper was told it was medication the doctor had prescribed and it was to be put in her tea or coffee twice a day, and when asked how much, she said it was a very small amount, and that she did it each time without the cook knowing. The cook was as yet not found, but the police were not in too much of a hurry to find her because what they could tell from what they knew, she was innocent of any crime but had got frightened when the other two left in such a hurry.

Oliver's solicitor had applied for bail, but it had been refused on the grounds that there was more than one offence to be investigated. Apparently, when the police mentioned gun-running, Oliver put on a show of not knowing what they were talking about, but he could not give an answer when asked if he didn't know two of his lorries had been modified.

Chief Superintendent Ormrod was true to his word when he had told James he would keep him and Fred in the loop. He telephoned and told them that Oliver and Andrews had both been arrested and officially charged, Oliver with the attempted murder of his mother and with aiding and abetting

Andrews, and Andrews for illegal gun-running. The latter going international as the police forces in France, Germany and other countries were investigating. This had become 'A big one' as he called it, and one that was to be kept within police restriction. Apparently, what Andrews was sending abroad using Oliver's lorries was small fry to what he was illegally manufacturing abroad, the big stuff, the likes of tanks, rocket launchers, etc. If all he will be charged with is proven, he can expect a very long prison sentence. But what about Oliver, James asked, when he got the chance.

The chief superintendent just said, 'It would be up to the courts when he goes in front of them, that he certainly will. However, these cases will take time to deal with, it will be many months before they are brought to a conclusion.'

They had both listened on their respective phones, and after thanking Chief Superintendant Ormrod, they hung up, and standing up, both shook hands. I think we can leave those two for the police to deal with now. However, we have to get back to rescuing the school.

Chapter 17

The first thing they had to do was to get the purchase of the school sorted out. They asked all the prospective buyers if they could meet at a hotel in Southampton, having realised their office would be far too small to have a meeting of this magnitude in it, where Oliver could be brought under escort. On contacting them all, they settled on a date and time for a meeting to be called.

They had received a call from Cunard telling them that the job they had agreed to on the Queen Mary had had to be deferred, and they would be contacted when it had been rescheduled. This was rather fortunate, as they could now concentrate entirely on the school and its outcome.

Before letters were sent out to those who James and Fred wanted at the meeting, James said he was going to speak to their old friend and publicist Joyce Sheen at The Times newspaper. They hadn't spoken to her for quite a long time, not since she had come to James' daughter Joyce's confirmation, being her godmother. When James telephoned her, she said she was aware of two respected businessmen having been arrested but not enough to go to print. James said it was a case they were working on, and they could give her the story so far if she could get permission from the police to let them have the story. She said she was more than interested and would seek police permission directly she had finished speaking to him, and she would let him know what the answer was. They agreed to meet her in her London office the day after tomorrow at eleven thirty, just in time for her to take them to lunch. James said how nice that would be and was looking forward to it already.

Date and time were set for the meeting to take place in a large hotel not far from the Bar Gate in Southampton. Two of them had booked a nights stay, saying it gave them an opportunity to see the liners that were in the port. It had been years since they had been there and they could recall some old memories. On the night in question James and Fred were joined by, John and Hazel Mountford, who were one of the couples staying overnight, and David Bright and his wife. The others, all going home after the meeting due to work commitments, were George Bateman, Joe Mather and Barry Keen. James had contacted Desmond Cave, the solicitor, and Stella Boulton, the school secretary, to take the minutes of the meeting. Oliver turned up with his police escort in a police van together with his solicitor. He looked ten years older since James had last seen him and seemed to be most uncomfortable. But then again, James thought, how would he feel if he was in as much trouble as Oliver's situation.

The meeting started by James introducing everybody although, of course, Oliver knew them all, with the exception of Cave. James explained why the meeting had been called and what he wanted to be sorted out before they left for home. He said Stella was taking minutes of the meeting as it may become an important document for the future.

He started by asking Oliver if he wanted to sell the school. Oliver said he had been advised by his solicitor not to sell it. This was a bit of a setback, as James had been told he would. Asking the solicitor why he had given this advice, he said it was an asset worth keeping. This brought Desmond Cave to ask what sort of asset is one where you don't want to keep it as a school, and as he has found out that he cannot sell it for development because it doesn't all belong to him, plus, of course, he may be in prison for a long time. Oliver, looking at his solicitor, said, 'What they are saying is very true; what do I want a school for? If I do have to go to prison, I have trusted people to keep the haulage and other businesses going, but the school I have no one. I would rather be rid of it and put it down to one of my business failures, adding, there hasn't been many of those.'

Having previously found out how much Oliver had paid each of the old board of governors for their shares, they knew what they each should offer. They all agreed to own the same amount of the ninety-five percent of shares, with John Mountford owning the other five per cent. The figure they offered was turned down flat by Oliver who said he wanted to sell the shares not give them away. The second and final offer, which when given, was said to be for a rundown school that was getting a bad reputation, was accepted. Oliver knew he was not in a good place and his reputation was in tatters.

He reluctantly signed over his shares to the men that were already school governors, and with head bowed and a face like thunder, with cheques worth thousands of pounds in his pocket, he was taken from the room by a policeman.

James now called upon John Mountford to offer guidance to those who had just purchased a private boys school that they wanted to make money from. He explained what he had agreed to do for James for one year, and that it would take that long to get the school back to where it was when he resigned from it. He said he would become the fifth governor if they required another one, but he would not become the headmaster again. They all agreed to what he proposed and sat and listened intently as he went on to say what they collectively had to agree to before the school reopened in two weeks time.

The first thing they had to do was to try and get any of the masters that had been sacked by Oliver back if they were in a position to return or if they wanted to. Then, when they had ascertained who would be returning, advertise for teachers highly qualified in subjects that were not covered by those who agreed to come back. He said that he, or they as school governors, would consider the applications and CVs and employ them directly, from the day the inferior masters were dismissed. A question was asked, what would they do about a new headmaster. John said he had given that a lot of thought, and he was sure that Gerald Good would be a changed man when Walter Brent was sacked. He said he was one of the only teachers Oliver had got right, albeit he was his brother-in-law, but with Brent, as one of his staff, he was never going to run the school as it should be run, and how John was sure he could manage it if he was allowed to do so. This agreed upon, he then went on to tell them letters had to be sent out as soon as possible to the parents or guardians of the boys attending the school, notifying them that changes were being made to the school, and that it was being returned to its previous standard. Looking over to Stella, she nodded, indicating she would see to the letters.

He, on behalf of the remaining governors, would arrange to meet all of the teachers the school had had complaints about, and those that he thought weren't properly or suitably qualified, and would notify them officially that their services were no longer required. He said this done, official letters of dismissal, signed by all of them, would be sent to them.

John, now in his element, then explained that all this would not take five minutes to achieve, but that it was necessary to get the parents on side.

The next thing that had to be done was to expel the pupils that were terrorising the school. Once again, he explained what James and Fred had told him about the head prefect and his bunch of henchmen. The prefects would be chosen by the headmaster, as was his way when he was the headmaster, on merit. He said, the school would have to open at the start of term as usual, but hopefully start to change directly his suggestions were put in place. He said, he would arrange with Gerald Good, who he found a very nice and understanding man to call a school assembly and with all the school in attendance announce the dismissal of Walter Brent and Edward Andrews (flashman) and his fellow prefects. This, hopefully, will humiliate them and be some retribution to the boys that had suffered under their bullying.

James butted in at this point and said he was going to arrange something for Brent but was not going to say what at this time.

As John Mountford and David Bright were staying in the hotel overnight they asked if any of them would like to join them for a drink and asked if they minded their wives joining them. Not being too late and the rest of them not having far to travel, they all agreed.

It turned out to be a very social evening when they could talk among themselves and to James and Fred in particular. James commented to John how he seemed to be getting an element of pleasure out of organising the near future of the running of the school, to which he said he was, and that he didn't realise how much he had missed the involvement since he had retired. Hazel, too, said quietly to Fred how she thought it had brought her husband back to life, not she said that he was ever boring. They started to leave when Stella said she should start thinking of getting home. She said she had a lot to do and was looking forward to working with her old boss again, giving him a cuddle as she left. She told James she would let him know each time she had got her tasks finished and would copy him all that she sent out.

He thanked her and said he looked forward to hearing from her.

As the last of them left, leaving John and David with their wives, James and Fred recapped on what the meeting had achieved and were satisfied with the outcome. John Mountford said he was pleased he was going to get rid of Walter Brent together with Edward Andrews. They both stood out from the rest when it came to being cruel. James smiled at this, knowing one could possibly be the father of the other but kept it to himself.

On getting home, James got the usual questioning of how did it go, to which he said very well. It would take quite a while to get the school to become one that parents were queuing to get their sons into, but with the way John Mountford was going to go about it, it should be sooner rather than later.

Both their children had gone to bed when James got home, so he said he would wait until tomorrow to tell Fredrick he had to go back to Radcliff's at the start of term.

He didn't know how he would take the news, but with what James was going to suggest to him might make him look forward to it.

After having breakfast, neither of the children were up, so before going to work, he woke Fredrick up and told him he wanted to talk to him. Wiping the sleep out of his eyes, Fredrick listened to what his father had to say. He reminded him he had asked if he was having to go back to Radcliff's before telling him he did. Fredrick looked genuinely put out, asking his dad if he must? James told him a little of what went on the night before but added, 'I don't think you will be caned any more; not if you can do what I suggest to you. If Mr Brent selects you, or any of the boys in your class, for an undeserved caning, when he gets his cane out from his desk or on top of it if he has already got it out, all of you pupils set on him. If you can wrestle the cane out of his grasp, you could use it on him. How many are there in your class?' he asked his son, and Fredrick replied, 'About eighteen usually.'

'Well, what you have to do is let all the other boys in the class know what you want them to do, and directly the cane is set for action set upon him.'

'But dad,' the boy exclaimed, 'that's not right.' James asked his son if caning him so much was right, and Fredrick said no.

'So then, what will Mr Brent be able to do about it, eighteen to one seems to me to be fair odds in this case. What will happen when we do this?' he asked his father and was told,

'Probably nothing, as long as you don't kill him and all undertake to give him a hiding. If you can get him down onto the floor, he will not be able to fight back very easily and will not be able to tell anyone because of making a laughing stock of himself. Just make sure he doesn't get hold of the cane again. He will not cane anyone else for fear of the same thing happening again.'

After talking to his son, he went off to work and getting there found Fred on the phone. He indicated to James to pick his phone up and listen in. It took James some time to gather who Fred was talking to before he realised that it was Ian Marks, the young soldier Brent had nearly killed and what he was discharged from the army for. He was explaining to Fred that he had been contacted by the police who asked him to stand witness for the prosecution to what Walter Brent was like before being dismissed from the army. Fred asked him if he would be prepared to go to court, and Ian said that was what he had rung for, to seek advice. Fred asked him to hang on a minute while he spoke to his partner.

Fred asked James why he thought he was being asked to go to court by the police, how was it anything to do with the army. James said he would like to talk to him. Fred nodded. James said hello and asked if he had become a train guard yet. He said he had and James and Fred congratulated him. He thanked them but said, 'What about going to court?' James explained what he thought the police wanted him for, it was to assure the judge when he gets to the court that Brent was a violent man. He said he thought this was to do with Mrs Brent going to the police telling them he was frequently beating her up. The police were following up on her complaint, and being certain she was telling the truth, they were going to prosecute him and wanted him, Ian, as a witness. He will not be in any trouble himself and will not lose money by going to court at the police's request. If found guilty, it should put Brent in prison for quite a long while. Ian thanked them and passed on his wife's good wishes before he rang off.

James said to Fred that what they had done in such a short time was amazing, and that their trip to London to visit Joyce Sheen was timed just right.

They got Susan to drop them off at Portsmouth Town Station, where they purchased their return tickets to Waterloo. Susan said she was going to call in to spend longer with her mum than she did when taking Fred to the station. The train was on time and only stopped at the usual four stops on the way. Crossing London by tube at that time of the day compared to rush hour was easy and they got to The Times newspaper's office in good time. They arrived at Joyce's office, with her name and 'Sub Editor' on the brass and polished door plaque on her door, ten minutes early. Her secretary said she would see if she was free yet, as she had been very busy that morning and they were early. She pressed a button on her phone as she picked up the receiver and asked her if she was able to accept her guests a bit early. She nodded as she put the receiver down and got up to show them into Joyce's office. Welcoming them and giving them each a hug before they sat down, she went back to her desk.

She said she had been in touch with Chief Superintendent Ormrod, and he had given her permission to go to print but she was only to print what she was told by Mr Royston and Mr Baker.

She asked how things were at home and how their families were and how business was going.

James told her all about the school he and Susan had sent Fredrick to, and how he had been caned so much and not complained to them. He said how the school had been purchased by an unscrupulous businessman who only wanted to sell it for development to make a huge profit on the purchase.

On investigating what he was up to, the army came into the equation, and that is where Andrews came into it, as well as Brent.

'We have an hour before we leave for lunch, so let me have it from the beginning.' She pressed a button on her phone and called her secretary in with notepad and pen. She invited her to sit in the last unoccupied chair in the office and said to James and Fred she would take it all down in shorthand, as she listened. She would edit it when Anne had typed it out. With Fred adding his bits, in between, James gave her the whole story up to where they were now.

Joyce told them they hadn't lost their touch and were still as good as they were when working on the Queen Mary and saving lives as well as catching their man. She said this would be the third exclusive they would have given her, and she was sure her newspaper would reward them handsomely. She asked when she could go to print and was told immediately, 'But please don't print anything about Brent other than the beatings he gave Fredrick. His forthcoming summons for wife-beating is not finalised yet, and I don't want him to know he will probably go to prison as well, which I feel sure he will, for the police are dealing with it right now, and most judges don't like wife-beaters if you get my drift.'

Joyce asked Anne if she had got all that, and being assured she had, she asked her to type it up, while they were at lunch, with a carbon copy.

Smiling, Anne left the room and Joyce reached for her rather expensive-looking jacket that went over the matching skirt. They walked to the restaurant she had taken them to before, where she was welcomed, and sat at the same table as on the other occasions they had been there.

They had a drink while ordering their main meal and talked while they waited for it to be served.

Joyce asked if either of them had started smoking again yet, and when being told no, she asked if they would mind if she did. She was still smoking Craven "A" filter tips. She ordered a bottle of wine that complimented the meals they had chosen and coffee to round things off.

Getting back to the office and making themselves comfortable again and James asking her when she was likely to become chief editor, she smiled and said she didn't think ever. The editor has said he is not going to retire yet, although he could; when he does retire, he will be replaced by the powers to be headhunting another man.

What would she do if that happens? and she just said 'Make the best of it, for my salary is more than adequate for my needs, and I cannot see me ever getting married again.'

Anne came in with the copies of what she had typed up and left for them to read. James said it was longer than he thought, but Joyce said it wouldn't be quite as long when she had edited down. She said it would make the front page and promised she would not dramatise it up, it would be printed as factually as it had been relayed to her by them. On thanking her for the lunch and telling her how nice it was to see her again, they said their goodbyes.

They caught the five-twenty train back to Portsmouth, as James had told Susan they would, and she was there to pick them up. She said her mum had got a cold coming and didn't feel just the thing but felt a little better when they had gone out and walked along Southsea seafront. The drive home was uneventful, and dropping Fred off, they headed for home.

While Susan prepared the family's evening meal, James got a phone call from Chief Superintendent Ormrod, telling him the police had called at Walter Brent's house to arrest him, and that they had to break in, after checking with a neighbour that he was in but would not answer the door. He said they had found him unconscious on the living room floor, with one empty bottle and a nearly empty one of whiskey on a table. He has been rushed to hospital where he is now recovering under police guard. The doctor that the police officer spoke to said if he had finished the second bottle, he would have probably died, and not be just unconscious. They checked the rest of the house and found Mrs Brent and her sister upstairs, also both unconscious, who also had to be hospitalised. They are both now recovered, but Mrs Brent has been knocked about rather badly.

She has been questioned and said she went to the house because she thought he would be out as he usually was, but she found him in. As she went into the bedroom to get some clothes she wanted, she woke him up and he set upon her. The sister who had driven her there had tried to stop him hitting her sister and was felled with one punch, so she could do no more to help. Apparently, he was very drunk, and after sort of realising what he had done, he went back to the bottle.

It was the neighbour that rang the local police station because, as she put it, she thought he was killing someone due to all the shouting and screaming that was coming from the house. The house, by the way, was absolutely filthy. The front door had been temporarily repaired with a police notice "Do not enter stuck across it". He said all three had been questioned, and that Mrs Brent and her sister had returned to her sister's house, while Brent will be put in a police cell when he is fit enough to be released. Did that mean he would not be going back to school at the start of term, James asked, and was told that he would remain in custody until his case comes up in court, which might take a few weeks, by the time we have enough evidence and witnesses to put him away for a long time.'

Thanking Ormrod and saying he would see him soon, he put the phone down. Susan, when he went to the kitchen with a glass of sherry for her, asked who it was on the phone.

He told her who it was and what the call was all about. She said she was glad but felt sorry for Brent's wife, but she asked as to what she was doing going back to the house for anything, let alone for some clothes.

When dinner was ready and both the children had come down from their bedrooms, James told Fredrick that Mr Brent would not be returning to the school. Fredrick's face lit up and he just said 'Good' and carried on eating his dinner.

James telephoned Fred and told him the chief superintendent had phoned and what it was about, and said he would see him in the office tomorrow morning. He said they could now put the case to bed, and that they could get back to earning some money.

Chapter 18

It was nearly nine o'clock when James got to the office, with Susan, and told Fred, who was already there, that he was going to ring John Mountford to see how far he had got. On getting through, John said a phone call would not be good enough and wanted to see him and Fred in person. They agreed to meet halfway between Southampton and where he lived. John suggested a hotel that he and Hazel had stopped at a few times and that he could recommend. They decided to take their wives, as a break for them, and nice to be able to meet each other.

John said he would make the booking and asked if they both wanted double rooms.

On confirming that they did and settled for the weekend, that was only two days away, John gave him the name of the hotel and the address and phone number. This arrangement, with Fred's nodded approval, was settled on.

Susan said she was ready, as they had spoken of what they would do next on the drive to the office, and was already on her feet and at the filing cabinet. They pulled Fred and James's desks together and getting every bit of paper, mostly in folders, that Susan had done as they went along, and spread them out along them as they took them out. It was surprising how much of it there was. Going through it all, they could see that they hadn't left a stone unturned.

What they wanted to speak to John about was how far he had got with contacting and arranging all he had to see to, to get the school back to what it used to be.

The call came through from Cunard giving the rescheduled date that had been arranged, for the job they wanted done, that gave them plenty of time to settle the school case.

Before they met up with John and Hazel, James wanted to visit Chief Superintendent Ormrod to see if he could find out how far he had got and if he had any idea if and when Oliver, Andrews and Brent's cases would be going to court.

He made an arrangement for them to go and see him the next day at ten o'clock. They spent the rest of that day going through all they had got out of the filing cabinet and had reminded themselves of every detail they had recorded. They laughed on a couple of occasions when it was brought back to memory what they had done. Susan, of course, had no idea what they were laughing about, but she realised it was taking some of the tension off what they must be feeling.

At ten o'clock the next day, they met up with the chief superintendant and learnt that Brent's case was being heard in a week's time, but that they were retaining him in a police cell until then. He asked if a definite time had been set for the hearing and what court it would be. The chief superintendent said it was far too serious to be a magistrate's court and was going direct to a criminal court. He gave the date, time and location of the court, and James said they would try to be there.

The other two, Oliver and Andrews, were a different kettle of fish, for a lot more investigation had to be made before they could go to trial. What they had uncovered with both of them was not enough to get them the sentences they deserved, and knowing they were both wealthy men, they could afford the best defence lawyers in the land.

Early on Saturday morning, after having taken the children to their grandparents the night before, they travelled in James's car to the hotel that John had booked and went to reception to say they had arrived, and to get their room numbers, keys and directions to get to them. They signed the register and could see from it that the Mountfords had already arrived. James asked if it was possible to speak to them, and the receptionist rang their room number and passed the phone to him. John answered it and they agreed to meet in the lounge for coffee in half an hour.

They all met and were casually dressed. The ladies were introduced to each other before a waiter came into the room and asked if they would like a beverage, tea, coffee or something a little stronger. They all agreed on coffee and said how they would like it. While the waiter went away to get it, they sat in very comfortable chairs in a bay window and the women talked together as did the men. John asked if they had good rooms and were told by James and Fred that their rooms were very comfortable and that they had a very pleasant outlook from their bedroom windows. The ladies seemed to be getting on famously, which gave the men the opportunity to talk about the school. The coffee came and was served from a tray containing everything they needed for their likings.

After coffee was finished, Hazel said she would take Susan and Amy out into the gardens, where they could stroll and chat while the men talked. They got up and left the men to it.

John said he had written to all six masters that were sacked by Oliver and had telephone replies from four of them, who all agreed to return to the school. Of the other two, he was waiting for a reply. He said he had contacted Gerald Good by phone and they had agreed to meet at the school. He said he was very hopeful that he would remain the headmaster. When I told him that Brent would not be there any more, he sounded delighted. Regarding the new owners, he liked what he had seen of them and thought they would be keen to see the school run properly. He told James he must have a very persuasive tongue, for all of them to agree to remain as school governors, thinking they would have to remain so if Oliver kept up his blackmail tactics.

He said he was prepared to become a fifth governor if they wanted him, when his year of advising was up and would be honoured to become one. So there were still some things that had yet to be sorted out, but also having contacted Margaret Gilbert, the school nurse, she to had agreed to return. Bob Singleton agreed to become school treasurer as he still felt an element of guilt about selling out to Oliver.

'The school is due to open again in a week's time, in which time I should have had replies from the other two teachers I wrote to, and have placed an advert in TheTime's newspaper advertising possible vacancies for masters at the school. Brent will definitely not be returning, and I will personally expel Edward Andrews and the other prefects he chose. So, hold on to your hats, for the first term of three months there will be all sorts of changes that will lead to me getting my old school back.' When you mentioned who you had spoken to when you first went to the school, David Wise, who said he was thinking of retiring early because of how the school was being run, well he too has now thought better of it and will remain with us.

Within such a short time John had performed miracles, he was, as Stella had said, a very popular and dedicated man. She was sure the school would be back on its feet in no time.

The talk finished, they went out and found their wives playing croquet on the lawn, they were getting on so well and being only halfway through their game, the men said they could pick them up in the bar where they were going. John showed them around the gardens on their way back and said what a lovely hotel it was. Getting to the bar, James asked what they would like to drink. When Fred said he would get them in, James laughed and said it doesn't matter which of the two of us gets them in, it will be coming out of our business account, as I am putting this and dinner tonight against our expenses.

It was over half an hour before the ladies joined them, saying what a change getting away like this was. James got them what they asked for from the bar and went back to the seats they had left in the lounge. There were a few other guests arriving as well as those in the bar, and so tonight at dinner, there should be a bit of atmosphere.

On Monday morning, they got down to breakfast at the arranged time, after packing, and after a hearty breakfast, they said their farewells to John and Hazel, adding they hoped to see them again soon, and that they have a safe journey home.

By having had an enjoyable break, getting back to work was like an anticlimax, but it had been, in fact, a great success, albeit that the police now had everything in hand. James telephoned Joyce at The Times and asked if she had gone to print yet. She said it was in that day's edition that James or Fred hadn't obviously read yet. He told her anything she wanted to write about she had to now go to the police. He knew she had already contacted them so didn't bother to give her any contact details. He advised her that if she wanted information on the case, she should contact Malcolm Oliver, and he gave her all that she would want to know about him and how to make contact if he was prepared to speak to her. He said he was going to telephone him so would mention it to him that she might ring. She thanked him again and passed on the thanks of her chief editor and said she would hope to visit them again soon.

He telephoned Malcolm Oliver and told him what trouble Anthony Oliver and Henry Andrews were in, and he said he had read some of it in that day's Times. James told him Joyce might be ringing him, and that it was up to him what he told her about the family. He said his mother would be more than satisfied after the way they treated her and would die a happy lady, knowing they had got what they deserved.

Chapter 19

The school term started on time, and Fredrick went with a far more optimistic outlook, knowing he was not going to get the cane. The masters John Mountford had contacted were in attendance, but they were short-staffed until the new masters were officially appointed. Although Dr Mountford had told James and Fred that he would never go back to teaching and certainly not as headmaster, he would board at the school for one month or until a relief was found sooner to take mathematics and English, but the relief would have to be well qualified. He told Gerald Good what his intentions were, and that he wanted him to call a special assembly so he could announce the expulsion of Edward Andrews and his band of merry men, in front of the whole school, and that he would not tolerate any more bullying.

James and Fred were invited to attend the school reopening by John Mountford, and so they took Fredrick with them. It transpired that he had also invited the board members, the new owners of the school.

He called the assembly just before lunch time so that everybody could be there. Gerald Good took centre stage with all invited guests, his secretary, school nurse, masters, school governors and James and Fred. They sat around him on the stage at the end of the big hall, as it was known as. He introduced each of them to the assembled boys and said what part they would take in running the school, with the exception of James and Fred. He left John Mountford until last. When he called his name, there was a tremendous cheer, especially from the older boys who were there as young men, as John used to call them before he resigned.

He said a few words explaining that he was only back temporarily but was now a school governor.

Before he finished and sat back down, he introduced James and Fred. He told the school who they were and what they had done for the school. It was then that Edward Andrews (Flashman), who had not yet been told he was expelled, shouted out, 'Why didn't they mind their own business and leave the school to run as it was?' James just said, 'If left alone, there could have been no school but a small housing estate, and boys would be caned without due cause and bullying would have continued.'

He sat down to a round of applause. It was then that Gerald Good expelled Edward Andrews and his cronies by name and asked them to leave the school immediately. Edward, not knowing, would not just accept this and went on to say his father would have something to say about it and was stopped in his tracts by James telling him that his father was going to prison and would probably be there for a long time. Edward, again, said his father was away on business with Mr Athony Oliver, and what they were being told was a load of bullshit. The boys booed as he and four other boys left.

It was then that Gerald Good as the headmaster told them that Mr Brent was not coming back to the school as he too was in a police cell and would probably go to prison. Hearing that news, the boys cheered at the top of their voices, as to did the rest of the people on the stage, although they tried to keep theirs a little more dignified.

After having lunch with Fredrick, his dad and his godfather told him to work hard and do the best he could at the school. He thanked them both and said he would not let them down, knowing all they had done to save the school and arrange for it to be run and managed properly again.

Chapter 20
One Year Later

Mrs Agatha Oliver never had a funeral because they found in her will that she wished her body to go to medical science, which was even more proof of what a kind lady she was, and it saved her family mourning over her at her funeral, they supposed, particularly her son; she must have really hated him because it was not in her previous will. She also left quite a large sum of money to Peggy Banks, her friend and nurse.

Walter Brent was sent down for five years for wife-beating and other charges that the police had discovered whilst making their enquiries. James was at the court when the sentence was passed, much to his satisfaction. The prosecution called, as well as Mrs Brent and her son, Ian Marks, who really laid it on the line how Brent was in the army. After the judgment was made and they were outside the courtroom, James asked Mrs Brent how her son was getting on, and she said, he was now in the airforce as a trainee officer and, subject to health and fitness, was going to train as a pilot and achieve his ambition. She said the divorce had gone through and was not contested. He also asked Ian Marks how he was getting on. He said he was an official Southern

Railway Guard and added that his wife was pregnant with the baby being due in a couple of weeks.

James and Fred went to both Oliver's and Andrews' court cases held in the high court where Oliver got ten years in prison for attempted murder, extortion, and for aiding and abetting an illegal gun-runner, while Andrews got twelve years. What the police got on Andrews, was far beyond what James and Fred had taken to them, but with the information they had given them, it certainly helped put them away for a long stretch each. Oliver's housekeeper was given an eighteen months' sentence and the Butler a year. They admitted their part in Mrs Oliver senior's death, but not of murder. The autopsy result came out as death by organ failure, aided by inadequate medication.

It was never proved beyond a shadow of a doubt that enough paraquat had been administered to kill her as quickly as it did. She was a frail old lady, and by doing what she did, Peggy Banks was commended but was told by the police that she should have reported her suspicions sooner. The doctor was struck off on the grounds of neglecting his patient and for taking bribes, so he had to retire, as he was then on the medical scrap heap.

It so happened that soon after being expelled from school, Edward Andrews was sent to Borstall for activities he undertook that broke the law. He was turning out to be a bad influence on the young society he mixed with, purely of being spoilt and uncontrolled by his parents.

Mrs Oliver's daughters, one of which was Mrs Good, one of the wives of Gerald Good, sold the house and grounds for a great deal of money, meaning their sister-in-law had to relocate which she did to France. As for Gerald, he divorced her and lived with his second wife. He got away with being a bigamist, how, James never found out, but he must have employed a very good lawyer who found some technicality to get him pardoned. All he knew, both from his son and from John Mountford, that he had become a very good and respected headmaster.

Peggy Banks and Inspector Richardson had become an item and were now engaged to be married next year. Peggy had gone back to hospital nursing and was one of the senior sisters where Mrs Oliver died.

Tommy Naylor had purchased the franchise for the forge on the Andrews' estate and was now working for himself and not for Andrews.

Lady Andrews was suing for divorce and was going to take Andrews to the cleaners as a settlement, but that was still ongoing.

Fredrick was now loving the school and is getting on extremely well.

He said Dr John Mountford took his class as form master for just over a month before a new master was appointed and was a very nice man. He said they don't see Mr Mountford very often, only at the parent-teacher meetings that he always attends, as do the other members of the board of governors. James and Susan always attended, and it was nice to get compliments from some of the parents they met there and to renew their acquaintance with the board of governors.

Fred and Amy, in particular, had become very good friends with John and Hazel Mountford and visited each other every month or so, and always enjoyed the company of Elizabeth when the Mountfords visited the Bakers.

With the work coming into the office, with the reputation they were getting, they were seriously considering taking on another partner, but that was still not settled on yet.

They had covered everything that had come into them, mostly these days working alone, but most of the shipborne jobs they did together whenever they could.

Thinking back on what they had achieved on the school case, they felt very satisfied and proud and had made a lot of new friends as well as some enemies on the way. Seeing it cost them quite a lot of their own money, they had deemed it well spent, although they were well rewarded by The Times newspaper.

Sitting in the office one morning, having just finished another case, James asked Fred if he and Amy would fancy going on a cruise. 'What a brilliant idea' was Fred's immediate reply.

'We can afford to close the office for two weeks and Elizabeth either close the shop or get the lady, that is now helping her, run it on her own for that time, and it would be like going back in time, to when we all first met.' James said he had been promising Susan he would take her on a cruise for years now, so why not?

'If we do it during the school holiday, the children can stay with their grandparents for a week with each, and they would love it.' And so it was arranged. They contacted Cunard, knowing who to speak to, of course, and got a hefty discount off their fare for better than average outboard cabins, two doubles and a single.

This gave them something to look forward to, and so it was.